T0315709

THE RISING OF THE SON

Giles Dawnay

Building futures, Bridging divides

THE RISING OF THE SON

By Giles Dawnay

© Giles Dawnay

ISBN: 9781912092208

First published in 2020 by Arkbound Foundation (Publishers)

Arkbound is a social enterprise that aims to promote social inclusion, community development and artistic talent. It sponsors publications by disadvantaged authors and covers issues that engage wider social concerns. Arkbound fully embraces sustainability and environmental protection. It endeavours to use material that is renewable, recyclable or sourced from sustainable forest.

Arkbound
Backfields House
Upper York Street
Bristol BS2 8QJ

www.arkbound.com

THE RISING OF THE SON

Prologue

Jonno stopped to catch his breath. The tears in his eyes and heavy gasping meant that he couldn't run as he wanted. There was none of the smoothness of action, no co-ordinated breathing or slick movements as was normally possible. Mind on fire and lungs burning, he wanted to rest. He knew he had to keep moving but for some reason he couldn't run. His chest felt tight, like someone was sitting on it. No matter how hard he gulped down the air, he couldn't take enough in.

Looking up, he saw nothing that reminded him of the human world; simply a wide-open space with a brightening, uninterrupted sky. The landscape seemed so still and unhurried, untouched by concrete and building. It just was. The ragged horizon of white peaks that stood behind him seemed like a menacing set of rocky gummed teeth.

He thought of a recent shark documentary he had seen with his family. He had been struck by the dead eyes and rows and rows of deadly white triangles that made these beasts so fearsome. There was an intensity of purpose about them, they were perfectly evolved to hunt and kill prey.

The mountains looked back at him impassively. He couldn't tell whether they too had the same dead eyes, the same hunger. Somewhere back there was his father, broken and in pain. He thought of injured seals and how they had no chance once the predator had locked on. He had to keep moving.

The light of the day was beginning to strengthen. He had left the camp later than he had wanted to. Dad had stayed asleep, finally calm despite the pain. Normally things would run like clockwork on these trips, but this one had been different from the start. Fragments of the day before attacked his mind as he ran. The little moments that, in hindsight, now pointed towards why he was running.

Nothing had been easy yesterday. Everything was a struggle, as though some sort of invisible force had asked them not to continue. But they had ignored it, this deeper intuition. Wading against a relentless, sticky tide of deep snow, poor weather and fatiguing bodies. These extra challenges wove themselves into a heroic narrative for the day; details of an epic expedition for father and son to recount when back in the safety of civilised life. The harder things became, the better the story.

Jonno continued moving, following the subtle and dusty path between enormous boulders. The thin air meant he couldn't just go hell for leather, he had to be smart with his movements. If he hurt himself as well then that would surely be it, they would both be lost.

He thought of what awaited him back home; Macie, his beautiful but annoying little sister who he loved. He hadn't yet found a way of telling her. Mum, and her endless public support and generous nature. He had occasionally heard her arguing with Dad about whether this trip was safe. He had his final year of school coming up. This trip was meant to be a last hurrah before knuckling down for important exams.

Jonno could feel the tacit enormity of what was happening knocking on his young mind. Responsibility and its consequences were becoming real rather than just boring things that adults endlessly droned on about. He had to find help and had to find it quick.

His father was back there and he was hurt. Badly. It was early in the day yet the sun would be getting viciously strong soon. He was in a strange, foreign country whose language he didn't speak. He didn't know exactly where he was, and he didn't know exactly where he was going. He just knew that it was now up to him.

Jonno stumbled on a loose stone and went sprawling, just saving a potential concussion by throwing his hands out in front of him. Tears came to his eyes as his brain connected the image of grazed skin with burning pain. This was suddenly all very real.

Chapter One - Leaving Home

"Wakey wakey, Jonny. Time to get up, it's time to get moving." The shadow of his father loomed in front Jonno's sleep-deprived eyes. He wasn't sure if he was still dreaming. He felt like he was in a nightmare he could not escape from.

"Wheerrr, whaaaa, now... really?" he groaned.

"Yep. Time, tide and airplanes wait for no man!" Dad chirped.

"Even at this ungodly time in the morning you have something clever to say," Jonno muttered to himself.

The morning of the great trip had arrived; plotted and planned for almost six months. Endless evenings of looking at maps and 3D Google Earth, researching kit, Inca history and making travel plans had finished. This was it. The talking was over; the day had come to go to Peru.

Jonno had hardly slept that night. A disturbing anticipation had dogged his thoughts; it had been impossible to properly relax. Among images of missing the alarm (although he knew Dad would set at least five of them) and the last minute worries of what he needed to take in his rucksack - whether it was too heavy for him to feasibly carry, whether he had taken too much or too little, whether they had toilet paper in Peru.

He had been overseas before, but never transatlantic. He knew that he should have been excited. This was a great opportunity, as everyone kept telling him, but he didn't feel it. His mates were off to the south of Spain this holiday, and even though it was a camp, he didn't want to lose out by not being with them.

Big stuff happens in your teens, he thought, *I don't want to miss any of it*. But his dad had been insistent. In fact, the build-up to this trip was possibly the most he had talked with his dad. That was a big part of the appeal.

Jonno rubbed his eyes. It was dark outside, and there was a stillness in the air. The world had yet to start its day. He felt a strange sense of this being a small secret: he and his father slipping out of comfortable suburbia under cover of darkness to fly across the Atlantic. The adventurous side of him began to win the battle for his heart and mind, defeating the terrified and hesitant side that he liked to keep hidden. A proper adventure, a real chance to do something that would make people listen to him!

He checked his phone. No messages of goodbye or good luck yet. *People must be waiting for before the plane leaves,* he thought. *Anyway Peru is bound to have Wi-Fi.* The main research he had done for the trip was whether there would be internet connection in the places they were staying.

It was 4 a.m. and the plane was leaving in five hours, though the taxi was arriving in half an hour. Jonno stumbled out of his room, heading for the bathroom. Half asleep, he pushed against the bathroom door, expecting it to give. But it didn't. He whacked his forehead against it with a loud "bang!"

"I'm in here," yelled Macie from inside, "why are you banging on the door?"

"Oh, come on Macie," barked Jonno, annoyed that his little sister would choose now of all moments to use the toilet.

"You can't rush these things," she sniggered back.

"Even today, you find a way to annoy me."

"Oh, get over yourself, Edmund Hilary."

"When are you just going to grow up!?"

"When you get a life!"

'Stop it, you two." The soft but strong frame of their mother appeared in the dimmed hallway, wrapped in her dressing gown. "For goodness sake, be quiet. You'll wake the neighbours!"

"But mum..." Jonno whined, "I need a shower."

"You always need a shower," called Macie. "You stink." He heard laughter mixed in with the flush of the toilet. Part of him hoped the flush might take her away as well.

There was a "*click*", and the door opened. Macie emerged, beaming, at the disruption she had caused her humourless and ungrateful older brother. Jonno thought back to how he and Macie had been practically inseparable when they were in junior school. They did everything together.

Now they couldn't be any more different. She had become the enemy, always teasing him, making fun of his attempts to be a man. He didn't give her the pleasure of eye contact as he walked head-down into the bathroom.

A quick shower later, he was changed and downstairs. His new rucksack was sitting on the kitchen floor. It had taken him an age to pack, deciding which clothes he needed and which he didn't. His favourite white surfing t-shirt hadn't made the cut; it was just too precious. Once packed, his heart both leapt and tensed up at the same time: this was really happening. The bag seemed full, not only of both clothes and kit, but also of adventure. As though sitting inside its cleverly stitched seams was a story that would soon be told.

His mother broke his concentration with a hug. "I love you so much," she told him. He was always amazed at how easy it was for her to say this.

"Thanks Mum, I love you too," he murmured, the final words seemed to congeal in his throat.

He saw Macie glaring at him. "Bye then," she said.

"Bye, Mace," he whispered. He wanted to say how much he loved her but it was just too complicated. He didn't want her to win. Not even with a hug.

"Give your sister a hug please, Jonny. Be the bigger person." Dad beamed, "You're *the* older brother, remember."

Jonno wasn't sure what annoyed him more: having to give his sister the satisfaction of victory, or the ever-present smile on his father's face. *Once again Dad does the right thing.*

He leaned forward and awkwardly put his arms around his younger sister. She softened in his embrace and whispered, "Please be careful. I really do love you, you know."

Caught off guard, he didn't know what to say and so just squeezed a little tighter. It felt good to give Macie a hug, Jonno couldn't remember the last time he had, but his throat was still dry and no words could come.

An awkward silence descended and seemed to drag on before it was mercifully broken by his dad's phone ringing. The taxi had arrived.

"Time to saddle up, Jonny," his dad jolted him on the shoulder. Jonno's thoughts drifted to a time when he used to love hearing his father say this, when they hiked and camped up in Scotland. There was a time when there was no better man than his father in the whole world, when there was nothing this superhero of a man couldn't do. Now most of what he said seemed to jar and grate, and this morning was no different.

Jonno pulled back from Macie, looking her in the eyes for a split second before dropping his gaze and moving to his mother. Macie had tears in her eyes, but she too was doing her best to look away, trying to hide her vulnerability, a little too late.

His mother came over and took him in her arms. "Good luck," she smiled through her own tears, "please come back safely. We love you both so much." Jonno felt so secure in her arms and partly wondered if he needed to go to Peru. But it was his mother that finally let go of him, and stepped back to say goodbye to Dad. "Please be careful over there James, no unnecessary risks. Mountains are dangerous places, there's no glory in being left on—"

"Please don't worry," said Dad putting his hand on her shoulder, "we've done the research, I'll be making the decisions, we'll be just fine." This felt like a slightly odd answer. Yet another of his father's seemingly generic cold responses to her that had become almost regular in months since Jonno's grandfather had died.

The taxi *beeped* from outside, breaking the moment. "Long goodbyes are expensive," his dad tried to joke, "taxis don't wait around for free!"

Jonno hiked his rucksack off of the floor. Heavier than he remembered, he almost lost balance as he heaved it onto his shoulder, sending the meat of the pack crashing into Macie.

'Some traveller you are," she sniggered. She regretted it later that day.

With a scowl, Jonno and his cheery father walked through the front door, put their things in the taxi, and quickly disappeared into the hushed pre-dawn, suburban morning.

Mum grabbed Macie and buried her in a huge but soft embrace. "Don't worry, Mace, he does love you, he just doesn't know how to say it."

Macie collapsed into her mother's arms, warm tears spilling down onto her mother's shoulder. As she began to regain her breath and settle, she heard the sound of a gentle sobbing that was not hers.

Chapter Two - Taxi Ride

Dad rode in the front, Jonno in the back. He couldn't help noticing how shiny and clean the leather seats were. The cab had a strange smell, an odd mix of new and old. It was a powerful car, and soon they were on the motorway heading for the airport.

Jonno looked out of the window at the changing scenery. A hazy blue light was appearing on the horizon as the sun neared the skyline. He had never seen the daybreak from a taxi window and this was what his dad had spoken so much of in the last few weeks. He went on about how amazing the mountains are at sunrise, the way the light creeps stealthily in and hits the white jagged peaks, setting them on fire. The pinks, the blues, the oranges. It sounded so exciting, the artist in him was looking forward to seeing these colours for himself. He wasn't sure about the climbing bit and how hard that was going to be, but the scenery, everyone kept telling him, will change his life. Whatever *that* meant.

The driver hit the brakes, jolting Jonno from his thoughts. He began to tune in to the conversation happening in the front; it all seemed quite excited. Dad had recently won a prestigious award for his contributions and advancement to surgery, and it looked like the taxi driver had recognised him from the local paper.

It was a familiar story for Jonno, being the son of the famous surgeon. "Oh you're Mr Cooper's son, how is your father? Please pass him my regards," was a very regular conversation in his life.

His dad was basically a hero, a hard-working surgeon who had changed and improved the lives of so many people. He worked in orthopaedics and had become one of the premier doctors in the country, with a private waiting list of six months. Though he still worked for the NHS a couple of days per week to "make sure he *remembered* his roots."

People loved Mr Cooper. He was talented, hard-working and charismatic: people were putty in his hands. Not to mention he was supremely clever, keeping himself at the forefront of his field by researching and writing papers. He was always winning an award for one thing or another.

Jonno was proud of his dad. But he was now finding himself in a tricky and argumentative situation with him. The heroic father of his youth had seemed to morph without warning into this grey workaholic who was rarely at home. He had really worshipped him when he was younger, looking up to him both physically and in terms of respect. He had loved being associated with a man that everyone loved.

But just like with Macie, things had changed in the last few years. Jonno had grown taller and was now almost at eye level with his father. Not only that but he was increasingly aware of his father's absence. He might be around on the odd Sunday, but then Dad was either tired or working on something important. Jonno could hardly remember the last time they did anything fun together.

In many ways the last nine months had been the worst. Jonno's recent report had indicated a growing lack of focus, something that his father had not reacted well to. While Mum was always there as a listening ear, he had begun to pine for some sort of older figure who could show him what becoming a man meant.

"You feeling excited Jonny?" his dad turned his attention to the back seat.

"Yeah... really excited, Dad," Jonno answered mechanically, "It's gonna be amazing."

He *was* starting to feel excited. He had a deep sense of excitement growing in his chest, but the butterflies were also dancing and weaving pretty patterns.

"But I feel pretty nervous as well," he bravely volunteered, "no idea what to expect. I've heard so much about Peru from you, and it sounded like you had such a good time all those years ago. It'll be great to meet the locals, I hope I have some time to draw and photograph them."

"That would be brilliant," added Dad, "you're good at that. Maybe I could join you?"

"I'd love that," said Jonny, caught slightly off-guard. He hadn't shared his artwork with his dad for quite some time, never sure if he was ever actually interested. *Maybe this trip is going to be OK.*

"You're an artist?" Piped up the cabbie, "what do you draw?"

"Oh, anything really, whatever is interesting." Jonno felt a bit embarrassed talking about his artistic interests with another older man, a stranger at that. He had hoped the conversation was going to be about the disastrous World Cup qualifier last weekend or something to do with Theresa May's latest horror show in Brussels.

"Go on," the cabbie turned down the radio.

"Well, I love to draw faces—and landscape type stuff, you know? I got into photography as well... we've got the good camera haven't we Dad?"

"Yep, in the bag you almost put Macie in hospital with! I hope you can carry that thing. These mountains don't have chair-lifts you know."

Jonno flushed, he felt a bit silly in front of the taxi driver, although he was loving this new form of conversation with his dad.

"I never went to Peru me, but I imagine you'll get loads of chances to do that over there," said the driver.

"I feel pretty nervous about the mountains, though," Jonno, starting to feel safe, allowed himself to continue this rare moment of public honesty, "apparently it will be just out of season when we go, meaning that there might be more snow than normal. The last time we went to the Cairngorms it was pretty snowy, wasn't it, Dad? That was tough. I got so cold!"

"Yes, but think, 'out of season' means we'll have the mountain to ourselves. Father and son climbing together, it'll be amazing. And the views from the top, we'll have them all to ourselves too. It's good that you're nervous, Jonny, shows that you have respect for what you're doing."

"But do you think it'll be OK? I was reading online the other day"

"It'll be absolutely fine," Dad interrupted, almost sternly, aware that the someone else was listening in to the conversation.

Jonno didn't bother replying. He knew that tone of voice. It meant things were not up for discussion. End of story. He had often wondered if this was a voice he used at work, when making important decisions

The glassy *ping* of the indicator brought his eyes back to focus. Signs for Heathrow appeared. They were getting closer.

Jonno, deep down, desperately wanted to be close to his father, to be respected and be his equal. Yet his father was a man of science, a man of answers. Jonno was choosing an artistic route and he felt an anxiety that his father might not approve. But Dad had never said anything one way or the other; it was the silence that disturbed Jonno the most.

As the cab drew up to the airport, he caught his father's eye in the mirror and he grinned back at him. "Vamos amigo, let's go!"

Chapter Three - Macie Saying Goodbye

I wish I could go with them. Mum says I'm not old enough. The classic excuse. I mean I'm nearly 13! Why isn't that enough for them? Anyway, me and Jonny used to do everything together, why has that changed recently? Mum and Dad keep calling it "maturing," something about the ways our bodies have changed has meant that we're becoming different from each other.

I have such happy memories and love him so much, but the last two years have been much harder. Ever since he suddenly got tall and could really look down at me, I don't feel like he is the same brother anymore. And he talks to me less, he smiles less, he doesn't ever seem to look at me anymore. I don't understand how it has all changed. I miss him. I don't know where he has gone.

And Mum looks sad too. Ever since Grandpa died, she and Dad don't seem so happy. They're very quiet together. Dad has been grumpy since, I haven't heard him laugh much.

I loved Grandpa but he's gone now, what can we do? I liked the way he would let me sit with him by the fire and ask me to tell stories about my favourite things. He would just smile and let me talk. I loved that.

And climbing mountains? I'd like to do that. Annabelle says her dad's happiest when he climbs. I hope it makes Dad and Jonny happy. Mum says men like climbing mountains, that it helps them feel confident. She says that men need to feel confident to be happy. And if they are not happy and feeling strong in themselves, then that can lead to lots of trouble.

Mum says men love winning. More like whining, if you ask me.

Men are strange I think, they seem to want different things to women. I'm not sure what, but they definitely do. Me and Jonny used to feel like the same person, when we were little. Like being a boy or a girl didn't matter. But now he is tall and his voice has changed, I feel different to him. I've changed a bit too, my body is becoming more like a woman Mum says, which makes me feel a bit shy. It's a bit annoying actually, I wish we could just be the same again, then I might have been able to go on this trip!

Chapter Four - Airport

The airport was unbelievably busy, and it was only half five in the morning. People of all shapes and sizes were spilling out of its seams. There were flights to practically all corners of the world. And then the queues: lines upon lines of people brandishing large cases and paper-cupped coffees for the long day ahead.

Jonno wondered if he had ever seen so many people in all his life. He had been to Paddington Train Station in London which pretty much blew his mind when he was 14, but this was on a completely different scale.

Looking around, he couldn't help but be intrigued by the different faces and ways people dressed. He was enthralled by the different appearances of the human body. He thought of a potential art project: photographing people from different cultures in black and white and asking them about their travels.

Some looked free and relaxed, others looked strained and hurried. Most, if not all, had the tell-tale marks of the 21st century; earphones in, smartphones gripped in clawed hands. There was a blankness about many of them, as though they were here only in body but not in mind, as though their phones were taking them for a walk, dragging them along by the hand.

Dad is really critical of smartphone culture, Jonno thought, *that people have lost their brains to them*. In moments like this he wondered, begrudgingly, if his father might have a point. The effect phones had on people was one of utter hypnosis.

He saw his dad coming back from the toilet, walking with his head held up, and taking in the world around him. Jonno couldn't help but admire his father's public persona. He seemed to wear an almost perma-grin something that wasn't always there at home. Yet in the outside world he gave off the aura of a man who knew what he was doing and that he enjoyed doing it.

Even though he must have felt tired, from a distance he looked alert and ready. Despite his greying hair, he still looked strong. His chestnut brown eyes looked intensely at his surroundings, his shoulders were wide and his arms had shape. Admittedly, there was a hint of fullness in the tummy and a softening of his clean shaven jawline, both of which Dad hoped to sort out on this adventure.

His fitness had taken a back seat recently, under work constraints and the loss of his own father. His face had aged, some of the lines by the corners of his eyes becoming deeper. One evening, months ago, Jonno thought he had caught a glimpse of true sadness in his father's eyes. As though something was missing.

There was so much he wanted to talk to his father about, but he had a way of dodging anything personal. His default position was that he was *"Fine, life is OK"* and that there were *"people worse off than us, so what is there to complain about*?" These stock answers had the deadening effect of shutting down a conversation rather than opening one up, which often left Jonno feeling cold when he wanted to explore more difficult topics with him. He was used to it now, but on occasion it made him mad that he couldn't be completely honest with his father.

"Oof, not a moment too soon," his dad grinned, "that's definitely one thing that'll be interesting over there. The state of the toilets. Enjoy these ones while you can. You can't flush the toilet paper over there, their pipes are too thin. If you do, it blows their system!"

"Seriously?"

"Yeah, it tends to freak people out to begin with. I mean, it's a pretty unpleasant sight."

"Gross. So, someone has to clean that?"

"Certainly do."

"Urgh."

Let's find our queue, we've made great time so no stress, just the way I like it." His dad smiled, more to himself than anyone "There it is, Block Q, Delta Airlines to Houston. Leaving in three and a half hours. Let's go and get checked in."

"Did we really have to be so early?" Jonno muttered, "what are we going to do for so long?"

"Don't start." His dad raised his chin, rounded his shoulders and began to make his way towards Block Q.

Jonno was entranced by the variety of people he saw on the way. Dark skinned women wearing incredible, bright outfits, looking like they were going to a wedding. Wrapped in cheerful and lively material, they moved with such poise and elegance, despite their huge suitcases.

Then there was the cluster of lighter skinned men who he thought were from the Middle East, donned in long flowing white robes with headdresses. There was a simplicity about their outfits, the material shining brightly under the sterile airport lights.

Jonno looked at his own clothes; his quick dry hiking trousers, slightly worn boots and trusted dark camping hoodie. He was tall and thin, he had grown quickly over the last few years and his limbs felt stretched rather than compact. This gangliness had made it hard to look or feel good in any kind of clothing. His token effort was to spike his short dark brown hair at the front. This morning, he felt the epitome of comfy and practical, the nemesis of style and culture.

They found the queue and went straight at the front.

"You see?" beamed Dad, "no waiting around for us."

"Aren't we just going to be waiting somewhere else anyway?"

"Please don't try and be smart, we've got a long day ahead."

A smiling desk clerk beckoned them forward. "Both to Lima via Houston?" Jonno recoiled at how awake and ready for the day she was. His own lack of sleep was starting to kick in again.

"Yes, please," said Dad.

"Anything dangerous in your luggage?" She asked, handing them a sheet of paper with potential explosive items on it.

"Just this guy's artwork," Dad smirked, looking at Jonno.

"Dad..."

"Please sir, this is a serious question," the assistant glared.

"Ok, sorry, no. And we've done all the packing ourselves."

"Thank you. Okay, and you can pick your luggage up in Lima, no need to pick up in Houston."

"Thank you," Dad replied. Was he flirting? Jonno's fatigue went up a level, and he felt a gurgling nausea in the pit of his stomach.

Through the barriers, they joined another queue, this time for luggage x-rays. Watery, anaemic-looking men and women with dark bags under their eyes manned the equipment. There was a sternness to them and their dark, starched uniforms. It was impossible to work out whether they liked their jobs or not.

A loud man was aggressively directing the traffic to the various machines. Dad talked about how 9/11 had changed air travel, had made it into an exercise in herding people and making them feel scared. Jonno always thought that was a bit conspiratorial but now he

couldn't help notice how authoritarian these people were being, and how automated the whole thing felt. In this metallic, shiny world, being human was frowned upon.

He reluctantly took off his headphones, put his bag in a tray, and removed his belt, shoes and jacket. He padded across the floor and waited to be called through. A guard on the other side beckoned him forth, in a way that seemed to look at him but not see him at all. He walked through and positioned his legs, slightly wider apart than was comfortable, while the guards patted him down. Jonno felt a surge of embarrassment, being touched by another person so close to his privates. Without so much as a word of acknowledgment. "Clear, thank you."

Jonno moved on to collect his bag.

There was time to kill, so Dad decided to set up "base camp" in one of the bland restaurants. Feeling restless, Jonno went for a walk, leaving his dad to his coffee and whatever he was reading. He was still irritated that they had arrived in the airport so early. He wasn't in the mood for sitting, checking messages or reading; he was going to be doing that all day. He'd look for an electronics shop instead; maybe see what kind of gadget he could feasibly get away with asking for Christmas.

When he was a good distance from the table, he turned to have a look at their seats. His love of drawing relied upon an appreciation of perspective and form. As he looked at his dad now, from a different angle, he remembered his teacher's instructions to keep changing his perspective on a subject to try and understand it better.

Through the jungle themed restaurant, in beneath the sterile wooden designs and the thicket of uniform table booths he caught his father staring into space. His book was down, and he didn't seem to be looking at anything in particular. Just staring.

Jonno hadn't seen this blank look on father's face before. His eyes didn't have their usual brightness, instead there was a look of melancholy.

He looked again, as though to prove himself wrong, but he was unmistaken. The face was pale, and his shoulders showed none of their normal strength nor width; he looked shrunken. Jonno felt a pang, even from this distance, he could see that this was not just his father, but also a person in his own right. He wondered how much he really knew about his dad.

How much does he know about me? We always talk about success and making the world seem positive. But what about when things are tough?

Jonno thought of his grandpa and the sudden way he had died. Was this what dad was thinking about? Jonno loved his grandpa but he had never felt close to him, never felt like he was really there when they spoke; his mind was elsewhere. He had always thought that the relationship between his father and grandfather was always a bit odd. They used to make time for each other, but then it felt awkward when they were together. Hearing them talking on the phone was like listening to people who didn't really know each other. As though both were talking but it didn't matter if the other was there.

Jonno caught himself. *I'm only just 17, what do I know about these things?* he thought. *I've got my own stuff going on. Final year coming up, and A Levels, and at some point, I've got to think about university. I've no idea what I want to do, no clue.*

Jonno knew he didn't have the same decisiveness as his father, the ability just to make a decision and make the best of it. Occasionally he just wished someone could make the decisions for him.

As the worries of life began to rain down, Jonno reached for his headphones. Ears filled with *Radio* 1's dance offerings, he turned back into the airport, ready to go explore.

He took a seat next by one of the enormous windows with a view of the runways. The sun was up now, and the sky was clear and pale blue. Every now and then planes would defy the logical mind and roar off into the sky, unaware that their great bulk looked far too heavy for flight. And then another terrifying metal-winged tube would descend gracefully from the blue and come to a slow, dignified halt.

No matter how many times he saw this; there was always a sense of awe and wonder. He often had thoughts like this, times when everyday things would stop him in his tracks. But he struggled to communicate this properly and ended up sounding naïve or silly. He had gotten used to keeping these sorts of things to himself to save embarrassment.

He closed his eyes for a moment, resting them from the incessant light of the windows. His head grew heavy, and he rested it for moment on the back of the chair.

"Jonno! Where have you been!?"

A strong hand was shaking his shoulder.

"Uh... wha... who..."

"Come on! For crying out loud, I've been looking for you for the last half-hour! You didn't answer your phone; you didn't come back to the booth. They're calling our flight! What are you playing at?"

Jonno opened his eyes to see his angry, red-faced dad. He checked his watch, "Oh God, I must have dozed off."

"You can be so irresponsible sometimes, Jonno," his dad said through clenched teeth, trying to hide his anger from passers-by.

'Sorry Dad, we've still got time though, haven't we?"

"That's not the point. Why are you sleeping over here? I might not have found you!"

"Why did we have to get up so stupidly early then?"

"Watch your mouth! Come on, get up. We're moving."

Jonno rubbed his eyes and stretched. These were the moments he was dreading. He knew there would be friction between the two of them. He didn't like the way his dad had caused such a fuss; they still had an hour, after all. It wasn't the first time he had done this, either. *He can get so uptight when things aren't done his way.*

Maybe Spain would have been more fun.

Still in a mood, Jonno spent the rest of the morning on his phone. It was easier that way. The departure gate was filling up when they arrived. They queued for the plane, showed their passports, and moved into the tunnel. But as the whining of the engine overpowered the music in his ears, he suddenly felt another flutter of excitement in his chest, and reflexively wanted to reach out to his dad and say thank you for organising everything.

Then he remembered that he was still annoyed and purposefully kept his gaze on the floor.

'Seats 23 A and B? Across the centre, sirs, and on your left."

And with that, the two men boarded, carrying not only their carry-on bags but also, unbeknownst to each other, plenty of extra weight about their own respective fathers.

Chapter Five - Ben, 23C

Gosh, what a morning. Saying goodbye to everyone and trying to make the plane on time. First day of the rest of my life, this; been looking forward to this trip for years. Been tough to say goodbye, though. I'm going to be gone for a while.

This trip hopefully holds answers to questions I've run out of steam trying to answer. I couldn't cope with the work anymore; never wanted to be involved in law anyway. Mum and Dad were so insistent that I should do it, to be like Dad. They paid for everything, but I hated it. I was miserable. Handing in my notice never felt so good.

The counselling really helped though. It's probably thanks to that that I'm here now.

Hopefully this'll give me some time to think. I feel like I've never really made any decisions for myself up until now. Being academic made things easy. I loved the status and praise that came with it. Who wouldn't in their early twenties? But it was hollow. Important, yes, but it lacked something real. These last few years spending, drinking, partying was all to escape the fact I didn't like what I was spending my time doing.

It's such a relief to have this year ahead to just see some of the places I've always dreamed of. No more excuses.

Just being on the plane is an experience. I wonder why these other people are travelling. The passengers next to me... a funny pair those two, the way they came on the plane. The older one, I guess the dad, smiling at everyone being friendly and jovial, while the younger one dragged his feet.

For all the bonhomie of the older man, there's little interaction between the two of them. The dad looks in control and confident, a people person. He was polite when he asked me to let them past. The younger one, music blaring, barely made eye contact, mumbling something resembling "thank you". Poor old Dad. I bet this trip won't be easy for him. No wonder he's by the window, could be a long flight.

Sometimes these trips come too early for people. Now, in my thirties, I can appreciate this journey. I'm not sure what I would have made of it as a teenager. At least this boy's dad wants to do these things with him, I guess. Dad was only ever interested in work. I almost fell for it as well, his world of endless hunger to be the best.

That kid should be grateful that his dad isn't like that.

Chapter Six – Flight and Stopover in Atlanta

The flight to Atlanta was uneventful. Jonno was crammed between his father and a man who seemed uninterested in his fellow passengers.

Occasionally Jonno took the chance to stretch his legs and walk up the gangway. He saw some air stewards grabbing a rare moment to chat to each other while preparing drinks. He was impressed by their immaculate uniforms. They made the job look fun and effortless, as though nothing was too much trouble, but he noticed they were not always spoken to with much respect.

It was as though some passengers felt they had the right to look down on them because they were paying customers. *I bet that gets irritating,* he thought.

But when he saw them laugh and joke their eyes sparkled and their faces crinkled with pleasure as though the smooth mask they normally wore had slipped, revealing a richly textured interior. He thought of his grandmother's favourite mantra: *"We are just people trying our best. Don't be fooled by how any of us look."* She would remind Jonno of this whenever he admitted to worrying about others' impressions of him, or how people always looked so much more in control.

Grandma would just smile and tell him to look deeper than the first layer. *"Don't always trust your eyes,"* she would offer. This always confused him, how could he ever draw or paint if he didn't trust what he was seeing?

When Jonno got back to his seat, he found some pale green cards awaiting him. He took it as a chance to break the silence with his dad.

"What do I do with these?"

"Simple, just fill in the relevant sections. Hang onto it until customs."

"OK, great, but it's just..."

"Just what?"

"Well some of the questions are a bit odd...."

"Are they?" His dad sat upright to have a look.

"Well there is one here that ask if I've ever *been convicted of an offence or crime involving moral turpitude...* I'm not sure, have I?", asked Jonno, trying hard to keep his face straight.

"Ah, well we did find you downstairs watching television at three in the morning when you were 10. That was pretty scandalous. Then there was the time you mercilessly hid all of Macie's socks!"

"So, do I put yes to that then?"

"On your conscience if you don't."

"And what about if I was *associated with the Nazi Party or involved in genocide*?"

"Were you?"

"Not between 1933 and 1945, no."

"Well then, tick 'no'."

"And am I a drug abuser?"

"You like drinking Coca Cola..."

"Oh man, I might not get past the States. You're going to have to go on without me."

"Like I keep telling you Jonno, the decisions you make in life will always come back to find you at some point. So be sure to keep making good ones."

They both broke into laughter. Jonno loved this side of Dad; fun and imaginative. This was the man he had grown up with. He felt strangely safe with him when he was like this, as though anything was possible. Since Grandpa's stroke, a lot of this man had vanished.

It had all been so sudden. One minute they were paying him a visit for his birthday, the next he was in a critical condition in hospital, and then dead. Gone, just like that. He was the second person Jonno had known to die. The first had been Grandma when he was much younger; he remembered that she had been ill before passing away, but he had been too young to really understand what that meant.

Yet Grandpa's death had shocked him deeply; how sudden it had all been. He didn't ever feel like he knew his grandfather that well. He was a man of few words but seemed to have a very strong and powerful presence. He had been a popular and well-known man. He seemed to have a drive to be the best, never satisfied. *When he did speak it normally involved asking how I could improve what I was doing*, thought Jonno. But rarely did he offer a simple "well done".

Dad hardly ever talked about him now. Jonno wanted to bring him up and ask Dad how was, but it never seemed like the right time.

Upon landing, the plane taxied slowly toward the airport. Jonno looked at his dad and saw a small grin dawning around the corners of his mouth. Although his eyes seemed to be looking into the middle distance, he could see there was an excitement in them.

It was the longest period of time he had spent in such close proximity with his father for quite a while. It had gone okay; they hadn't fallen out or disagreed heavily. In fact, it had been more silent than he had anticipated. Jonno had noticed his dad was happy to be quiet and reflective, content to read, listen to music or just doze. He seemed to come to life when the staff offered him a drink or food, bringing out his familiar energy and charm, but when they had gone, he would rest back into his seat.

Jonno, hadn't felt that talkative himself. He sensed the brooding presence of the passenger to his left, feeling a sense of discomfort and lack of privacy having him so close. Even though the stranger spent most of the flight asleep or watching the in-flight entertainment, Jonno had the strangest feeling that he was also being studied.

As the plane came to a halt, the atmosphere switched from sedate to bustling as passengers sprung to their feet, grabbing at bags and rushing for the exit. Jonno saw one man wrench his bag from the top locker with such force that it flew out and caught another passenger on the shoulder. The two looked at each other with a combination of surprise and aggression.

"I'm so sorry," the hasty passenger seemed to say. "That's okay," the other mouthed, his eyes not matching his face.

Jonno thought it best not to join the stampede there was no point adding another set of flailing limbs to the ever-decreasing space.

Finally, when the plane had started to clear, Jonno stood up and stretched his legs. It felt good to be upright again and with some space to move. He reached for both his and Dad's bags.

"Thank you, Jonny," his dad yawned, stretching his arms wide. "How was the flight?"

"A bit long and cramped but okay. I don't think I've ever been on such a long journey before. Makes you think how big the world must be if it took 10 hours to get *here* and we're not even *there* yet."

"Wait for the bus journeys over there, that's another story all together."

"What was the longest one you ever went on?"

"Oh, once we travelled from Quito to Lima. My God, it was two separate buses of 16 hours each, back to back, with a five-hour stop at the border in the middle. Two nights on a bus. The worst part was I had just bought a pair of traveller-type trousers as I wanted to look the part. Very tight, very itchy, and *not* breathable. Pretty sure they harmed my chances of ever having future children."

"Dad!" Jonno laughed.

"Horrendous. There was no air con and the windows hardly opened. It's amazing, some of the life lessons that travel teaches you, and they're not always what you might be expecting."

It was good to hear his dad open up a little. Jonno didn't know much about his father before he had started a family. He found it surreal and slightly mind-bending to think of his father as a young person just like him, a young man with his own life and thoughts. He had always thought of his father as some sort of permanent edifice, strong and in control, occasionally too much so, but not as a wannabe hippy stuck sweating himself into infertility on-cramped South American buses.

In the airport, Jonno couldn't help noticing the size of people; their height, physique and waistlines. America seemed like a land of giants, and him and his father seemed so small in comparison.

Not that they were all obese, as everyone loved to say, but everyone and everything just felt bigger. Men dressed in black, holding guns, were directing traffic. Jonno had never seen a gun in real life, and he found it hard not to stare. They were so powerful and terrifying. *Do they really make you safer?*

The armed men seemed strong and tough, as though they had it all under control. They didn't talk much; their eyes locked in concentration. They were clean shaven, with short, neat hair, and smartly pressed uniforms. Jonno was reminded of *The Matrix* and Agent Smith searching for Neo. This was a welcome.

A star-spangled sign told of its pledge to *"cordially greet and welcome travelers to the USA"*, and that all would be treated with courtesy, dignity and respect. Yet the vast queues of people were being herded through like cattle, with little interaction or welcome. The sentries were intimidating rather than receiving, giving off the impression that everything would be fine as long as you did it on their terms. The "Land of the Free" was not feeling quite so free.

The queue thinned and finally it was their turn with the stern, pale man in the customs booth.

"Good morning sirs, and how are you today?"

"Good morning, fine thank you," Dad answered formally, "and, how are you?"

"Where are you going?" The man replied, ignoring Dad.

"To Lima, Peru," Dad replied, his body tightening.

"Father and son?"

"Yes."

"Nature of your business there?"

"To go to the mountains."

"How long will you be there?"

"Just over 3 weeks."

"Documents please."

There was silence as the man gestured for their passports. He looked down at their pictures, and then up to examine their faces. His blue, icy eyes met Jonno's in a detached stare. He looked down again before tapping something into the computer. He then paused, as though mulling over something very important.

He handed back the passports, hesitating just as Dad reached out to take them back. Slowly, quietly, with a peculiar mix of authority and southern drawl, he said, "I went to the mountains once, but they weren't for me. Now I go to the beach instead. Y'all be careful up there. Welcome to America, sirs."

And with that, he let go of the passports and looked over their shoulders to whoever was next in line. "Next!"

"What was all that about?" Asked Jonno, once he felt they had made safe distance from the booth.

"These people are crazy," Dad whispered. "Come on, let's move before they change their mind or start accusing us of moral turpitude."

They wandered through the polished and immense corridors of the airport, looking for their next flight.

While close to his mother, Jonno yearned for an older brother or another man who could give him some advice on how to be. The world of being a man felt strange and contradictory, on the one hand chasing success, fame, strength and on the other being asked to show more emotion and vulnerability. But in his groups of friends, being openly vulnerable always led to ridicule, which left him feeling confused.

He had so many questions about the world that he was afraid to ask, so many musings about how to behave, what he was meant to do, who he was meant to be attracted to. He felt he couldn't answer these on his own, but that his mother wasn't the right person to provide the answers or guidance. She was not a man, and while she repeatedly said that she understood men and how they thought, he had a strong suspicion that she did not.

He felt envious of her relationship with Macie, it seemed a lot more harmonious. Even if they bickered there was constant contact. Macie had her role model, Jonno felt at a loss for his.

Jonno at least knew now that he didn't want to be a doctor, no matter how worthy a job it was. Not if it meant that he would have no life outside of it. No, there was too much to see in the world without being stuck indoors all day with the broken and unwell.

Jonno wanted to create, not fix. Hopefully this trip would afford the opportunity to finally tell Dad this. But the thought still made him anxious. Would he still gain his father's pride? Respect? Even, paradoxically, have his father look up to him?

He wanted his actions to have impact and meaning, he wanted to hold his own in the world. It was all so confusing; there was a building pressure to become *someone*. But who?

***

They settled in one of the coffee shops, putting their backs to the wall so they could people-watch.

"Are you excited Dad?" Jonno ventured. The question fell from his mouth.

"How do you mean?"

"Well, you know, the trip, the holiday, the adventure, the coffee? I dunno..."

"Yes! Of course." Dad slightly blurted out the words. "It's wonderful to be able to do this. To have this much time off from work is a rare thing these days."

"Do you like work?" Again, the words seemed to accidentally slip from Jonno's tongue.

"Do I like work?" his father looked at him incredulously, "whatever do you mean?"

"Sorry..." Jonno turned away from his father's strong gaze. "I just mean, what's work like? I just wanted to know a little more, that's all."

"My work is a great privilege, Jonno. It's a great honour to care for and help others. I work hard, and yes I stay late, but that's the sacrifice of joining the medical profession."

"Dad... I wasn't trying to get at you."

"Don't you let your mother get to you please, don't let her use you to get at me. I work jolly hard for everyone, all of us. Please respect that."

"I do, I really do Dad," Jonno felt the inside of his nose begin burn and his eyes heating up.

"Thank you. If I can be honest with you, I don't want to talk about that right now. If anything, I just want to enjoy this coffee."

Jonno felt cold, this had completely caught him off guard. He had pushed his luck too far. Why did he ask about work? Feeling slightly sick, he clamped his headphones back on and buried himself in his phone.

Now and again he would look up and see his father reading or watching the traffic. He remembered the advice of his mother: sometimes if things go wrong or backfire, it's better to do nothing. If you're lucky, they'll just fix themselves.

Jonno was surprised to hear both English and Spanish coming from the departure gate loudspeaker, having always thought of the United States as an English-speaking country.

"Are they speaking Spanish because we're heading to a Spanish speaking country?"

"America has a history with Mexico and the Spanish speaking world," his dad replied, almost relishing the chance to speak about something that might not cause an argument.

"Yeah, it's really interesting," his father continued, "I was reading somewhere that there about 40 million native speakers of Spanish here, not far off the size of Spain!"

"How come?"

"Well this is what I find interesting, it's a big part of their history. You see, back in around 1848, or so I was reading, there was a war with Mexico which resulted in the US winning almost 500,000 square miles of Mexican territory and making it part of America. States like California, New Mexico, Nevada and Utah all went from being part of Mexico to then being American. Can you imagine it? One day you are from one country, the next day you are from another! Of course it's never that simple and you cannot lose your cultural identity overnight, so there is a huge Hispanic influence in the States as a result. There has been a lot of immigration from the Latin American worlds ever since. "

"So what, one day people were Mexican, the next day they were American?"

"Something like that, yes"

"But that's mad, how does that work?"

"Well, not always smoothly is the best answer. A massive land grab, essentially, and the people just came with it."

"But you can't just be Mexican one day and not the other, surely?"

"Exactly, it's an intriguing idea isn't it? That one day you can be from somewhere, the next from somewhere else."

"I can't really get my head around it."

"Makes you think about countries and who is really from where? What does a passport mean? Think of Britain, who is from Britain? Someone with a British passport? But Britain was only created as a political entity in 1707, not that long ago relatively speaking. So what does that make of the Welsh, Scottish, Northern Irish and English all sharing the same country. And then what of the many immigrants who have come to live and make their homes there? Once they have their passports they too are entitled to say they come from Britain, even if their links to the land only go back a few generations. I think it's wonderful, all that diversity, it makes for a wonderful country to live in, but who is really *from* Great Britain? Especially when you think it is an island of people that have been conquered at least four times; the Romans, the Anglo Saxons, the Vikings and the Normans. That means we must be such a mix of peoples..."

Jonno had stopped listening. Occasionally he wondered if his dad needed him for these conversations or if he simply enjoyed going off on one. *Besides, the past was over, why did it matter anymore?* He had never had much time for history, too many dates to learn and too much looking backwards *What did it matter, these days, who was originally from where?*

The departure gate was busy and had a different feel to the one back at Heathrow. Jonno felt a small thrill looking around at his fellow travellers. The size of the people caught his attention; he suddenly had a sense of feeling tall. Walking among them, he did his best to look without staring. He saw people of dark and pale skin, and if he wasn't mistaken there was a hint of something almost oriental in their faces. Smooth skinned, mostly dark haired and in modern clothes.

For some reason he hadn't thought that Peruvians might wear similar clothes to himself. There were solo travellers and groups which looked like families, people with an air of wealth, and those who seemed poor. Some looked smart enough to be business men and others looked relaxed and casual. There was something disconcerting about the familiarity, though he wasn't sure why. It was as though part of his brain had built the trip up to be something incredibly different and other-worldly. In some ways this was true, but in many others, it wasn't true at all.

* * *

Chapter Seven – Elijah, Barista

Another day serving the travelling folk, seeing 'em all come and go. Y'know, they all love having a coffee or something before getting on their planes. I wish I could travel, that'd be nice. At least this job gets me closer to them planes. I got this job to get me closer to them planes, If I can't actually go then I might as well get some satisfaction from watching others go.

It's amazing how many people jump on these here planes, so many people wanting to travel. They say that the smoke is starting to hurt the earth, making it sweat. Some folk get real angry saying it's all made-up, others get real angry saying no-one listening. I dunno who's right and who's wrong, but I do know them engines make one helluva racket noise when they take off and land. I hear them from my house at night. Sometimes, when I can't sleep, I hear 'em. But them people obviously need to travel, they need to move. I know I can't stay still for too long, makes my mind go a bit crazy. I guess there must be some type of freedom in moving around. Maybe we feel like we being locked up when we sit too still for too long. I never left the States yet; I don't know no-one outside these borders. We only got Mexico and Canada next door. Too much the same to the north and too much difference to the south. I'm happy here I say, stick with what I got.

I sometimes watch the folk have their coffee and try and work out who they are, where they going, what they moving from. Sometimes it's real clear, other times I ain't got no clue who's who. Take these two sitting over there, I reckon they must be father and son or something like that. They look real familiar to each other. The younger boy, he got the same features as his old man. They come in smiling and looking real light and all, but then they sit down and he says something to his old man and it all changes. Temperature kinda goes a bit cold between them. I couldn't see all of it because missy over here was getting kinda irate about how much change I gave her, so I had to concentrate. But then I saw them just sitting and not talking. Looks like one got offended with the other, but hard to tell who. Then the look on their faces, like the milk in their drink went sour or something.

Reminds me of my daddy, how he used to beat on me and Momma. We could never say anything right to him, he just had some temper. I thank God every day he left us when he did, we couldn't take it no more. I still wish I had a daddy though, even though I love my momma so, she amazing and all that. But it's not the same when you only have one to raise you, it's like you missing something. They say single mommas ain't good for society, that their children get brought up all broken, get brought up all angry an' all. I don't think it's the fault of single mommas though, they ain't breaking no one. It's the daddy that does all the breaking. But I ain't angry, I can tell you that, but I still feel like something ain't there, like a part of me never happened. There's only so much you can learn from your momma how to be a man. The rest, you gotta just work it out, and that's the tough part now, cos I ain't so sure how to do it.

I see them two and I just hope they can mend it, whatever it is that's making them sad. The older man, he looks real preoccupied by something, he just looks ahead but not at all at anything in particular. The younger one, well he just keeps looking at his daddy like he trying to work him out or something. I can't work out where they from. I like to play that game. I can see they ain't from Japan, that's for sure. Although they might be, I ain't never been there, how do I know what every Japanese person look like?

Well I wish 'em well, I wish everyone and their daddies well. There not a day gone by when I wish it had been different, when I don't think how much better it would have been if I had had a proper daddy. Y'know a daddy to teach me stuff, how to be a man an' all. But for now, I gotta work that part out for myself. Some days it make sense, others I ain't got no clue. This job keeps me plenty busy though, gives me time to make some moneys and think about what I want. These travel people love their coffee, so I get to meet and say hello to a lot of people. I like to think I play my part in getting them from A to B. One day maybe someone like me will get *me* a coffee, when I have to go somewhere exotic. That'd be real swell.

* * *

Chapter Eight – Arriving in Lima

'Señores y señoras, pasajeros y pasajeras, bienvenidos a Peru. Bienvenidos a Lima!"
"Ladies and Gentlemen, welcome to Peru, welcome to Lima!"

The words sizzled through the plane's already electric atmosphere. Only minutes before, applause and whoops of joy had greeted the landing of the plane. Jonno hadn't been expecting that, in fact he had never even heard of that being done before. He looked at his father who just shrugged his shoulders and smiled. He didn't try and give an answer or an explanation, but instead joined in. Jonno imagined applauding the bus driver or train driver every time people got to their destination, or even applauding his mum or dad next time they drove him somewhere. Maybe Macie could be trained to applaud him every time he entered the house. He laughed to himself as he collected his bags from the overhead locker.

The journey had felt long and wasn't as comfortable as the first flight of the day. There had been no personalised in-flight entertainment, and he found it harder to get settled. The thought of actually being in Peru was beginning to make him feel nervous. He had heard so many stories about South America and rumours that Lima could be dangerous. It was one thing to say you were going somewhere but something else entirely to actually *go.* He had read about Lima's shanty towns in Lima, which held almost 35% of the population with some residents earning as little as $250 US per month. Jonno thought of the bike his parents that had bought him last Christmas which cost over twice that amount.

He was out of his comfort zone with his lack of Spanish, and he begrudgingly admitted that he was going to have to rely on his dad – something he had been proud of avoiding over the last few years. Dad had passed the flight chatting to a Peruvian chap on their row. Ernesto, he was called, and he was apparently coming back from the States visiting his brother who had emigrated there. He worked in Lima in a bank and was glad to be coming back. He said the American food was not as good as at home and he missed eating fresh fish! He lived with his whole family, children and parents. Family was really important to him, as was dancing salsa. He even offered Jonno and Dad to come and stay but Dad politely declined. Jonno's mind boggled, since when did strangers ever offer anyone to come and stay?!

They disembarked into the cold, damp Lima night air. Jonno drew in a big breath, his first in Peru, and felt energised. They were here now, finally.

He looked out over the landscape and saw twinkling orange lights in the distance. *Who lives out there?*

They clambered down the rickety metal steps and–boarded the arrivals bus. Everybody crammed in, the bus lurched off, sending its occupants flying into each other; Jonno was surprised to see the passengers smiling to one another and laughing it off, something that would never have happened on the tube.

The stories that his dad had told him, had conjured up the image of some sort of Latino Wild West, but the airport seemed up-to-date and slick, even if the wall were butterscotch colour.

On the approach to the immigrations queue, Dad could barely hide his smile. His eyes were taking in the surroundings, but also seemed to be looking at something beyond the walls of the airport.

"Excited to be back Dad?"

"Very. Part of me wondered if I ever would," he replied.

"How come?"

"I don't know, I guess life has moved on so much, and I wasn't sure if I'd ever have the time again."

"You loved it here, right?"

"So much, this place totally set me on fire back then. But already it feels a bit different, like it's lost something. The airport seems a bit odd. I mean it feels modern, not quite as chaotic as I remember."

"Is that a bad thing?"

"Well, no, but it's different."

"But like you always say, nothing stays still forever."

"True," he sighed, "I can't argue." His words tailed off as though he wasn't only thinking about the airport.

Everywhere, signs showed a mixture of images. Some showed menacing military-type figures standing before huge words blaring out warnings about drugs, others depicted soaring Peruvian vistas – the mountains, the jungles, and the people.

Come and enjoy yourself and spend all your money, they seemed to say, *but we will make your life hell if we catch you doing anything we don't want.*

They waited by the bag carousel for longer than was comfortable before their rucksacks finally appeared. Jonno found that the zip on his was open, which was odd as he definitely remembered closing them all before leaving.

They exited the airport walking through the glass sliding doors to be met by a wave of official taxi drivers, all touting business. Big confident smiles, "Hello sirs, welcome to Peru... you speaking English... how can we help? ... good prices to Miraflores, central Lima."

Dad immediately started haggling with one of them for a price to the hotel. He seemed a little aggressive to begin with, suggesting a price far below the taxi driver's estimate. Eventually a combination of getting nowhere and Jonno's unimpressed expression persuaded him.

"OK, amigo... vamos."

"Very good sir, we go now."

And with that they followed the driver, a man named Manolo, through the main arrivals area. Jonno was struck by how many people were there. It was two or three bodies deep behind the barriers. A dizzying array of signs, people, banners and excited eyes barraged the over-travelled senses of anyone walking through the main doors.

Whole families waited, tense with excitement, for the arrival of a loved one. There were tears for the reunions and great shouts of joy when eyes had locked onto a familiar loved one. Great displays of emotion and affection seemed to accompany each meeting, nothing seemed as though it was held back.

For some reason, Jonno had felt tense about leaving the airport, as though he might be attacked or mugged in this new and strange land. But instead all he saw was happy people greeting other happy people.

They were taken to a stylish, fresh-looking white Hyundai, which looked to be in better condition than most cars on their street back in England. They both jumped in, Dad in the front and Jonno in the back, a mixture of excitement and exhaustion gripping them both. The travelling was done, they were here now, and it was beginning, the adventure that had been so long in the making.

The taxi pulled quietly out of the airport, and Jonno stared out of the window, trying to make sense of this new world he had arrived in. Dad was busy in conversation with Manolo, and Jonno didn't fancy trying to work out what they were saying, but the adrenaline of being somewhere new kept him alert and keen to stay awake.

The car pulled into the hectic Lima traffic and was almost collided into by a rickety local bus driving far too fast. It was lit up in bright neon lights, pumping rumbling smoke from its exhaust and blaring out vibrant salsa music. It was crammed inside, and a thin man with a young face stood by the door yelling *"Lima, Lima!"* to anyone and everyone in the outside world.

Manolo, seamlessly anticipating this kind of thing, gently moved the car out the way to let the bus pass. He turned to Dad and shook his head, "This is Leema, very crayzee people," before laughing and returning to Spanish.

Dad turned to Jonno and smiled, "I think it's actually improved since I was last here!"

Jonno sat back, unsure as to whether he *did* want to look out the window anymore. The traffic was firing along at an unusually fast speed, and the aggression on the roads combined with the pace unnerved him. At least another ten buses screamed past them on the way, some looking like they didn't have many journeys left in them. He noticed a crucifix swinging from the rear-view mirror and a picture of what must have been the Virgin Mary stuck near the dashboard. Just below her, on the glovebox, was a Real Madrid Football Club sticker. Jonno had heard that Peru was passionately Catholic. *No wonder,* he thought, *if they all drive like this.*

Religion had never really been part of his and Macie's upbringing, Dad always made a point of telling them that he believed in hard science and not in stories. Their parents said it was important to live a good and honest life, doing your best for those around you. But Dad bristled at the idea that people would give up responsibility for their own actions and ask God to sort it out for them. He thought it made people lazy and too fatalistic, as though they could just use God as an excuse for all the rights and wrongs in their lives. He believed in taking hold of yourself and not passing the responsibility on to someone, or something else.

As they drove, Jonno saw how relaxed his dad was in the front seat, the chaos of the traffic and manic overtaking didn't even seem to register with him. He was lost in conversation, relishing the chance to speak Spanish again after so long. While it didn't flow as well as his English, Manolo was patient and friendly with him. At some point he heard the inevitable "doctor" word, and the driver seemed to be impressed just like everyone back home was.

Jonno felt a familiar nausea in the pit of his stomach, he couldn't escape the power of his father. Here he was in the back seat in darkness while his father was having a laugh in front and gaining the respect of the driver. A part of him wanted to be in the front, the centre of attention, being respected. His gaze drifted back over the swinging crucifix, and he caught Manolo's eyes in the process. "You OK?" the driver asked.

"OK, thank you, gracias."

"Oh gracias, very gooood!" the man smiled, "Haha, you speaking Spanish now!"

"Haha, poco, poco," Jonno said, joining in.

"I think you like Peru very much," the man said, "you have good time here. Many nice beer, and Peruana chica verrrryyy beautiful."

"Oh, haha, I hope," Jonno replied, not really knowing what to say. He hadn't thought about this trip along those lines. He just smiled, hoping the darkness of the back seat would hide his blushing. He returned his eyes to the window, content to let his dad carry on without him.

Eventually they pulled up to a building on the corner of a well-lit street. Early morning air was still, despite the nearby dual carriageway. Across the well-maintained road was a bright Dunkin Donuts sign standing next to a Starbucks. On the car ride, they had passed a modern sports shop with an obscenely large picture of a preened Cristiano Ronaldo staring out the windows. Jonno wondered if he was hallucinating, perhaps his mind was superimposing some sense of familiarity onto this new world. Everything seemed far too normal.

Manolo got out the taxi and strode towards the metal fence surrounding the building. Barbed wire and shards of broken glass glittered from the top of the metal railings, which seemed a little excessive given how quiet this area was. He rang the buzzer but there was no answer.

"Is this the right place?" Jonno whispered to his dad still in the front seat.

"I hope so," his voice betrayed some elements of fatigue. "The driver seemed to know the address when I showed it to him."

Manolo rang the bell again and this time a very tired voice answered. After a brief exchange, the metal gate made a whirring noise and clicked open. Manolo came back with a triumphant look on his face.

"OK, señores, Casa de Miraflores. Aqui Estamos!"

"Dad?"

"We're here!"

"Fantastic," yawned Jonno, "I can't wait for my bed."

"Almost there now," said James gently.

They grabbed their bags from the boot and walked through the gate to be met by a small, soft faced man in pyjamas who looked half asleep. James turned to Manolo as though he was an old friend, smiling and thanking him, before paying him the agreed price.

Manolo shook James and Jonno's hands before heading

back to his car and quietly pulling off into the empty road. Jonno watched him through the slits in the fence before turning back to the man in his pyjamas.

He motioned for them both to come inside, still half-asleep. The hotel looked more like a modest square house than anything else. They walked through a dimly lit corridor into a main living area. A collection of eclectic artefacts hung on the walls, ranging from large spiders mounted in glass boxes to carved masks and spears. A selection of pan pipes hung behind an enormous plasma TV which was surrounded by DVDs. A battered copy of the *Economist* lay next to an issue of *Cosmopolitan* on a small coffee table. It all felt so familiar yet utterly bizarre to the travellers' sleep deprived minds.

The man led them up a narrow flight of creaking stairs whose dark green walls were adorned with a picture of the Virgin Mary. On the landing, they passed a small statue of a fat, smiling Buddha before reaching the door to their smallish en-suite room. There were two single beds.

"We're sharing?" asked Jonno, slightly bemused.

"Of course. What did you think, that you would have the presidential suite?"

"Well... I guess it never hurts to dream."

"Let's just get to bed. It's been a long day," replied James, whose resources of humour had seemingly run out.

"Good idea, I'm done."

The pyjamaed hotelier looked at James to see if he needed anything else. James smiled and shook his head, making the universal pillow sign with his hands pressed at the side of his head. The man nodded and left father and son in the room.

James placed his bags on the bed by the window, leaving Jonno no doubt as to which bed his bed was. Without a word, he opened his rucksack and pulled out the old t-shirt and shorts that he always slept in. The clothes were freshly washed, and as he quickly changed while his dad had his back turned, he caught an aching trace of home.

Jonno was under the duvet and asleep before his dad had the chance to tell him to pick up his discarded travel clothes and place them neatly somewhere else.

Chapter Nine – Manolo, Taxista

Here come the gringos, in their new and bright colours. They must have so much money to leave work and come here for so long. I know I love Jesus and his cross is in my car, but I find it hard not to mentally throw stones at these people. They come here and just take from us, like they've always done. More white people in the footsteps of Cortes and Pizarro, coming here for their own glory, nothing to do with us.

Then they have the *cojones* to argue with us about taxi money. We don't even set the price, but they still argue. Have they got any idea how hard it is to live in Lima these days? I've got my family to think of, every sol counts these days. It takes me most of the day just to get enough fares to pay off the car rental for the company I work for!

Look at these two, they've got all the mountain gear. Must be father and son. The boy looks scared and suspicious, glancing around everywhere. Apparently the guide-books warn gringos about the taxi men at the airports. *Madre de Dios!*

I miss the old life in the mountains, the life of the pueblo. The air was so clean, the white cumbres looking over us. Simpler times. Simpler than the dirt and grime of Lima now. This place is such a rat race, and we're all racing. But there was no money in the mountains, no security, only beauty. I'm not going to work in the fields, I don't want my children to be campesinos. They have a chance here; they can get the education I didn't. That's their only escape. I wish I had listened when our elders told us to go to school when I was younger. I love them so much, my hijos. I hope they don't think too badly of their padre being a taxista.

OK, this father speaks some Spanish, seems like a nice man. A doctor and a surgeon, he must help many people. He came here 20 years ago and wanted to bring his son. He even likes Roxette!

His son is quiet but he speaks no Spanish, so who knows what he thinks. OK, maybe I'll charge them the correct fair, no extra tax this time. What's life if we can't look after those who do some good?

Chapter Ten – First Morning

Jonno awoke with the sound of traffic in his ears. He had had a long, deep dreamless sleep but opened his eyes with no idea where he was. He sat up in bed and looked around. The room was light, and the bed next to him was empty and fully made. He saw his pile of clothes on the floor and glanced back at his dad's neatly arranged bags in the corner.

The bathroom door was ajar, with nobody inside. He rubbed his eyes, stretched his arms, and took in a long breath while trying to piece together his situation. A glossy framed picture of Machu Picchu on the wall above the other bed sharpened his mind. *Of course*, he thought, *I'm in Peru!*

He looked at his phone and the time said it was 4pm in the afternoon, which took him a little by surprise. Rolling out from under the duvet, he sat on the side of the bed gathering his thoughts. The air felt moist and he felt a little cold, not quite the tropical temperatures he was expecting. Jonno could see no trace of his father and so assumed that he had gone downstairs. He spent the next five minutes debating whether to go and look for him or wait for him to come back. Part of Jonno wanted to explore, another part wanted to stay in bed. He heard the sound of traffic in the distance, interlaced with beeps and growls of engines. The atmosphere of the place had a dank and unfamiliar quality to it and the sky appeared grey though the blinds on the window. He stared ahead summoning the courage to walk out the door and start his Peru adventure properly, but it all still felt daunting. A pang of loneliness ran through him as he thought how far away he suddenly was.

Finally, after coming to the conclusion that his father was not coming back any time soon, he got to his feet and went to take a shower. It felt good to wash off the day's travel from yesterday and the hot water brought a bit more life to his weary mind. Feeling cleaner and presentable he went back to the room only to then put the same clothes back on that he wore yesterday. They were only staying one day in Lima and Jonno didn't really fancy the effort of unpacking and the repacking everything. He gave the clothes a smell and decided that they were acceptable, at least for now. With no other excuse to keep him in the room, he made the bold move of opening the door and heading out to the landing.

Outside in the corridor he heard the sound of voices coming from downstairs. There was the unmistakable voice of his father, laughing and speaking loudly with other voices that sounded from a mixture of languages. They all sounded like they were having a great time with James' voice definitely at the centre. Jonno headed down the stairs and entered the main living area they had walked through when they arrived to see his father sitting on one of the sofas chatting with a group of three people who were also perched on various chairs around. It was hard to tell their ages but they all gave off the impression that they had been travelling for some time. One was a man in a hoodie with a shaved head and big beard, another a woman in hiking gear with dark, plaited dreadlocks and a nose piercing, and another older man with thick glasses wearing jeans with a red and grey chequered shirt. There were some other people in the room too, but they were fully absorbed in their mini laptops or smartphones and clearly not part of the conversation. Bob Marley was playing the background, decorating the background silence with his soft and gentle redemptive tones. It wasn't the music he had been expecting to hear in Latin America but he immediately felt at ease with its timeless familiarity.

"Ah, there he is, the beast has arisen. Buenos dias, Jonny." James immediately stopped the conversation to welcome his son to the room.

"Hey Dad," Jonno responded, not quite sure where to put his gaze as the others looked at him. "Hey everyone," he added shyly.

The others nodded at him, smiling welcomingly.

"I was wondering if you were ever going to wake up."

"Well. I guess...." Jonno wasn't sure what to say, acutely aware that others were listening to this conversation and annoyed at his father for putting him on the spot like this. "What time is it? My phone said 4pm."

"It's 10am man," said the man in glasses, kindly.

"Oh..."

"Don't forget the time difference Jonny," James interjected. Jonno winced.

"Ah...of course. We are 6 hours behind here aren't we?"

"Correct," James added unnecessarily triumphantly. Jonno felt his toes curl. "Well this is Jonas, Sofia and Emilio. From Sweden, Spain and Argentina. All been travelling independently but now are here."

"Hey guys," Jonno did his best to look them all in the eye.

"Your dad is amazing," the man with the beard said, "he has been telling us so much."

"Yes, and also lots about you," the woman added, smiling.

"Oh?" said Jonno, his face feeling hot.

"And that you are both going climbing," she added, "Huaraz is amazing; I have just come from there."

"Cool." Jonno added, feeling like there must be a better word to say.

"But what I love," the bearded man said, "is that you guys don't go to Machu Picchu. You come all this way. To Peru for the first time and you go to the mountains, you do your own thing. That is so fricking cool."

"Yeah man, it's awesome," the man in glasses added. Jonno had no idea what anyone's name was at this moment.

"Well, we do try," James grinned. "Not always a good thing to follow the crowd is it Jonny?"

"I think I am just following you actually." Jonno said, allowing himself to enjoy the ensuing laughter.

"Ha! Fair enough," James loudly retorted.

"But it is nice," said the woman who Jonno felt confident must be called Sofia, "I was there two weeks ago. Really great, but so many tourists. We did the Inca Trail; it was so good. But then so many people they come on the bus just for the day. I think they don't appreciate it as much. Too many tourists, you know?"

"But Sofia, you are a tourist too, no?" The man with the beard said with a mischievous glint in his eye.

"Ah, Jonas, you are so difficult. No, I am traveller, not like the tourist."

"What's the difference?" the bearded man asked.

"Travellers work hard for their experience, tourists do not," she added, sitting back.

"Haha, I think you are in denial" he said.

"And I think you are a *cabron*." Sofia snapped back. "OK I go and sort some things out. Nice to meet you, Juanito." And with that she got abruptly and left the small group, leaving the other men at a brief loss of what to say next.

"So Jonny," James finally broke the silence, "let's get some breakfast and head out. What do you think?"

"Sounds good, Dad. What's the plan?"

"Well, good question. We've only got the day here before getting the bus tomorrow and we're both a little tired after yesterday, I imagine?" Jonno clenched his jaw. "So I was thinking about grabbing a bit of breakfast here and then getting a taxi into the old town. We could go for a wander and then come back here for some dinner and then get an early night."

"The old town is great," chipped in the bearded man, who had since taken out his iPad and had appeared to be doing something very important on it. "Yeah, you'll love it. A bit different to Miraflores."

'Sounds good Dad," Jonno answered weakly.

"Great!" James said enthusiastically. Then pointing to the corner of the room, he showed Jonno a table with breads, jams and eggs with some flasks with looked like hot water in them. Pots of coffee and tea were just next to them. "Grab yourself some breakfast from there and let's meet back here at 11am, see the clock there. Then we'll go."

"What are you going to do now?" asked Jonno picking up that his father wasn't going to be joining him for the aforementioned meal.

"Ah yes, don't worry about me, I had breakfast ages ago, I'm going to go and sort a few things, check emails and ring your mother. Make sure she isn't panicking too much thinking we have been abducted."

"Ha! OK. It wouldn't surprise me if she had already contacted the Peruvian authorities to come and check we are still alive."

"Exactly! Did you want to speak to her?"

"Not so much, I did only speak to her over 24 hours ago, but send her my love."

"Of course. And to your sister?"

"Ummm, well…. Yeah, why not? Say hello to her too."

"Very open minded of you."

"Well they say travel broadens the mind, don't they?"

"I'll pass on your warm regards, see you in a bit."

And with that James got up and silently left the room, leaving Jonno in the company of the bearded man and the man with glasses. With his father gone, the two of them then both smiled and the man in glasses then said, "He is a lovely man your father, I bet you must be happy to go travelling with him? He had so many amazing stories this morning."

"Yeah, he's quite something my Dad," Jonno replied.

"A great experience to share this with you Dad you know?" He continued, "my father is never interested in my travels, always telling me to get a job."

"Really?" Jonno asked, slightly disarmed at this sudden honesty from a man whose name he couldn't even remember, who must have been at least double his age and that he had never met before.

"Yeah, never easy when your father does not respect your life, does not respect your decisions."

"Wow… it's like that for you?"

"Yeah, all my life. I just want different things; he never gets that."

'So how do you cope?"

"Haha…" the man paused, looking Jonno deeply in the eyes, "I just keep travelling."

"Fair enough, you must have had such an interesting life?" Jonno immediately wished he hadn't sounded so wooden.

"Well…perhaps. But who hasn't?" He smiled enigmatically before rising from his chair and tucking in his shirt. "Nice to meet you and enjoy your time in Peru. I think you will have a great trip."

"Thank you. Likewise, I hope things go well for you."

"Haha, me too, my brother, me too." And with that he too was gone, leaving Jonno to his breakfast, accompanied by Bob Marley and a room full of people who seemed to be using their dark screens to be anywhere but the place they were currently in.

11am finally came around, and before he knew it Jonno and his father were back on the same street that they had arrived on the night before. Only this time it was like a flowing river, almost bursting its banks with cars, buses and bikes, all seeming hell bent on getting to where they needed to get to as fast as possible. Buses of all shapes and sizes, bright coloured and with some of their signs appearing hand-written roared past. Each one with its own *chico* in the doorway, balanced perilously between vehicle and tarmac exhorting all those on the pavement that his was to be their bus of choice today. The sky was heavy and grey, Jonno coughed from the thick and smoky breath he took. The fumes from some of the buses only added to the already darkened the air.

James put his hand out and within seconds a small, squat yellow car appeared as though from nowhere, pulling up right next to them. The paintwork looked battered and it seemed improbable that anyone could fit in it, let alone a driver with two passengers. The driver looked out of the window and smiled at them both.

"Hola Gringos!" he said loudly above the noise of the traffic.

"Hola Señor" James responded. "Al centro?"

"Vamos!"

"OK let's go," James said with the look of a man who had just achieved something quite significant and was openly allowing himself to feel quite good about it.

They opened the back doors and folded themselves into the small yellow box. James again taking his place in the front, while Jonno made himself comfortable in the back. The site of his father crammed into the front seat with his knees almost up to dashboard more than made up for the fact that he once again was in the backseat.

The traffic seemed to be endless and just before Jonno had wondered how the taxi driver would get himself back in the flow, he spotted an improbable gap and powered the small yellow box on wheels into it at surprising speed. "OK Señores, vamos" the driver said turning around and giving them both a big grin, with no apparent care that he was also driving in a busy road at the same time. A car slowed down abruptly in front and just as Jonno and James were about to yell out he quickly turned around again and pulled the wheel hard left and then right again to avoid it.

"Leema, people very crayzeee," he said out loud smiling to himself, shaking his head. As it turned out at that moment, all three men in the car were thinking roughly the same thing.

Chapter Eleven - Mum

A slightly strange phone-call. Obviously I'm glad they are both there safe and Jonno is settling in fine. This is such a big event in his young life, and mine! I miss him already, so much. To be away from him for over three weeks is a form of torture. It's not that I love him any more than Macie, far from it. I just miss him. He's been in my life almost 17 years and I have never spent so long apart from him. At some point they say we have to let our children go and fly the nest. I am dreading this to be honest, I know it has to be done for him to continue his growth into the fine and beautiful man I see him becoming. But oh, my heart aches.

His father was on good form which I'm glad of, although it is always hard to ever get an accurate version of the story from him. He just seems to always see everything as positive and there are never any problems. Yes, this is inspiring when you don't know someone very well, but when you live with them and want to share your life with them it becomes hard. He has always been an inspirational man, a real leader in many ways. I see how dedicated he is with his patients, how much time he puts in, how much he cares about doing the right thing. They must love his capacity to reframe things and make them look rosy. But what they don't see is the impact this has on his home life. Apart from not being here as much as we'd like, when he is it is often like seeing a very two-dimensional cut-out. It is hard to really know his inner world. I try and share mine but he is often so quick to offer solutions, not to just let me open up. I ask him about his and he says he is fine and things like, "you should see some of the lives of the people I meet at work, I have nothing to complain about." Yes, of course I agree, but an intimate relationship needs more fuel to its flame than just positivity.

These last few months seem to have put him on over-drive. The death of his father was haunting. A very successful man in business who had such an incredible and driven work ethic. To see him struck down so savagely by that stroke and then be gone from our lives five days later was horrifying. A man who was the epitome of strength and resilience, suddenly reduced like that before our eyes. Then gone. It was heart-breaking, His loss still brings tears to my eyes. But James, he has hardly mentioned it. In fact, he seems to have become even more upbeat about life and motivated. I ask him to slow down and talk to me, but he says he hasn't got time. I can't help but worry.

I know he had his issues with his own father. What's so sad is that I don't think they were ever resolved, so much was left unsaid. Ever since I've known James he has always held his father in such high regard but I never felt them to be close. They both would talk so much about their respective successes, but the conversations never went into vulnerable territory. I see this repeating itself again with Jonny, he is so sensitive and yearns to explore the questions of life, but James doesn't like this. Science has given him so many answers, sometimes I wonder if these help him feel safe. Jonno is at such a sensitive point in his life, and to have such a capable and successful father himself must feel a burden. I see him wrestling with how to be sometimes, how much he wants his father's attention and to be well thought of, but also of the creative and different path he perhaps wants to take. James, without meaning to, casts a large shadow on those of us who are closest to him. I'm not sure he even realises but it affects his children deeply. He is amazing at never telling his children what they should do, part of him feels his own father did that and forced him into choices he might not have made. But the irony is that his silence combined with his brilliance makes it even more confusing for Jonny and Macie.

James is such a wonderful man, but he is as closed as I have ever known him. To have seen his own father suffer like that and not be able to talk to him in those final days must have been beyond awful for him. I often wonder if he felt truly loved and accepted by his father, maybe he hoped to resolve this at some point. And then the opportunity was gone. I remember his face the first time he saw his father in the hospital, he went so pale and ashen coloured. So many of his patients he must have seen in those beds, on oxygen, with drips, with broken and breaking families at the beside. And then it was his turn, in his own hospital as well, where people knew him. I always wondered if that put extra pressure on him to "rise to the occasion" and come out looking strong as he loves to do.

It is amazing that he has managed to take the time off for this trip. Three weeks! I can't remember the last time he took so much time off. But I do worry about this trip, it has taken on a slightly obsessive bent. The mountains, the idea of climbing a peak with Jonny, the desire to do it without a guide, it unsettles me. I'm not sure his motivation is completely healthy.

But what can I do? If I ask him or demand he opens up, it makes him retreat even more. It doesn't work, it never has done. I have to look for the positives myself now or the worry will kill me. He has taken time off; he is with our son on an amazing adventure that will hopefully be something they talk about for years. The potential is all there. Half of me jumps for joy for them, yet the other feels a deep sickness in the pit of my stomach. I miss them both so much.

* * *

Chapter Twelve - Lima

The taxi journey into the centre of Lima was one of the most hair-raising experiences of Jonno's young life. All the seemingly normal conventions of how to drive and how to share the road with others had been either ignored or hadn't made it to this part of the world yet. The taxi driver seemed to take great glee from his opportunity to show the new arrivals some of his skills and abilities behind the wheel. Jonno noticed how many of the other cars had dents in them, and how old and crumbly so many of them looked. After snaking around the roads of Miraflores they dropped onto a thick three-lane main road that must have been the main artery of the city. Cars, buses and bikes all competing for space and all seemingly in a race with one another to get wherever they were going first. The driver handled the conditions as though his small flimsy yellow box was some sort of high-speed tank, as if others should watch out for him rather than the other way around.

Occasionally at traffic lights they would stop and catch their collective breath, only to then be greeted by another sight that took Jonno's breath away. Children who were no older than ten, with darkened skin that must have been a mixture of natural tone and dirt, wearing clothes that clearly hadn't been washed for a while, seemed to appear from nowhere holding all sorts of things to sell. They roamed in and swarmed around the stationary cars holding their wares, from sweets to domestic products for the drivers to buy. Some even came with buckets of water and wipers and began to offer an impromptu window cleaning service.

Jonno was transfixed. The children managed to look so old yet so painfully young. They moved and danced through the fume-belching cars with all the grace, elegance and curiosity of people their age. Yet when he looked closer their faces appeared hardened with squinting eyes. None of the softness and innocence that he had thought was normal in the face of a child, but narrow eyes that glinted with vigilance and awareness. At one point one child came and put his face to the window, looking in. Jonny looked back and for a timeless moment their gaze met, as though both humans on either side of the glass were trying to look into the mind of the other. The child then scrunched his expression before relaxing his face, smiling at Jonno. Jonno smiled back as the child then lifted the packet of chewing gum he was holding to the window.

"Don't take it," a voice came softly from the front, "do not open the window."

"Really? But"

"No, never open the window at traffic lights."

"But"

"No, Jonny," the car become silent.

Jonno grimaced back at the child and shrugged his shoulders. The child stared back for a brief moment and also shrugged his shoulders. Jonno smiled. The child's whole demeanour then changed and his face narrowed and he gave Jonno a deep scowl. He then pirouetted, turning his back on the car and headed off to the next car. Jonno felt his chest tighten.

The lights changed and the cars began to move. He saw the other children run for cover as it didn't appear that other cars were that interested in moving for them. They quickly scattered back to the centre of the road, laughing and jostling each other to get off the road. Jonno looked back to see if he could see the child who had come to the car but his view was blocked by the other vehicles in the road.

"It's just best not to get involved."

"They do this to earn money?" Jonno asked, still coming to terms with what he had just seen.

"Sadly so."

"But who looks after them?"

"Some live at home, others in shelters, some literally live by the side of the river."

"But how?" Jonno's stomach tensed.

"Well. There is so much urban migration and poverty here. So many families come looking for work they live in the *barrios,* shanty towns on the outskirts. Things don't always work out well and children leave because they think they have more safety on the streets. They come to the street to earn money during the day. When I was here last time I met a five-year-old selling ice creams, he would spend the day selling them and take the money home to his parents to help them."

"That's beyond unbelievable," Jonno stammered. "How is this allowed to happen?"

"Because this country isn't set up well to cope with these situations. It doesn't have the money or the organisation to protect its people as well as one like ours does."

"That's awful."

"It's horrendous."

"What can be done?"

"That's the million-dollar question."

"I feel sick."

"Good that you have seen that though Jonny," James then added after a brief pause. "It helps put your own life into perspective, doesn't it?"

"Dad... you don't always have to turn everything into a learning point you know. I can work this stuff out for myself. I am not incapable of thinking and feeling things for myself without being told." Jonno hesitated. "I can think for myself," he snapped before turning his whole body to face away from the front seats. He hoped that the driver didn't understand the conversation they were having.

James took a deep breath, "OK" he exhaled slowly, returning his gaze to the front window. Silence again returned to the inside of the cab.

Eventually the taxi pulled up at an enormous square filled with palm trees and surrounded by large, ornate, and mainly yellow buildings.

"OK señores, aqui estamos." The driver grinned.

"Bueno, gracias," replied his father before getting his wallet out.

"Cincuenta soles" the taxi driver beamed.

"Como!?" James responded.

"Cincuenta soles," the taxi driver repeated, with no intention to dip his beaming smile.

"What's happening Dad?" Jonno asked, unsettled by the agitation in this voice.

"Hang on Jonno, he's trying to overcharge us."

"What?"

James then began a heated conversation with the man at the wheel who appeared to have no interest in changing his mind. Jonno didn't need to understand exactly what was being said. His father was at first patient but as he proceeded to get nowhere became more and more irate. At one point the driver threateningly pointed to a police officer languidly sitting on a horse in the distance.

James eventually gave up and after yet another long period of two men sitting in an awkward silence and staring ahead, he opened his wallet and gave the man a note without looking at him. "Gracias Señor." James's eyes narrowed.

"OK Jonny, let's get out," he said and opened his door. They both shut the door and the taxi driver drove off without any pretence of the usual civic formalities of either side wishing each other well.

"What happened there, Dad?" Jonno asked, doing his best to neutralise the tone of his voice as much as possible so as not to irritate his father any further.

James took in another deep breath and let it out slowly. "I made the most basic of errors Jonny."

"What?"

"I forgot to agree the price before we got in the cab."

"And?"

"And that man will be eating very well tonight."

"Oh...."

"Exactly. Oh!"

"How much extra did he charge?"

"About 25 Soles."

"Which is how much in Pounds."

"About 5 pounds extra." Some of James' dry phlegm spat out.

"So not the end of the world. I was thinking from the way you were talking to him it was loads." Jonno chuckled, he couldn't help himself, it all seemed a bit ridiculous to get upset over such a relatively small amount. *Nothing better than when dad gets it wrong.*

"That is not the point!" James said exasperatedly. "That is not the point!"

"Oh..."

"Right, moving on, let's go have a wander."

"Good plan, Dad."

The next few hours were spent wandering around the enormous plaza and taking in the various sights. Jonno was taken by the faded grandeur of some of the buildings that lined the plaza. He noticed that those on the square looked pristinely maintained, but if you were to look down a side street, they quickly became dirty and dishevelled. At one point they walked past the Presidential Palace (according to James, who was doing his best to have the answers to all Jonno's questions) and saw a small crowd forming. As they went over there was a group of men dressed in military best of deep red jackets, electric blue trousers, knee-high leather riding boots and pith helmet, marching with sabres, instruments and Peruvian flags. To the outsider it had the effect of watching a group of toy soldiers having all been wound up and then let free, but Jonno wondered if that is what all military drills look like to people that are from outside the country and culture. He found it both interesting and pointless, and wasn't sure which one of the two observations he would remember it by.

At one point they wandered down a side street where the buildings began to take on a shabbier appearance and more rubbish began to appear in the street as they approached the River Rimac. The atmosphere away from the square didn't feel quite as easy and safe as the big open plan plaza with its any police, in fact there were none here, even though it was only less than 200 meters away. Jonno felt the eyes of those he walked by on him and for the first time that day began to feel aware of his presence as an obvious outsider. His father, however, kept proudly marching on with his head high and shoulders back. They stopped at the side of the river. Jonno was shocked at the amount of rubbish that was piled up by its brown sides and the smell of garbage that wafted up from its flow. He had always thought the Thames was dirty but it was practically Alpine Spring water compared to this. There were people milling around them and he noticed that as they stopped they seemed to attract more attention, which made him feel uncomfortable. A couple of young children wandered over with sad looking faces holding out more chewing gum to buy. Jonno looked at his father who gave a stern "no" to them. At first they paid no attention to him and carried on pushing their wares, but after a few more barks from James they quickly dispersed, laughing and joking with each other.

They eventually moved back towards the wide open plaza where Jonno began to relax, and they sat on one of the benches. It seems there were people from all places here, Asian to African, white and tall to squat and dark all milling about. There was an obvious police presence circulating the plaza which struck Jonno as a good thing but also made him wonder so many were needed. As though reading his thoughts James said,

"You know they have two different types of police here; one for tourists and one for Peruvians."

"Yeah? How come?" Jonno said still keeping his eyes people watching.

"Well, tourism is massive here, it is the third biggest industry here."

"The third? Seriously?"

"Yes, if you compare to us in the UK, I think it is IT that is our third biggest in terms of what it brings in. Tourism accounts for about 20 billion US dollars a year and employs 10% of the people."

'So basically they have to look after the tourists?"

"Correct. It makes you think what sort of state financially the country is in if it relies so heavily on tourism."

"And?" Jonno did his best not to exhale too loudly, wondering how he had managed to tune into *Dad FM* again.

"Well it means they are relying on the money coming in from outside all the time, they need people to physically come here in order to bring in money. Whereas other countries make things and then sell them to make money, Peru needs people to actually come. The travel market can be fickle so it is a less guaranteed income."

"Bonkers." Jonno added, not really knowing what else to say.

"Something like that." James added, with a hint of disappointment in his voice. "Let's go check out the cathedral if you like, then get some food?"

"Sounds good."

Ahead of them stood the cathedral's two imposing towers with a large wooden door in between. They climbed the steps and entered inside. It felt quiet and cool, its high-arched ceiling and smooth black-and-white-checked marble floor giving a sense of order and calm. The predominant colours were of white and gold with ornate carved wooden pews facing towards a golden altar. It was hard not to be impressed.

"I think they'd be better off spending the money on their people than decorating a building," his father whispered to him. "You know Napoleon said a hilarious thing once."

"Go on," Jonny added knowing that his father didn't actually need an invitation to continue.

"He said '*the only thing that stops the poor from killing the rich is religion, and vice versa',* which I think remains pretty true."

"Sorry?" Jonno asked feeling a bit puzzled and also not really wanting to have this conversation in such a seemingly holy space.

"Well...because of the moral code drawn up by religion, it means that you have to love your neighbour, forgive them and know that there is more to this world than just material things. It works both ways. It allows the poor to forgive the rich for their mistreatment and not be envious of their wealth. And it encourages the rich to feel sorry for the poor and want to help them as it is part of their duty in order to get access to Heaven. Along with not just killing them off because they are a nuisance."

"That all seems a bit cynical."

"I guess when you've really studied science, it is hard to take religion seriously."

"That's just your opinion Dad," Jonno replied, "and a bit of a narrow one at that."

"Well..."

"Please, Dad. I am just quite enjoying the silence in here. I might go and sit down for a bit if that's OK. I just want to go and soak it up."

"Fine, I might go and have a wander then. Have a look at a few of the different bits of artwork in here."

"Sounds good."

"So meet back in around ten minutes?"

Jonno exhaled slowly and audibly. "Sure, that'd be great."

Jonno left his father standing and went to sit on one of the empty wooden pews. He had no idea what he thought of God or any of the bigger questions, but he did feel drawn to buildings like this. It wasn't necessarily the unrelenting imagery of Jesus on the cross that appealed, it was more the calm and silence it provoked. There was a sense of space in building like this that allowed a calm clarity to settle on the mind. These were places to sit and be, not necessarily do anything else. He sat back and shut his eyes just to experience the space and found himself unable to really work out where the edges of cathedral were. There was soft movement of people all around but even their footsteps became absorbed in the overwhelming peacefulness of the place. He found when he opened his eyes he would become distracted by the various images that were present all around, but when his eyes were shut it was the endless sense of space that seemed to envelop him and make him feel relaxed. No wonder people believe, he thought, if they can come and find peace in buildings like these.

Just as he was starting to feel at ease, he felt a tap on his shoulder with his father standing above him, "OK San Juan, let's go. I'm hungry."

Outside the cathedral down one of the side streets they found a smart looking restaurant with a covered area outside for them to sit. James seemed keen to be outside even though it was little on the chilly side saying that this was "mountain training," getting used to less than comfortable temperatures. Jonno was at a loss of what to order, with the menu utterly foreign to him, so he let his father take the lead. James insisted on a fish dish called *ceviche*, something he had been raving about ever since the decision had been made to come to Peru. A cold dish of raw fish that had been soaked in lime juice with chillies, garlic, onion, coriander and served with soft and warm sweet potato and sweetcorn. Jonno was surprised at how delicious it was, especially as his stomach seemed to beg him not to eat it when his father had originally mentioned the fish was raw. It was soft, tangy and energising. The limes and chillies left a sparkling effect in his mouth and the fish seemed to slip down. They sat enjoying the food, not saying much.

Jonno saw something move beyond the glass barrier between them and the street. Another group of three young children approached having spotted them from the far end of the street. They looked similar to the ones he had seen at the traffic lights but Jonno didn't recognise them as the same boys. They walked with the same mixture of vigilance and confidence, as though they owned the streets but also that they were not safe. Their faces and clothes grubby and their eyes had the poignant look of being years older than their young faces and frames suggested. Jonno couldn't stop looking, until today he had never seen children like this. There was something so together about them yet so vulnerable. Spotting his gaze, they silently moved up to the other side of the glass holding out the packets of chewing gum and, even more shockingly for Jonno, the cigarettes they were selling. They couldn't have been more than seven years old he thought. The leader of the three, or the most confident as it was hard to tell, came close to the glass looking at Jonno with big wide eyes. Jonno could see him mouthing the words "gringo" and offering an expression that looked both pitiful but also detached. The child held out the cigarettes offering to sell them.

Then a loud shout, a waiter who had been inside moved aggressively outside the glass barricade and began moving menacingly towards the children yelling something at them. Like pigeons in a town square when approached too close and quickly, the children scattered and were gone in the blink of an eye. Jonno was left looking through the scrupulously clean window to a shabby looking yellow coloured colonial building that stood opposite the street.

The waiter came as though embarrassed and began to apologise to them at the table for their interruption. James simply smiled and thanked the man. He apologised again before moving inside.

"Those poor children." Jonno broke the silence.

"I know, it's awful isn't it?"

"I don't know what to make of this, I don't know what to think."

"It's heart breaking. I don't know if it still happens but when I was here last there used to be people employed to go around the tourist parts of the city and literally scoop the homeless and street children, put them in a van and drive them to the outside of the city. To stop them from being a nuisance to the tourists. To make the place look clean and safe."

"That's crazy. I thought the homeless were badly treated in our country...but I just can't get my head around seeing children working on the street. I wasn't ready for this."

"I'm not sure anyone is." James said softly, "I'm not sure anyone can be."

"Shall we go back now Dad?" Jonno asked. "I'm suddenly feeling quite tired."

"Don't want to see anymore? James asked.

"No thanks," Jonno said staring ahead, "I think I'd just like to get back and rest. I suddenly feel a bit light-headed."

"OK fine, I'll get the bill and we'll grab a cab home."

James settled up and they headed back to the square to look for a taxi. A whole swarm of yellow cars were there and it took less than a minute to attract one's attention. This time

James made a point of agreeing that price before they got in. Although not as straight forward as he would have liked, once both driver and he agreed on a price that was roughly fair to both of them they jumped in.

Back in amongst the weaving and chaos of the traffic Jonno looked out of the window at the passing scenery. The sky was thick with cloud and the sense of concrete was overpowering. Occasionally they were stuck in heavy traffic as the mass of cars seemed to congeal into a huge metal blob, all hooting and honking at no one in particular. Jonno had the feeling of a city that was bursting with energy but had yet to know how to make it flow in a useful way. Full of people all doing their best to get by in conditions that offered nothing to help. Meanwhile he turned his attention to the front to see his father locked in yet another lively conversation with the man driving.

***

That evening ended up being a quiet one, Jonno and his father both tired from the day's exertions the previous day's travel. As James had already organised tomorrow's tickets to Huaraz, they decided to take it easy. James suggested a pizza, which Jonno couldn't say no to. Despite feeling a little guilty that they were in Peru and perhaps should be a little more adventurous, he also felt a desire for some familiarity, even though it had been less than 24 hours.

There was a shopping mall down on the coast, about ten-minute walk away so they decided to go there. Out on the street again Jonno found the constant movement disorientating and also was conscious of the fact that him and his father looked like anything but locals. Not only were they taller than everyone, they wore their hiking clothes and had markedly paler skin. He felt local eyes crawl, rub and glide over his skin as he walked and found himself unable to merge into the background as he often preferred to do when out in public. James, however, strode down the street with his head held high often saying "hola" to people who caught his eye and smiling. Jonno found that he both hated and admired his father in almost equal measure in these moments.

Along the way were large adverts on the billboards by the roads. They almost all showed pictures of a happy family life, either based around certain mobile telephone companies, or sweets and foods. What Jonno couldn't quite grasp was that the people in the pictures looked long, tall and pale skinned, even blond. This was a far cry from the people who they were walking past. They were shorter, darker skinned, dark haired and less angular in their appearance. The adverts seemed to be offering some sort of other worldly ideal of what happiness was in comparison to what daily life was perhaps like. How people could fall for that, he wondered, as they were offering something that seemed so clearly different from the reality that was being lived in.

They finally arrived at the shopping mall, a vast three floor affair cut into the side of the cliffs overlooking the sea. Looking down on it there was an air of familiarity but also incongruity about it. Jonno recognised many of the outlets from back at home and the place had a very shiny, plastic and modern feel. But based on what he had seen earlier in the day it felt a little out of place. There were security guards on every corner holding guns and the complex seemed immaculate. The people inside looked well dressed, smart and purposeful. Some of them even looked very close to the figures he had seen in the adverts. It all seemed a million miles away from the dirt and poverty he had experienced earlier, there was something surreal and counterfeit about it.

They descended down one of the escalators and went looking for somewhere to eat. James saw a bright pizza outlet and suggested they go there. It was on the edge of the complex overlooking the ocean and immediately appealed to both of them. Sitting down with their pizza that they ordered in English from a very friendly young waiter, Jonno turned to his father and said,

"Dad, this place feels weird. I don't get it"

"How do you mean?" James answered, mouth half full.

"I mean... it's hard to say but... this place just feels odd."

"In what way?"

"Like...It shouldn't really be here. Like... it has nothing to do with what Lima is like. It doesn't feel very Peruvian"

"How do you know what Lima is like? How do you know what is Peruvian?" James asked back, softening his shoulders and leaning in.

"Well I don't... It's just.. I can't really get those street children out of my mind from earlier. I just can't believe that can happen. That there is no money and support for them. That they have to roam the streets and traffic jams for money. But now we are here, and it feels so different, as though they do not exist."

"I see what you mean," James added thoughtfully. "If it's any consolation, it's so much better than when I was first here. Lima was really struggling then. It feels much safer now."

"It was worse than this?"

"Oh yes.. the roads were terrible, the cars and buses were so old and falling to bits. There were street children everywhere, you could feel the poverty so much more."

"But... isn't a place like this just hiding it? Aren't we just pretending it doesn't exist by sitting here?

"Perhaps... but this is the reality of countries like Peru. There are so many extremes, different to where we come from. In the UK, often the poverty is more subtle or harder to see as we are so used to living there. But here it is so obvious. It is much more in your face. The daily hardships of people are not hidden or helped like where we live. There is little real infrastructure that can support them."

"Should we be eating in a place like this, just putting our heads in the sand? I feel quite guilty eating this pizza if I had to be honest."

"Jonno..." smiled James, "you are so like your mother. I think you have a wonderful sense of other people and what you do and don't have. But try not to overthink things like this, it will only tear you apart. You have to remember that this is just as much Peru as anywhere else in Peru. It is part of life here, not for everyone but for some. Everywhere in the world there is both privilege and there is poverty. What is important to concentrate on is not feeling guilty for where you are from but for what you can do with what you have been given."

"How do you mean?" Jonno dropped the crust of his pizza with a slight thump.

"Well...look.... You cannot choose where you are born or who you are born to. That is just luck and fortune, either good or bad depending your circumstance. What you can do is make the best of the hand of cards you have been dealt. This is what life is about, not feeling guilty that you had a better start than others."

"But I feel like I have so much, I want to help, do something."

"That's great," James said, putting some more pizza into his mouth, "that's really great."

"Is that why you are a Doctor?" Jonno asked, his eyes lingering on his father's whose were looking elsewhere.

"Amongst many reasons, I think so. I loved the idea of helping people, I love the idea of putting my skills to good use for others." James looked strongly back at his son, aware that he was looking right at him. "I am no religious man, but growing up I always liked the parable of the talents that Jesus talks about in the Bible, don't bury them in the ground, go use them. Make them multiply."

"But how about the pain? How about the sadness of seeing these people? How about the fact that we have more than them?"

"Look Jonno... these are good questions, but what can you do? Do you give all you have away so to be like them? Or do you do your best to help? Life is unfair, in my opinion, people who say it isn't are just naïve or not paying attention. But to feel guilty for what you've been given and not use it? That, in my opinion is just self-indulgent, ego driven immaturity."

"Hmmm...fair enough, but I still don't like it. I feel awkward being here."

"That's up to you" James said sharply. "I don't and I'm enjoying this pizza."

"Fine Dad, as always you are right."

"Jonno... please, don't be like that."

"It's just...."

"Jonno," James interrupted, "enough."

Jonno stopped what he was saying and looked away from his father. He hated the way his father took control of conversation and just gave an answer, a way that things just are. There was no freedom to look at anything another way. He fixed his eyes out of the window and saw the dark silhouettes of the waves in the ocean rise and fall in the moonlight. The sea appeared both dark and foreboding, capable of anything, yet at the same time vast and inviting. The pulses of the swell rose and fell, crashing into a ghostly white foam before being swept up in the immense tableau and absorbed again into the darkness. Its movement calmed his agitated mind as his father continued to eat his pizza. He felt a familiar tightness in his chest as his thoughts wandered to the next three weeks they were to spend together.

They finished the meal saying little else. James asked for the bill and paid without much extra fuss. He left a small tip despite complaining how expensive it had been. Jonno didn't comment. He just wanted to get back to the hostel and get to bed. Fatigue had multiplied after the pizza had reached his stomach and he was ready to sleep. They left and walked back thought the streets both in their own thoughts. Upon arrival, there was no one in the main area of the hostel as they passed through which was a relief to Jonno as he had literally run out of anything to say. He took the key and head up to their small room, hoping to be asleep before his father came up. James stayed downstairs saying that he had something to check online.

As it happened Jonno was snoring within seconds of hitting the pillow, and James crept silently in so as not to wake him. Before turning off the light he allowed himself a long look at his sleeping son, of whom he couldn't help but feel so proud. He smiled as he thought of how Jonno had challenged him, but it didn't once cross his mind as he flicked the switch that his son might like to know this.

Chapter Thirteen - Arriving in Huaraz

The bus began to pull into the station after what had been a long day. Jonno had been spellbound by the scenery as they travelled from the dust bowl of Lima up into the bright blue sky mountainous arena of the Ancash as they headed towards Huaraz. The day had begun early with his father practically marching him out of bed at a time that seemed neither reasonable nor remotely sociable. His father seemed a little different in the morning and he kept saying things like "this is where it begins" as though they were heading to the base camp of Casharaju that day.

They had left the hostel while it was still dark and the streets were once again calm and empty. Jonno liked this aspect of the Lima he had seen. He had found the general noise and chaos of the day before a little intense and enjoyed the sense of space that seemed to open up now the roads were somewhat calmer. A taxi was waiting for them and they renewed the now familiar positions of Jonno sitting in the back with James in the front chatting to the driver. Within seconds he heard the word "doctor" and so sunk back into his seat losing himself to what was outside of the window.

They arrived at a very smart bus station in good time; Jonno was again caught off guard by the appearance of the place with its sleek and enormous black buses sitting in well-lit bays, awaiting their human cargo. He had not been expecting the general sense of order and abundance of dark uniformed security guards with batons and guns on all sides. *Why so much protection?*

They paid the driver and swung their heavy packs onto their backs to walk in. James seemed to manage his pack with great aptitude yet Jonno was still struggling to pick his up, it just felt far too heavy. James noticed this but wisely decided to not say anything. They found a small café and sat waiting with a coffee and packet of cheap biscuits to the pass the time. The terminal, despite the fact it was still dark outside, was already alive with people and movement. Buses seemed to be traveling to almost everywhere in Peru.

Finally, they were called and checked in their bags at a special area as though they were at an airport. The men in the area gladly received the bags and then studiously weighed them before writing down their various findings. From there they headed into the vast spaceship-like bus that awaited them. Jonno had never been in anything like it, with two floors and seats that reclined to practically being like beds, it was quite something. A smartly dressed and extremely attractive, yet still heavily made up, stewardess welcomed them on board as they passed through the doors. James couldn't resist but greet her back in a similar way to how he spoke in the airport to the stewardess. Jonno cringed.

They had seats right at the front of the bus at the top, "only the best for us" James had said more than once until he had finally elicited a perfunctory "thank you" from Jonno and they settled back for the journey. The giant black spaceship moved effortlessly out of the terminal as the dark sky was beginning to lighten to a flat grey and make its way on the mountains. The bus made its way along the coast, heading out of dry and dusty Lima. Jonno couldn't believe how long it took them to leave Lima, not for the traffic but just how the city seemed to sprawl and sprawl. As they left the inner urbanised part, then came the passing through of what seemed like one large shanty town. Thousands and thousands of small shacks with corrugated tin roofs all clumped together in what seemed to be an ordered chaos. Everywhere was so dry and barren, with these proud yet pitiable shacks looking like they had been dropped from the sky. People were milling around all of them, both adults and children beginning their day. There were open rubbish pits and Jonno gasped out loud when he saw a group of children running and playing through one. The sky was pale and dreary, the land waterless, the shacks and poverty seemed to go on forever.

Finally, free of the oppressiveness of Lima, they wandered along the coastal aspect of the road looking down the enormous dunes that spilled into the pacific. They continued until turning inland and rising high up into the foothills of the Andes traversing seemingly endless narrow switchbacks that the bus elegantly lurched one way and the other to make it onto a higher plateau. At this point the heavy gloom appeared to be penetrated and slowly was replaced by a cloudless blue expanse. James nudged Jonno as they both saw the sun for the first time on the trip, hanging effortlessly in the ocean of deep cobalt sky having been hidden by the clouds all this time. It was exhilarating to see such a colour change and brought a completely different atmosphere to the scenery. The brightness itself was uplifting and the intensity of colour from both land and sky flooded into their eyes. The first of the snow peaked mountains came into view after about six hours and James nudged Jonno again with a massive wide-eyed grin on his face. Small triangles in the distance broke the horizon and reached their peaks to the heavens. The white of their sharp summits made great contrast against the open heavens above them and their shapes played the familiar trick on the eye making them seem easy to climb. From far, like so many things, they looked incredibly straight forward.

The journey had been otherwise pleasant with Jonno experiencing his first taste of the famous Inca Kola. A bright neon yellow fizzy concoction which all the guidebooks had been raving about. The bubble gum flavour was appealing but he wasn't entirely convinced he would necessarily thirst for more. James leaned in when he was drinking and suggested that this was one of the best pick-me-ups if Jonno had some issues with his stomach later in the trip and not to discount it just yet. They also chatted about where they were going to be staying in Huaraz.

When James had been before so many years ago he had made friends with a local lad named Rodrigo. He had been the son of the guide on one of his climbing trips and they had gotten on really well. Rodrigo had had grand ambitions to make something of his life, and they had chatted long into the mountain nights about life may or may not hold for them. They had bonded though their own sense of ambition and prospects. James had shared his hopes for what the medical world might bring him, and Rodrigo had wanted to go into business. He had seen how physically hard the life was of his father, even though it was spectacular, and knew that he did not want that. They were both young and had the world ahead of them. James had kept in sporadic contact over the years, initially by letter but when email came in it had become easier. Rodrigo had worked hard over the years and established a hotel in the centre of Huaraz from which he helped organise trekking and climbing. This was where they would be staying for the trip and despite not having seen him for so long, James seemed very excited to see Rodrigo again.

But Rodrigo's story had been one stained with tragedy. Rodrigo had met a Spanish woman who had been travelling through soon after James had left. They had fallen in love and she stayed to make a life with him. They married and set up life in Huaraz full of hope and possibility, and they soon had a daughter. It seemed that nothing could go any better. However, their happiness was short-lived as on a trip to Lima, his wife was tragically killed in a road accident. James had remembered feeling devastated for his friend at the time. But Rodrigo managed to come though this and met a local woman and fell in love again later on, this time having two more children. The tone of their correspondence had since changed, James told his son, after the death of his first wife, and Rodrigo had become a lot more serious and far less speculative about the future. A heaviness had appeared in his writing that belied a lack of faith or trust in the world around him.

It all sounded very complicated to Jonno as he struggled to fully take it all in. His father had a very matter-of-fact way of telling the stories of other people lives. He told them as though they were simple truths that had come and gone. Perhaps, as his mother occasionally told him, his father has seen too much emotion and sadness at work and had become numb as a way of coping with it. But his young mind was caught by the sorrow of the story, whereas his fathers seemed to focus on the success Rodrigo had made of his life to pick himself back up and move on. Jonno tentatively asked a few questions about what that must have been like to go through, but James didn't seem interested in exploring, he simply said that he had moved on and should be congratulated for that.

The majority of the journey had been speaking about the mountain; the principle reason that they had come to Peru. James sounded very eager about the challenge they had set themselves. He talked through with Jonno all the research he had done and the strict acclimatisation plan he had put together. Time was tight and this trip was shorter than he would like for them to get ready to climb the mountain but he felt that it should be fine. He had climbed this mountain before and felt he could remember it well; they were not going to be using guides as he wanted this to be a self-supported mission. It was important, he kept saying, to be able to do things for yourself in life. Jonno didn't have anything to add but just listened to his father as he explained in painstaking detail the research he had done and how they were going to achieve their aims. The mountain was called Casharaju and should be a great beginner's peaks for someone like Jonno. There shouldn't be any need to for anything too technical like ice climbing but they would need ropes and crampons.

Jonno watched his father's face while talking. His eyes became very focussed when discussing the detail of what they would do. There was little place for humour - what they were embarking on was something deadly serious. None of this seemed open to debate, James had planned it and his word was final. They had climbed and trekked together in Scotland a few years before, which Jonno had loved, but it brought back memories of how strict and authoritarian he could be come in these situations. He had set the itinerary for the next few weeks with day trips, day hikes, and then a longer trek for four days through the Santa Cruz valley. Jonno remembered some of the pictures his father had shown him of the incredible opal and deep turquoise lakes that were that they would see on their way. Then finally they would take to the mountains to attempt Casharaju for the last week of the trip. This was to be the pinnacle of what they were doing and everything now, James kept saying, was in preparation for this. He stressed over and over again that he wanted Jonno to begin focussing on the task in hand. Mountains are serious places, he said, and we need to be serious when we are in them. While Jonno couldn't help but agree he found the intensity of his father a little too much, especially as they were both sitting in a bus, not yet on the mountain itself. Jonno felt the cramp of self-consciousness distract him from his father's words, worrying what others on the bus may think of this man talking in such impassioned and obsessive terms.

Finally, they began to snake their way through the outskirts of Huaraz, outside of the window people were just going about their business. Jonno saw that there was a shift in the way people dressed here, away from the almost ubiquitous urban uniform of jeans and t-shirt, he saw men and women walking in much more traditional dress. At the side of the road were women in a large broad brimmed hats and heavily plaited ponytails that reached all the way down their back to their below their waistlines. They had large colourful and striped blankets full to the brim of something he couldn't see wrapped onto their backs. They had multi-coloured billowing skirts with dark leggings underneath and were busy trying to sell the vegetables that were laid out in front of them. Small children, almost identically dressed, sat with them helping them in their day's work. The faces of the women were heavier than the faces he had seen in Lima, the lines seemed deeper and the skin colour darker. All along the street as the bus came into the city he saw this scene repeated. James told him that they had come down from the villages to sell their produce.

The bus finally slowed down outside a small blue gated complex. A man in the uniform of the bus company came out from inside and waved at the driver. He then hauled open the gates and the bus performed an unbelievably skilful three-point turn that allowed it to reverse into the space behind the open gate. It then stopped and the gentle voice of the stewardess boomed out over the speaker system that was a little louder than it needed to be, announcing that they had arrived at their destination.

The bus had pulled into a gated-off courtyard and the passengers all went through their individual routines of stretching and making loud yawning noises as though to wake themselves up. The bus was full of mainly foreign looking people, not many Peruvians seemed to be on the bus with them. Jonno was definitely the youngest though, which gave him a small thrill, the others on the bus were much closer to his father's age. They had an interesting mixture of tiredness but focussed excitement in their eyes. There had been plenty of animated chatter on the journey as the first mountains had come into view.

They descended down and off the bus, thanking the ever-smiling and immaculately dressed stewardess on the way, then out into the bright sunshine of Huaraz. Jonno took a deep breath as he got off the bus and found that his lungs didn't fill as much as he might have expected. The sun caught his face and he let himself feel wrapped in its warmth, it was the first time since they had arrived in Peru that he had felt its heat. They were led to a small area inside where their bags were brought to and then had to show their ticket to prove whose bag was whose. The local men on the other side of the counter, who were young and powerful looking, seemed to take great pleasure in lifting the invariably heavy bags of the passengers and passing them over as though they weighed nothing. Only for the recipients to then struggle a little, losing balance putting them on. Jonno was no exception, slightly over-swinging his bag and toppling a little to one side. James caught him and smiled, telling him to go easy, "the altitude changes things a little up here". Jonno noticed he didn't feel quite a strong as when he got on the bus, his body seemed to be straining with just managing the pack.

They walked out from where the protected bag space was into an entrance to see a group of more local men waiting holding signs up. Either hand-written or printed, had signs suggesting they were waiting for someone. James scanned the faces before finally his eyes lit up,

"Rodrigo!" he called out.

"Jaime!" one of the men boomed back. He looked about the same age as James, was smaller but broad shouldered and strong looking. Wearing a dark leather jacket and simple pair of jeans with dark shiny shoes. His face was dark and its lines bore the hint of a smile, his hair also jet black and neatly combed into side parting. Yet there was a mild heaviness to the eyes Jonno couldn't help but notice.

"Fantastico," said James, "he's here," and he strode purposefully towards him. Jonno followed, not quite sure what was going on but that it probably best to go with his father. Standing next to him was a young-looking woman, perhaps about Jonno's age also smiling confidently at them both. Jonno caught her eye and she smiled right at him, her face open and full of confidence. She was in a simple pair of jeans and light blue tunic. Her thick, dark hair fell to her shoulders and her eyes seemed to sparkle in the afternoon light. Jonno had absolutely no idea how to respond but by the time he had gone through all the possible permutations they were already standing together as a group.

"Señor Jaime, welcome!" said Rodrigo, giving James a big bear hug. Jonno watched as his father tried to adjust his held-out hand.

"So good to see you again," James said, recovering his composure, "you look well Rodrigo, really well."

"Señor Jaime! How long has it been? You look well but maybe you not running around so much now?" Rodrigo laughed, patting his father on his stomach.

"Ha!" James snorted, "this is why I came back to the mountains. Maybe they can take this back!"

"Haha, well this depends how much Peruvian beer you will be drinking and how much guinea pig you want to be eating." Rodrigo smiled a deep and genuine smile.

"Rodrigo," James changed the flow of conversation, "this is my son, Jonny. I thought it was time to show him the most beautiful place on earth."

Jonno flinched. Jonny was a name that made him feel like a child and it irritated him every time his father used it.

"Ah mucho gusto Señor Juanito!" Rodrigo boomed, giving Jonno a strong but curiously respectful handshake. "Bienvenido a Peru. I see you look like your great father, you have the look of adventure in your eyes."

"Mucho gusto Señor" Jonno replied, already feeling at ease in this man's warm and effusive company. He leaned forward and shook his hand.

"And this…is my eldest daughter, Magdalena. She wanted to come and meet you both."

"Buenos tardes señores, very nice to meet you. I hear many nice things from Papi about you," she said smiling widely and shaking hands with them both. Jonno was instantly impressed by her self-assurance and how smooth she seemed to be in the situation.

"Well, Jaime, how things have changed. I think it is maybe twenty years since I last see you. We have many things to say. But I am not sure if you have changed so much, except in the trousers you need to wear!"

"Ha!" Jonno couldn't help himself let out a small laugh.

"Well perhaps Rodrigo, but at least I am not wearing a leather jacket yet," James shot back.

"Ha! Only a matter of time amigo, only a matter of time," Rodrigo chuckled. "OK, enough of the welcomes and insults. I think time to leave this bus station and take you both back to the hotel."

"That would be great," said James, "it's been a long few days."

"OK Magdalena, let's help these caballeros with their bags"

"Si Papi."

"It's OK Rodrigo, we'll carry them. I think we need the training. We have a few adventures ahead of us."

"Yes, so I hear Señor, we have lots to talk about."

And with that he led them to a smart looking white saloon car that was waiting at the gates. As they drove an enormous vista of mountains came into view dominating the skyline of Huaraz, rising up from above a smattering of clouds at their base. They seemed to loom over the town, looking down curiously at the inhabitants that were living their lives below. Five peaks side by side with the biggest in the middle that dwarfed everything else in their vicinity.

"That's Huascaran," James nudged Jonno in the ribs," biggest mountain in Peru."

"We're not are we?" Jonno gasped.

"Haha, maybe not on this trip," James grinned.

Jonno stared and stared. Half in awe and half in utter fear.

Chapter Fourteen – Magdalena

He seems nice this new gringo chico that has arrived with his father. My Papi has been excited for some time to welcome his old friend back; they knew each other before I was born, even though he doesn't like to talk about that time much. But he has been really excited to see him again; I think they maybe climbed some mountains together when they were young chavales.

We have so many gringos coming here to trek and climb; it is a good way of meeting new people from the world. They bring new ideas. Ah! Peru can be so backwards sometimes and our traditions can be so overpowering, especially when you are female. It makes me so mad sometimes, the way the men get preferential treatment here! But it is good to meet others from outside where we are from, they bring new energia and stories, they show us that there is a world beyond.

I don't think I can stay here forever, I love the mountains and my country, but part of me does not to accept this. I am a type of mulata, my mamacita was never from here. She too came travelling and met my father and they fell in love. It is a beautiful story with such a sad ending as she then died in a road accident when I was three. I never really knew her, just the stories that Papi tells me. I am not sure if I miss her or not, because I never met her. But something is missing and I feel like I need to find it. Not only that but then Papi met Adriana a few years later and now I do have a real Peruvian mamacita who is a good person but she is still not my mother. Not to mention Ernesto and Beatriz, my half-brother and sister! I love them all, I do, but they do not feel mine.

I am only half Peruvian but I feel like full Peruana most of the time. Mamacita's family all live far away and we have such minimal contact. Growing up was strange as I never looked quite like the other girls, my skin was a bit lighter. They all thought I was just a rich girl from Lima. I am no different to them but they wouldn't let me believe that. So it was like I have to be extra Peruana to fit in! Then there are the boys, I think they find me interesting but are also not sure what to make of me. Anyway they can be so jealous and immature sometimes that I am not sure if I want to date any more of them. I mean some of the looks they give, when I walk around town here with the people who come and stay when showing them around, are almost scary.

Then you hear the stories of the abuse behind closed doors, it doesn't always feel safe. I know Papi has always been respectful of Adriana but even he loses his temper. He never has done anything but I know how passionate arguments can be. Not everyone is able to hold themselves back like my Papi. Everyone knows someone at college who knows someone who has been hit. It happens. Then, how aggressive some of the men are on the street, the problem is that men can never see this; they think we make it up. Violencia is not only physical you know. But other women, we all see even if our voice is still small. It can be dangerous to stick up for yourself. Make life harder. But then what else should you do!? 'Ni una menos', as we say amongst ourselves.

But I am not sure what will happen. Right now, I want to help Papi, he has always been such a support to me and now his hostel is really taking off. The guests love this place and I love working here. But I also feel a bit trapped. I don't want to be just another well behaved hija that stays at home with her family; I want to get out there. I know I should feel grateful for all I have been given and there are those who much less, but I feel there is more; maybe in Lima, maybe in the United States, maybe in the rest of the world. For now, I need to study hard, that much I know. There is no way to do anything if you come from a place like this if you don't get smart, you'll never leave. That might not be the worst thing, but to die always wondering what else was out there, I can't do that to myself.

Sometimes I want to travel and never come back, go and find a country that respects and makes the women there feel safe. Other times I look at the sun rising behind Huascaran and think there is nowhere more perfect in the world. I think Papi understands, he knows that deep down I am not only from here and that one day I might go. He says he sees my real mamacita in me and it makes him both happy and sad. He says I have her looks and spirit and I see him look like he might cry. Then I want to cry too, not just for me but for all of us. It is sad, but what can I do, I can't spend my life feeling sorry for myself, things happen that are not fair. That is life.

But he does look like a nice boy this chico, I hope I get to speak to him more. Papi speaks so highly of his father and so I hope his son is from the same material. He has a different look to his father though; there is softness in his face whereas his father looks hardened, like he has been in the fields too long. I know this look, when men have become tough and forgotten how to be gentle. I see many of the boys at college practicing this look; like they need to show the world how strong they are to be taken seriously. And I think it is good that a man is tough, he needs to be. But not always, otherwise he spends his life crashing and bumping into everything.

Anyway, enough day-dreaming; I have my jobs in the hostel to do before Papi gets back and then my homework. Life is busy but it has to be. The only person who will sort my life out is me. Otherwise I will die in Huaraz!

* * *

Chapter Fifteen – Huaraz

There was a palpable change in James. It had begun early on the first full day and continued in a way that alarmed Jonno. They had been sitting having breakfast in the hotel restaurant with Rodrigo and were discussing their plans. James was telling him about the mountain they were going to climb and how he had studied the route and was excited to be going there. Rodrigo had also been excited as he knew lots of mountaineers who had climbed it recently and had a good experience. Yet when he started offering advice, Jonno noticed that his father did not seem interested in taking any of it. For every suggestion it seemed that James had a quick answer to the point where it became a little uncomfortable to listen to. The idea of a guide was mentioned but James seemed adamant that he knew what he was doing, he had studied the route so well. Rodrigo, to his credit as perhaps James was not the first know-it-all mountaineer he had met, backed off a little and deftly changed the subject away from it. It appeared that a little of the spark that he had upon sitting down to talk with his old friend had dampened somewhat by the end of the conversation. Both men seemed to be interested in entirely different things, one in catching up and offering advice and the other in laying out his grand plan.

It was strange seeing the two men catch up with each other. They clearly seemed fond of each other but also Jonno was acutely aware of how little they really knew of each other's lives. Rodrigo shared his story of the loss of his first wife which had been terrible but then quickly moved on to the new life he had established, marrying again and now running this hotel which was doing well. He seemed to want to focus on the good things of life rather than dwell on anything that may have seemed sad and painful. At one point, Jonno saw a shape move in the background and looked up, he saw Magdalena looking at her father from behind the counter in the kitchen. She seemed to be listening to him as he was telling the story of his life, yet her expression did not seem to match her fathers as he spoke.

James too, told his story since they last met. From what Jonno tuned in to, it appeared that he had had a quite a life, with his achievements in being a surgeon, marrying and having Jonno and Macie as children. To be fair to him, he told his story in a non-boastful way, more there was an element of surprise to how well he had done, but he seemed happy to keep going with the positive narrative anyway. There a was an odd moment when Rodrigo asked about how James' parents were, to which he then seemed to lose momentum. James simply said that his father had died nine months ago, which was very sad but that they are all moving on with their lives. Rodrigo simply listened before saying that he was sorry for the loss.

Despite their mutual respect and affection for each other, Jonno could sense a line of tension had been drawn after Rodrigo had suggested other ideas to James's grand plan that he had worked on for climbing Casharaju. Rodrigo seemed a little shocked when he discovered that they were not going to use a guide, especially as it was the end of the season and the quality of the slopes would be changing soon under more snow. James did not want to know, saying he had it all under control. Again Rodrigo said little extra but Jonno was sure he saw him wince slightly when he heard the plan. He loved the plan James had prepared, but clearly not the idea of climbing unsupported. Eventually he looked at his watch and said that he had to go and attend to some business, but if he could help in any way, he would love to. James thanked him but said he felt he had it covered. Rodrigo then turned to Jonno and shook his hand, again offering him any help while he was here. Jonno thanked him and simply said he too was going to go with 'Dad's plan.'

The early days in Huaraz were challenging. James had designed quite a strict itinerary which he was working on sorting out and arranging. This left Jonno with quite a bit of time on his own to both wander and wonder about what he was doing when his father was away from the hotel. He always invited Jonno to come with him, but Jonno didn't feel up for it initially, he had found that he didn't feel so well physically. One of the most challenging aspects was the altitude itself. Huaraz stands at roughly 3000 meters above sea level and it showed on every staircase and lift of a heavy bag. Within twenty-four hours he had a banging headache and constant queasiness in the pit of his stomach. He had never been this high before and had not remotely prepared for this. James too suffered with headaches but made very little show of them. His advice was to drink lots of water and rest. Both of which Jonno did his best with but it made little difference. Sleep was tough as he would wake breathless and his heart pounding, his father seemingly peacefully slumbering next to him. Even getting upstairs proved a challenge, needing to take a good rest at the top if he forgot himself and went up them too quickly. Jonno noticed that if he did anything too quickly that he really paid for it, there just wasn't enough oxygen in the noticeably thin air. He learned quickly to slow down and make much more premeditated movements rather than rush everywhere, as he was in the unhelpful habit of frequently doing. But for the most part he was dogged by the sense that there was no way he was going to be able to climb any mountain in the next few weeks if he was struggling with the small task of going up stairs. He mentioned this to his father who simply replied that it would be fine, and not to worry.

In quiet moments in the hotel, when his father was busy or away organising things, Jonno bumped into Magdalena a few times. It turned out she helped in the hotel outside of going to college. This was pretty normal in Peru, she said, for children to help the business of their parents. Jonno would be sitting in the lobby reading a leftover magazine or in the shiny corridors when he met her. Initially it was only a shy smile and a "hola" but they soon began to talk a little more. He noticed that she always had time despite what she was doing, but also kept a degree of distance between them. She always asked how he was and how preparations for the mountain were going; she seemed excited for them both. She gave him some details about her life and what she was up to, but never so much that he felt he had an insight into who she was. Their meetings were fleeting but as the time in Huaraz increased and Jonno felt some of the loneliness of only knowing his father, he began to hope to bump into her more and more. Despite not always feeling that they were ever able to talk about anything below the surface, he felt a strange sense of ease with her. She had a smile and way of looking right into his eyes when she spoke that occasionally made him wonder where his legs were. As they came and went from their small walks and treks, she had a habit of popping up just when he needed her. On the rare occasions when Jonno wondered if she had a particular interest in him, he would see her talking with some of the other guests behaving in a very similar way, which brought him unceremoniously back to terra firma.

The hotel also had other trekkers and climbers. Most coming back from their expeditions rather than preparing for them. Breakfast time was always interesting meeting the various characters who they were sharing the building with. There was an American church group from the southern states who had come for a mixture of walking and contemplation. They were incredibly welcoming and entertaining, but couldn't resist any chance to see if Jonno or his father would like to join them in a prayer session later that day. Jonno was impressed by the way they seemed to live their faith and it permeated most of what they said or did. But he also felt uneasy as it occasionally seemed a competition over who could quote the most bible chapters and verses in any one sitting.

Then there was Dietrich and Günter the two lean, dark haired and skinned Austrians who had come to climb. They had just got back from a mountain called Alpa Mayo and were ecstatic. It had long been on their list to climb and the conditions had been incredible, they said. Jonno sat in awe as they told of their adventures of camping on a glacier and then ice climbing four hundred meters to get them to the summit. It sounded such an adventure that he could almost feel his body yearning to do something similar. But what he loved most about them was how they didn't appear to take themselves too seriously. Clearly they had done something extraordinary, James confirmed this later with great excitement, in climbing this mountain that was meant to be one of the most beautiful mountains in the world. But the way they spoke of themselves was hilarious. Having reduced both James and Jonno to silence with the story of the summit, Günter, brushing away his floppy dark hair from his brow, turned to Dietrich and said,

"But you know...we are crazy Dietrich. You know... I think, why do we do this? Why climb the mountains?"

"It is true Günter, we could do any sport, we could be heroes anywhere, we spend so much time and money. And why do we do it?" Dietrich chimed in.

"I think we must be honest. Why do we do this? We do it for the girls!" Günter roared with laughter, "so that they will love us!"

"It is true! But where are the girls? There are no girls! We never find any in the mountains. And if we do they are too cold or too busy to talk to us!" Dietrich bronzed face grinned into the middle distance.

"The girls, they are elsewhere. They are at the beach, they are at the lake, some are on the bicycle. But here in the mountains, there are none! We spend all this time to impress them, but they do not see us!"

At which point they both collapsed in hysterics. These were the sorts of climbers Jonno loved to meet, not the distant ones who were always obsessed with the next peak they would conquer.

Jonno enjoyed wandering around Huaraz, it felt very different to the claustrophobic urban chaos of Lima. A lot of it, he discovered had been destroyed by an earthquake in the seventies which had reduced much of the city to rubble. As a result, many of the houses had a slight functional concrete and box-like appearance that he didn't find particularly attractive. But there were much less cars and people along with an endless supply of fresh mountain air. He loved the fact that no matter where he was, at any given moment, there was a mountain that could be seen in the distance. Huascaran appeared to hang on the horizon overlooking them all. One afternoon he sat in a plaza doing his best to try and sketch it. The more he looked the more gigantic and other-worldly it appeared, so much so it was hard to truly understand the scale. There was something about being so close to mountains, Jonno thought, that made one feel very small. Back home in the flat suburban life, in the rows and rows of houses, small unimportant things had the capacity to become very big stressful things. There was nothing bigger than the cars or houses to make people think beyond themselves. Yet here, surrounded by such awe-inspiring uprisings of the planet, who were far older than human beings, rising up and into the sky couldn't help but make those who lived under their presence aware of their own relative smallness to the earth, let alone the universe.

He had gone to do some drawing after a particularly difficult lunch with his father. Sketching in his own time gave Jonno a chance to breathe again and as he let his gaze settle on the great peaks in the distance, a chance to see them as things of beauty, not only to be climbed. The way their faces were full of ridges with gentle and harsh sliding contours. There was a softness to their enormous faces and sense of great patience and calm in them, that seemed in direct contrast to the stories of adventure, terror and bravery that were part and parcel of the climbing world. A small wrapping of light cloud would adorn the base, which only seemed to accentuate the summit. As he looked and contemplated, he found emerging in him a fascinating contradicting feeling of both wanting to be at the top but also being happy simply to look and witness. The mountain looked like it was there not only to be claimed but also respected. Were both possible, he wondered?

Jonno brought himself to this plaza a few times during the build-up to the climb. It was a chance to be alone with his thoughts and see the mountains in his way, rather than always through the adversarial lens of climbing them and the techniques needed to be safe.

He went to the plaza on one particular morning the day after they had been on a spectacular trip to a high lake called Laguna 69. It had been a good day but he was feeling exhausted and still not remotely comfortable with the thin air and had come home with a blazing headache. James had been irritatingly upbeat through the day and gave off the impression that it was all very easy for him. But at the same time it had been impossible to talk to him about anything apart from mountains and the one they were going to climb. Jonno had tried to talk about other things but found himself consistently shut down by his father's seemingly bullet-proof positivity. James seemed to have no trouble talking to the other trekkers they met and giving a good impression of himself to them, but when it was just the two of them the words seemed to dry up. It was not only the altitude that was making Jonno feel breathless.

As he sat there hunched over he saw a figure on the opposite corner of the small red bricked plaza that caught his eye. The figure was walking towards him, on her own, carrying some small bags. As she got closer he saw it was Magdalena. Immediately in a reflex action of protecting his drawings he turned them over and grabbed the book he had brought with him and begun to try appear as if he was reading from it.

"Hola Gringo," her cheery voice greeted him as she came near.

"Hey," Jonno said doing his best to smile naturally.

"Que pasa tio?" She said as she sat down next to him but not too close, gracefully and quietly letting her bags rest upon the floor next to them.

"Eh?" Jonno blurted out.

"Haha, oh… what's up?" Magdalena beamed.

"Ah, just chilling, today's a rest day. Yesterday we went to Laguna 69 and so Dad says we can have the day off."

"Que Bueno. I never went there, but they say it is so hermosa, so beautiful."

"You never went there?"

"No, haha, I know, everyone goes, but I never made the time. I am too busy."

"Oh. You should go, it was stunning. I never saw colours in water like that before."

"Si! People say the lakes here look like precious jewels scattered in the crown on the mountains. I have seen some, but not Laguna 69. You have inspired me, I must go!"

"Ha, I bet you say that to all the guests." Jonno then added, immediately not sure why he said that. The midday sun suddenly felt very bright in his eyes.

"Ha! It is true, I say many things to the guests. But I never lie to them. That would be bad."

"Haha, fair enough."

"You are drawing? I see you before you see me, you looked like you are concentrating very much. Can I see?"

"Er…. I was just…." Jonno fumbled for something to say.

"Oh I see, you are one of the timidos, you want the world to see you as a tough man and in control, climb the mountains and be a hero. That way you can hide your sensitivity. Then you can draw in peace and not let anyone see." Her tone did not seem to match her ever present sweet smile.

"Sorry!?" Jonno spluttered.

"Haha, it's OK gringuito, I am only playing. It's OK if you don't want to show me what you draw."

"It's just... I never feel happy sharing my stuff, I am never satisfied with it."

"Ah... then you must be an artist. Because what you do makes you suffer."

"Haha, I think you are very forward." Jonno sitting up a bit straighter and leaning forward.

"Haha, si tio, you are right. I have a bad habit of saying what I feel. Occasionally it gets me into trouble. Please forgive me."

"Haha I bet," Jonno replied loudly, his throat relaxing. "But I think I won't show you today if that's OK, it is not finished yet."

"Ha! The torture of the great artist, when to know when their work is finished and walk away from it!"

"Ha! Who are you? You sound like someone from an art philosophy book!"

"Haha, OK you catch me, I am reading a book on artists at the moment. I love it, I love the wild creativity of them. I think you are more an artist than a mountain climber."

"Sorry?" Jonno shook his head and scrunched his eyes against the bright sunlight.

"Haha, OK tio, maybe I say too much. But I see you with your father in the hotel and see you are two different people, that maybe you want different things. I think this must be hard for you, and him. You have both come to the mountains but you are climbing different ones."

"Wow...." Jonno stared at her.

"But it's OK, I see many people like you come here. They think they are coming for one thing and leave with another. So I feel it will be OK for you."

"I don't know what you mean?"

"Haha, I think I am just talking too much. But I must go now, my Papi needs me back at the hotel to help. He sent me out for a quick shopping today. Now I am late. Oh... he can get so cross!" Her eyes glowed as she stood up regathering her bags.

"OK, better get back to him then."

"Good to see you gringuito, keep drawing. One day you will show me! Haha!"

"Ha...only when it is finished," Jonno retorted. But by then Magdalena had gone, already on the other side of the plaza walking jauntily along back to the hotel and out of sight. And he was left alone again in his thoughts. As he came back to his body, he realised that there was a mild ache in his jaw and on further examination that he had a huge smile imprinted deeply across his face.

Over the two weeks of preparation James had meticulously prepared what he called an 'acclimatisation itinerary' that took him and Jonno for the heights of the mountain which involved visiting some of the local attractions as day trips and also a small four-day trek to get them both used to the kit they would carry and the weight. These trips passed well and without much incident and Jonno found himself gradually beginning to cope with the thin air and slowly adapt to what he was trying to do. Initially any quick or aggressive footsteps with his pack reduced him to a panting mess as he couldn't draw enough air in, but he soon learned to work with this rather than against it. Learning to make smaller steps and not let his mind get ahead of his body so the two moved in synchrony rather than the latter trying to get up the hills as fast as possible to catch up with the former.

***

They had some great days visiting the Laguna 69 and also Lake Churup which had the bonus of walking through a local village on the way. Jonno was taken by the feeling of going back in time as they walked through. Local men working in the fields, women in local dress of large hats, big bright skirts and colourful cardigans dotted throughout the villages with also some in the fields as well. Many had large shawls on their back carrying impressive weights, often accompanied by small children who also wore almost identical outfits. Everyone seemed friendly to them as they passed through and just carried on their business as though it was not a big event for them to be there. Many flashed big smiles before then going back to their business. It was a nice change from the hustle and bustle of Huaraz where Jonno was never totally sure if eye contact would then mean potentially being offered something to buy. The young children all seemed to have as much responsibility as the adults and at one point they had to take evasive action to abandon the path as a child no older than ten years' olds sauntered through with a herd of cows. He smiled at the gringos before yelling various commands to his herd to keep them in order. Life in the village seemed peaceful and welcoming and was framed by the now familiar yet still spectacular white tipped mountains that were consistently visible in the peripheries.

James kept a quick march up not seeming to ever want to spend too long to pause.

"Come on son, we've got a lake to get to."

"I know Dad, I'm coming."

"This is all good training for Casharaju"

"Phew Dad... I know but I'm just trying to take some of this in, it's incredible. Do we have to rush through?"

"I know what you're saying but we have to keep to schedule, we are trying to acclimatise quickly, don't forget."

"It's as though nothing else exists but this mountain." Jonno kicked at an innocent stone by his foot.

"I heard that Jonny. Please, I appreciate what you are saying but this is serious stuff. I would love to sit around all day sketching this stuff too, but we have to remember our main objective."

"You make it sound like something out of 'Call of Duty'." Jonno said quietly to himself, puffing his cheeks out an exhaling loudly.

"What was that?"

"Nothing." He took a deep breath, shrugged his daypack back on his shoulders and started moving his feet again.

For James it kept coming back to the mountain and how amazing it would be when they finally climbed it. He kept talking about altitude and the various tips and tricks he had for coping with it, then he would keep chipping away about techniques for walking on the snow and how they would cope with certain situations should they arise. Jonno began to feel like his father was missing the point let alone the majestic and wide-open scenery that they were walking though. Occasionally the conversation moved onto other areas and there was chance to just talk about life but it soon all worked its way back to do with something about Casharaju. Whenever Jonno asked about whether they should consider a guide the conversation quickly became cold or difficult and so after a while he just decided not to bother. Jonno began to find it easier to walk in silence and enjoy the company of his own thoughts, he trusted his father not to take any risks with them that he couldn't handle, but the process made for an increasingly isolated experience.

There were highlights though, seeing the colours of the lake in Churup were unforgettable. The deep blues and clear greens of Churup with the ragged and imposing peak of the same name standing over it. They had a wonderful picnic up there and then also braved a quick swim in the icy temperatures. Diving in, both father and son roared with a mixture of delight and sheer cold as they came up for air. In the subsequent picnic they had a good conversation about the importance of just enjoying life as they shivered themselves warm in the strong sunshine. The cold water seemed to momentarily snap James out of Casharaju obsession and they were able to have a laugh and reminiscence about the time when they went swimming in the sea on New Year's Day in Devon a few years previously. How the definition of swim had been taken to its limit by running in, dunking their heads underneath the water and then running out screaming again. Both Mum and Macie had held back as Jonno and his father had stripped off and run in, and both had refused to acknowledge their efforts as a swim which had almost caused a family meltdown later in the evening with Jonno and Macie almost coming to blows.

The four-day trek to Santa Cruz was their first experience carrying all their own kit and navigating together. After the long and bumpy bus journey to get there Jonno couldn't help but feel a little envy for the other trekkers who were starting at the same time as them but were with guides and donkeys meaning their packs were minimal. They all walked off at a good pace leaving him and his father behind under the weight of their extra tents and food supplies to share between them. The straps of his rucksack rubbed into his shoulders and the belt strap occasionally bit into his hips. They were consistently offered a guide or donkey but James seemed to revel in refusing them. Jonno noticed that the locals found his attitude a little irritating as though he might be denying them work and money by wanting to be independent.

The trek was their first experience of tenting together. James seemed to step up the intensity even more, consistently talking about how it was a warm up for the "main event." His focus seemed even more sharp and attentive to the details of being self-sufficient. The irony that Jonno found was that he enjoyed and took pleasure in the fact that they were carrying everything and doing their own cooking, even if it meant very simple food each night. Porridge in the morning and then high energy packets of food packets that hot water could be poured into for lunch and dinner which James had brought with him form the UK. It was basic and he supplemented the nagging hunger with the trail mix he had brought as well full of nuts, chocolate and raisins. It was the first long trek he had been on and soon got into the swing of setting up camp and finding a water source by which they could cook, clean and purify. There was a sense of pride of seeing him and his father doing it all for themselves in contrast to some of the other groups they met along the way who seemed accompanied by a large entourage of cooks, porters and donkeys. But there was also a part of him that felt he was missing out slightly seeing the groups eating together and sharing the evening with their Peruvian guides and helpers.

In their tent at night after they had eaten he could hear the laughter and shared experience from the other groups. James would be reading or generally plotting the next day, writing in his journal or keeping his thoughts to himself. Conversation was possible but there remained a feeling of something that was not being said or talked about and it hung heavy in the air.

The walking was challenging but the views more than counter-balanced the incessant breathlessness that came with such a heavy pack. James gave Jonno advice early on to make small steps, not big ones as a way of saving energy which he found really helpful. James seemed to talk it all in his stride, carrying a load that was significantly heavier than Jonno's but seeming to take great pride in this. There was an indefatigable attitude in how he approached the trek which was both motivating and grating. Every time Jonno mentioned that he was tired or finding it difficult it was met with a series of comments such as "well this will be nothing compared to next week" or "imagine if you had to carry my pack." When Jonno wanted to be vulnerable and open up about his doubts and fears, that if he was struggling on this trek then there was no way that he would get up Casharaju, the conversation would be shut down. James did not want to talk about weakness or failure, only adventure and possibility.

The trek took them over the famous Punta Union Pass. It was a tough and demanding day with each footstep getting harder towards the top. Not to mention seeing the other walkers without any extra weight who seemed to effortless float their way up and through. The view was worth it though, as Jonno and his father arrived gasping for air together at the small notch that separated the two valleys. To the left and right both valleys spilled back downwards flanked by rocky spurs that seemed to interlace endlessly into a descending horizon. The floor of the valley was studded by more opal lakes which look other-worldly with their deep and pastel like palette of blues and greens. The view was made sweeter by the physical toil that it had taken to get there. Both father and son exchanged a sweaty hug at the top which made it even more meaningful for Jonno, even if James then went on to talk about how Casharaju was going to be so much harder and they needed to stay focussed.

After the trek was done there was a chance for two days' rest and final preparation. Jonno returned to Huaraz feeling tired but much more used to his pack and the weight and so was feeling a little more confident than when he started. He had learnt with the altitude that there was nothing gained by trying to push things and that he just had to keep moving in a slow and steady way. Father and son had, despite the heavily one-sided conversations, developed a good rhythm together and had discussed endlessly how they were going to approach the climb. If anything, James' obsession and attention to detail meant that Jonno felt safe with him. They spent one whole morning trying on all the right kit, with crampons, boots, harnesses, ropes, clips, helmets, ice axes, snow gear and jackets all being thoughtfully chosen. James, to his credit, did not try and skimp and save money and made sure that they only had the best. Jonno gulped as each new item was added, aware that it was only going to add more weight, but he was impressed that his father was being so meticulous. He felt confident that nothing had been left to chance.

The owner of shop they went to seemed to be a little surprised when James mentioned they did not have a guide, especially, as he said, the weather was not going to be so good in the next few days. But James seemed to win his confidence back when he began speaking about all the planning he had done and the experience he had. The conversation then moved into what James did for a living and soon Jonno could see the familiar sight of a stranger looking up to his father for what he did. Jonno even found himself, for the first time in years, feeling the same way.

Chapter Sixteen - Getting Going

James had decided that it would be easier to hire a taxi to take them to the start. As much as he wanted to take local buses, it was just going too long and be too much hassle he said. The alarm went early and, having quickly showered, they went down for a breakfast in the dark hotel lobby. Rodrigo was there with a steaming pot of coffee and two plates of eggs and bread.

"Buenos Dias Señores!"

"Rodrigo!" James smiled, "Buenos dias amigo."

"So today is the day? You are excited?"

"Si Señor. We have been looking forward and preparing for this for some time now. I think we are ready."

"I think so too, I see all your preparation, and I feel you will have a great experience. Juanito, how are you?"

"Good morning Rodrigo, thank you for this," Jonno croaked in the dry air.

"De nada amigos. I will return to bed now but I come to wish you luck. All I say is please be careful. The mountains can be cruel places, no matter how much you have prepared. There is no shame if you must turn ba..."

"Thank you Rodrigo," James interjected. "We are feeling ready and excited. The maps are good, the kit is good and we are feeling strong. It will be a great adventure."

"Bueno, amigo" Rodrigo smiled slightly tensing his tired, early morning eyes. "I wish you both good fortune. Magdalena also sends her best wished to you both, she asked me to tell you."

"Thank you" said Jonno, feeling a little towards his father.

"OK Caballeros, I think your taxi is coming in ten minutes. I will leave you and welcome you home soon to celebrate!"

"Haha, thank you Rodrigo, you have been very kind." James spoke again, straightening both his and his son's cutlery.

Rodrigo then stood up, made a small bow and then quietly left them, his bare feet gently padding against the smooth and shiny floor of the lobby. Jonno and his father then both ate quietly. Jonno tied to steal the odd glance at his father trying to work out what he might be thinking but his face was blank, like it often was. Eyes locked into a middle distance and the sense that the was working through some sort of puzzle or other, trying to solve something. The occasional faint movement of an eyebrow was enough to signal that deep inside; some great thought process was whirring away. Jonno assumed that it was about the days ahead so left him to it.

The taxi arrived and they pulled out of Huaraz as the light of dawn was beginning to flood the valley. The streets were still mainly empty, which gave the place a ghost town feel. Normally thronging with people from the nearby villages who had come in to sell and trade, it felt unusual to see them so vacated. They passed through the various grid like streets until they made it through the city limits onto the main roads. The ride reminded Jonno of when they had left from Heathrow what seemed like an eternity ago. So much had happened even though it had been only two weeks. The sun had been rising then and the whole unknown of the adventure had lain out in front of them. Now they were finally leaving for Casharaju and the talking and planning was more-or-less over. As he looked at the sides of the valleys that were beginning to emerge from darkness, with their soft browns and greens revealing themselves, he remembered the uniform, indistinct suburban houses they had passed that day, with their occupants still dozing. It had felt like a secret with them both sneaking out of the UK early before the world awoke and got on with its daily mundane business, and this same day was feeling very similar.

The taxi ride passed in somewhat of a blur. The roads led away from Huaraz towards the imposing presence of Huascaran that seemed to hover regally above all that was below. The sky was clear and but there were some clouds to the east that seemed to be gathering. The weather had seemed to be changing in the last week and both James and Jonno had been frequently reminded that they were attempting this mountain not at the best time of year. The hotel had been quieter just before they had left and they met less mountaineers as when they had arrived. Undeterred James had brushed this off saying that they were more likely to have the mountain to themselves. As it was a 'trekking' mountain and that they should have little in the way of technical climbing to do, he seemed deeply unconcerned about where they were heading. The ice axe would just be for walking with and using to arrest themselves on the ice should they slip, otherwise it was more of a glorified walking stick he kept saying with a satisfied grin on his face.

The journey became increasingly bumpy as they got closer to the where they had agreed to be let off. After passing through a small town that seemed directly under the enormous gaze of Huascaran they turned onto a less finished track, meaning that the car had to slow to navigate the relative assortment of large rocks and crumbling pot holes that lay ahead. The driver huffed and puffed as his poor vehicle made passage though the obstacles, repeating over and over in Spanish how bad this was for his car. James however did not enter into conversation about it. Jonno heard him mutter under his breath on numerous occasions, he assumed it was something along the lines that the taxista "shouldn't have accepted the ride" if he knew it was going to be that bad. It created a slightly tense atmosphere in the car especially as the customary positions were taken of father in the front and son in the back. Jonno occupied his time listening to some music through his headphones and gazing out of the window, trying to take in the increasingly vast and seemingly endless scenery. Reading anything was out of the question as the car bumped, jumped and swerved its way along the road.

Out the window at one point he saw something that made him look again. On the corner of a forthcoming bed he saw a local woman, dressed in the classical big skirt and colourful cardigan, with her dark hair heavily plaited wearing a high visibility jacket and a yellow hard hat instead of the normal wide brim one he had seen so often in Huaraz. She was carrying something that looked heavy. As they came closer he saw that there more women, all who must have been at least 40 or older, carrying spades and other tools. Jonno had to take a second look as his eyes did not match anything that he could compute with in his brain. They looked as though they were working on the road.

"Dad, have you seen that?" he exclaimed. "What is going on here?"

"Wow" said James "I have no literally no idea. I thought the men were a little lazy in this country but this is taking it to a new level. Let me ask the driver. I've never seen this before."

After a few minutes of lively chat James turned back to face Jonno and said,

"OK, so it's a bit more interesting than first appears. It turns out that this is part of a government initiative. Basically it is a way of allowing women to empower themselves and reduce the social and economic gap between them and their male counterparts."

"Sorry?! By maintaining roads? I don't get it."

"So... as I understand this is done so that women can find more work, rather than just being in the fields or at home, and also gives them a sense of a life outside of the village. And it pays them. So it gives them another way of earning money, a way of becoming independent of the heavy traditional structure of the business. The driver here thinks it's a great idea."

"And they want to do this? Is it not really heavy work?"

"So it seems, it makes you wonder how bad their lives must be if they would prefer to do this. Across the developing world, if I am allowed to still use that phrase, there is great initiative to educate women and empower them more. To help them break the super structural environment of their villages and traditions, to help them challenge the traditional male cultural authority. It is being increasingly thought that to end poverty, the key is to educate women."

"Really, how so?"

"Jonny, you have to remember that the country we live in is very fortunate in that it has a great appreciation of women's rights and a desire to empower them as equal parts of society. Yes, there are problems and lots of work to be done, but great progress has been made. But in countries like this, they are miles behind. For so many people, women included, it is culturally seen that women are there to marry and have babies with. That they have no higher purpose. Because of this female education rates are low and pregnancy rates are high. This then leads to health issues as giving birth is so dangerous, especially in isolated communities. And then think about it, if women are always mothers and in a cycle of being pregnant and giving birth, it is harder for them to have the time to do anything for themselves as they are always looking after others. Their horizons are narrow before they have even got going. Their expectations of who they are and what they could achieve with their lives are already minimal. As a result, little is done to change the overwhelmingly male-orientated approach to how things are done."

"So schemes like this, show women that they are more capable than they believe themselves to be?"

"Exactly! It shows them they can earn some money, be independent of men and that there is possibility of doing something outside of the village."

"Amazing. So it is not that the men are being lazy. In fact, this isn't about men at all?"

"That's it. Imagine Macie out here, do you think she'd do this?"

"Haha, I think she'd like the hard boots to kick me with!"

"Ha!"

They drove past the women who stopped what they were doing to smile and waved at the passers-by. Light glinted from their golden teeth replacements as they offered broad and outwardly happy smiles to those in the car. Just as they passed them and were far enough away they driver made a comment that made him and James laugh.

"What was that? What did he say?" Jonno asked, not wanting to be left out.

"He said 'this road is terrible; you can tell a woman made it.'" James chuckled.

"Dad!" Jonno said, his face blushing. "You're just part of the problem if you are laughing at that."

"Oh Jonny, don't take life so seriously."

"Dad, honestly, that's not cool." Jonno said coldly. "People like you are actually part of the problem. And you don't even realise it!"

"Oh Jonny, just calm down. No I am not."

But Jonno didn't respond, he put his headphones back in and tried to calm himself down. He found this lurching between looking up to his father and being deeply disappointed him exhausting, let alone the car journey.

They eventually arrived at a small village at the entrance of the national park. Pulling up Jonno saw some small children with reddened cheeks and faded clothes coming running towards them. "Gringo!" they cried out in unison and came bounding towards them, over their shoulder he saw some older looking children in football shirts who were sitting on a stack of chopped wood holding back, eyeing them suspiciously. They came to the car windows smiling though, holding out their hands and yelling "caramello" and "un estilo" while laughing amongst themselves. Jonno, opened the door and stepped out, greeting them all with a friendly "hola." The driver then got out and made various hand movements and noises to shoo them away. They ran away in hysterics, laughing and pushing each other as they went.

The taxi driver then started to unpack their bags. Heaving them out onto the floor. They were both heavy, full of all the food and equipment they were going to need for the next few days. Jonno looked at the size of his rucksack and his fathers, and then took a deep breath. Thankfully James had organised the itinerary that they had time, and not far to travel each day. The weight wouldn't allow them to travel quickly, and in moving slower they would acclimatise better, which was his rationale. An elderly woman, dressed in bright orange with a red shawl wrapped around her hat with a kind and deeply lined face, sauntered over, she said something to the driver and then looked with a hopeful face to James and his son. James smiled and then said a firm "no" to her.

"She wants us to rent her donkeys," James turned to Jonno,

"Why don't we? Those bags look heavy I was thinking."

"No chance, we are doing this ourselves I'm afraid." James replied quickly, his eyes again looking to somewhere beyond the actual point in space and time where Jonno was stood. "The plan is a good one and we are going to be self-sufficient, that is *the* challenge."

"But...are you sure? I mean is it not a good idea to get some help?"

"Jonno, please. Everything I have done in my life I have managed to do myself, no help from anyone. That's what gives you confidence in yourself, when you know you can look after yourself and not rely on anyone else."

The woman, who didn't appear that she understood English then shot James an aggressive look and shook her head. Jonno wondered if maybe she didn't need words to understand his father, the tone of his voice and body language probably said it all. She then said one more thing to the taxi driver before turning her back on them and heading back into the village.

"What did she say then?" Jonno asked.

"Weather is turning bad." James said.

"Really? I thought it was going to be OK?"

"Jonno, it's fine. She's just grumpy that we are not giving her any money. Don't worry about it. Speaking of which, I'll pay the driver and we better be on our way. We have Camp One to get to!"

James turned and settled up with the driver. The man smiled, shook his hand, patted him on the shoulder and then made his leave. The engine noise of the car puncturing the airy village stillness before fading as he disappeared down the track. James turned excitedly to his son, "OK amigo, vamos. Let's do this!"

With their heavy packs on they followed a path through the main village. Despite the reception that the orange woman had given them, the rest of the village seemed friendly enough. More small children ran to them asking them for gifts as they passed through the dilapidated concrete and adobe buildings. Running nimbly in their sandals over the uneven ground, they looked very at home in this far flung environment. Further up the track a young boy with a small herd of cows came towards them. James and Jonno had to step quickly out of the way so as not to be knocked flying. The boy ambled on, calling out to the cows every now and again, hitting the odd one with a stick and throwing stones. He looked as though he had been doing this all his life.

"This place is just so different, isn't it Dad?" Jonno said as they started to reach the edge of the village. "I mean how do they live here? It feels like nothing has changed for years."

"This is why it's so important to come to places like this Jonny," James replied. His enduring signature habit of answering questions that he wanted to answer but that hadn't necessarily been asked. "You never see where you are from in the same way after you have seen how people live elsewhere, in such different conditions."

"How do you mean?"

"I mean... well I found that when I came back from traveling the first time, seeing how little some people had, it had a huge effect on my life. It helped me appreciate what I *had* back at home, where often had thought about what I didn't have."

"I guess..."

"It's a perspective thing. It's always easy to think about what you don't have, so many people spend their whole lives doing this. But when you actually rub shoulders with people, human beings just like you, who have so little and make the best of it, it makes you think. We are extremely lucky to live where we do and have the lives we do. I hoped this would come out on this trip."

"Yeah," Jonno replied breathing deeply as he struggled to walk with the heavy pack and talk at the same time in the thin air. "It's one thing seeing it on the internet or television I suppose, another actually seeing it for yourself."

"Exactly."

The walking took them from the village following a river which was flowing the opposite way to their own movement. They followed a well-marked path but with James stopping every now again to make sure they were where he wanted them to be on his map. They took lunch in the shade by the river and rested before saddling up again and walking on slowly to where they would camp that evening. After so long in the making and the thinking, both men felt secretly relived to be on the trail at last. Even the sight of clouds beginning to creep surreptitiously across the open sky did nothing to dampen their enthusiasm, the weight of expectation and imagination had now been transformed into the physical reality of their packs. Neither wanted to admit to the other they felt too heavy and so they plodded on, breathless but relieved to have finally started.

Chapter Seventeen - Justino, Campesino

I'm not sure I'll ever understand these Gringos, either in speaking to them or why they do what they do. I mean look at them, carrying such heavy bags, breathing hard, looking always at the mountains, dreaming of being at the top. It doesn't make any sense to me.

I have always been from this area, growing up in one of the pueblitos. My family have been here as far back as the stories. My Father, his father, his father, they all worked the land. Now that is what I do and bring my sons with me to learn so that they will know how and survive. That said, more of the young of the village are leaving, going to the cities like Huaraz and Lima to look for what they think is a better life. More money, mas plata. I suppose I can't blame them, we thought about going, getting away from the intense physical life here. But in the end I couldn't, this is my home, our home. We are meant to be here.

But I see the westerners come, they walk through our villages with big bags, shiny sunglasses yelling their "holas" and taking pictures of our wives hanging out our washing. The children love them though, they find them endlessly fascinating, they love having their picture taken and seeing their own faces on the dark screens. It is these interactions that we fear will inspire our children to leave us, go explore the world outside the village, to end up as taxi drivers in Lima because they think it will be better there.

These two walking now, they seem a typical couple. Big bags and cameras. They drink water out of a pipe attached to the bag, it can't all be water in there can it?! They walk with purpose and determination; eyes focused slightly beyond where they are now. It is hard to read their expressions, their faces are so much softer than ours, and their glasses hide their eyes. It hard to know what they might be thinking. But even while resting you can see them looking at the mountains to the snow. Imagining themselves to be up there on the summit.

I never understand this, when life is hard enough, why take such risks? For us the mountains are beautiful, for some even sacred. But for all of us they are dangerous and not for living. Why would you go up there, how can you live there? These foreigners must have very strange lives if they want to risk them to be on the top of them. My one life is so tiring, why would I spend my free time to use up even more energy and put myself in danger. We often laugh amongst ourselves that these white people must have gone mad in their cities, that in having finally achieved all the money, comfort and safety they could have ever wanted, they want to risk it all to stand on the top of a mountain. Every day is dangerous for us here in the mountains, we have to be careful, people get hurt, get sick and might quickly die. Yet these gringos are inviting these things upon them by climbing these mountains. It doesn't make any sense, they have such amazing lives, lives we can only dream of yet still they come. I wonder if they are unhappy, is that why they come? What do they search for? Or do they have no fear of death?

I wonder if these two are father and son, they look similar. Maybe the father is teaching his son about life the way I teach mine. Maybe the son wants to follow him, and grow up to be like him. Or does he, like many of our children, think life will be better elsewhere? I don't speak any Spanish or other language but Quechua so I cannot ever talk to them, but I smile, wave and try and wish them well. Even though I think they are mad, I don't wish them any harm.

And now they go again, the taller, stronger man taking the lead. He seems like he has purpose in his movement, the smaller one looks like this is hard for him even though his bag is smaller. Both look at their watches, it always amazed me how important timepieces are to these gringos. They all have these big boxes on their wrists. For us it is just the sun, when it is up we work and when it is down we rest. I wish them well I suppose, they are not with a guide which is a bit strange, but maybe they are very experienced. Anyway, I have rested now, I better carry on.

* * *

Chapter Eighteen - Base Camp

"Almost there!" shouted James as they came over the steep ridge. Jonno was breathing hard about 30 meters behind his father a little further down the track. The climb up the path to here had been exhausting and he was soaked through from the rain. Jonno looked up to see his father beaming a familiar broad smile against a backdrop of grey cloud in amongst the boulders. He had found the spot he wanted to camp in and was looking very pleased with himself.

"How do you know?" Jonno panted back.

"It matches the pictures and research I did perfectly," James yelled. "Come on, let's get set up and get dry!"

The walk up had been laborious and pain staking this morning. Having left their camp in the valley floor the ascent had become a lot more vertical as they had to climb another 800 meters skywards to the level of the moraine field. Up until today the walking had been more or less at a gentle gradient deeper into the valleys, but today it involved taking a much sharper incline. The base camp of Casharaju was based in the rocky moraine fields that are the last bit of the mountain before the snow begins. The ascent from the valley floor meant snaking up the switch-back trails of the mountain, leaving behind any vegetation and growth and moving increasingly into this new rocky world. The track became increasingly less certain underfoot as packed earth became replaced with shale-like stone. Each step required not only balance but the capacity not to let each foot slide backwards in moving forwards. The day had been frustrating and exhausting, the packs feeling heavy and uncomfortable. James had marched energetically ahead, Jonno had kept having to stop and catch his breath.

This was compounded by the fact that the clouds had moved in, obscuring the view of the mountains. Over the last few days it had become cloudier and gloomier as the day went on. The days tended to begin with a clear blue sky but it was full of dark heavy cloud by mid-morning. The incredible views of the jagged white peaks that had taken both their breaths away when they first saw them were hidden from sight, leaving little inspiration to catch their eye as they trudged on, weighed down by their packs.

Jonno tried to cast his mind back to when he first saw Casharaju as they cleared the forest they were walking in yesterday. They had passed through another village and then a thick forest up on to a high plane. The sky was still gloriously empty and in the distance was Casharaju's beautiful triangular looking peak straining towards the sky. The contrast of its white purity, enormity and how it stood alone rising up against the clear blue had stopped him in his tracks. It was magnificent and he dropped his pack and sat to catch his breath and simply look. It had been the first moment since they had left that he thought this adventure might be worthwhile. He had been feeling fed up and irritable. His father, despite carrying a much heavier pack than him, had been pushing ahead and making this all look very easy. Jonno's shoulders and hips were screaming at him from the weight and he was genuinely wondering whether he might be doing his back some damage. The frustration of this was boiling over towards his father and he was finding himself unable to have any sort of conversation with him without snapping at him. James had wisely realised to keep his distance and say as little as needed.

But when they finally witnessed the object of their striving, Jonno found himself transfixed. He was stunned at how beautiful this white triangle looked, that stood alone and higher and that the other peaks near it. This was not the highest mountain in Peru, not even close, but from this angle it had no competition. It appeared to just be sitting there, patient yet majestic. Waiting to be discovered. It's size and grandeur only intensified by the electricity of the cobalt heavens that were behind it. The question crossed his mind - how on earth were they going to be standing on top of that? - the idea seemed ridiculous. But then another thought appeared, he saw the mountain as something to be taken, to be conquered. He felt a deeper longing to be victorious, to win out against its size and might. For the first time on the trip he felt an appreciation of the fascination and madness that must come with mountains, the desire to risk it all to make it to their summits. He had been reading about Mallory's expedition to Everest after the First World War and the siren-like hold it seemed to have. Despite having survived the horrors of the trenches and returning safely to his family, he would then leave his wife and children and go back three times in four years to claim it. His obsession was so great that he lost his life pursuing it. Now faced with the mountain he was to climb, Jonno felt a similar yearning take over his body. He took his gaze from the peak and looked at his father, who too was staring at the mountain. Looking wide eyed and excited, the hint of a smile appearing at the corners of his stubbling face.

"There she blows" James pointed his walking stick.

"Incredible" Jonno replied. "And we're going to climb that?"

"Certainly are." James said, his voice sounding deeper than normal.

"Wow."

"Wow indeed," James laughed. To which Jonno, in his exhaustion and fatigue, had no resistance and started chuckling himself. Both men sat on their heavy bags chuckling together as beads of sweat poured from their faces.

But today had been different after the hope and excitement of yesterday. The clouds had closed in quickly and Casharaju had been lost early from view. They both woke up feeling sore from their efforts and it took time to eat and break camp. The path was well signposted with a red wooden sign with Casharaju written on it pointing the way. The climb to high camp was going to steep and strenuous James had warned. But they had time and there was no need to rush. A rocky path scored into the landscape that snaked forward and back on the side of the mountain. It made for slow going as they rose up from the valley floor but what had made it harder was that the weather had taken a turn for the worse. With the clouds coming in also brought rain and they had both become increasingly soaked through. Rain normally meant snow further up, but he tried not to think about this and what it might mean for the expedition. The increased greying of the land was becoming matched by a slate drab of the sky, after the inspiration of yesterday the old aches and pain roared back with nothing to distract or pacify the eye or mind.

Straining against the loads of their packs they pushed on, following the trail that was obvious and well-marked with small piles of stones that other climbers had left. It surprised Jonno seeing how many cairns they saw yet they did not see any other climbers. He knew this mountain was a popular trekkers' mountains from what he had spoken to his father and read about it, yet it felt strange that if that was the case, they had seen no other climbers since they had been dropped off by the taxi. They had passed through a second smaller village and seen some other local men out farming the fields but otherwise that had been more or less it. Jonno had been expecting to see others on this mountain and it felt odd that they were alone. When he had asked his father, James had simply focussed on how lucky they were to be able to have this all to themselves.

The moraine field was the final stop before the snow. Acres and acres of large boulders scattered at the edges of the snowline. They weaved their way through this, needing to take regular small breaks as the air was now noticeably thinner. The path seemed obvious however by virtue of the cairns and smaller stones that appeared to have been well trodden. Finally arriving at a small flattened area where they could see the echoes of previous tents from the arrangement of small but heavy rocks that must have been used to tie the ropes onto. The rain had stopped now but both men were wet and the first priority was getting the tent up and getting dry. This they did silently but quickly, used to the rhythm of doing this together regularly over the previous few weeks.

Once the tent was up, James told Jonno to get inside and change his clothes, as he went to fetch some water so they could have something to drink. Jonno quickly took his layers off in the cramped tent and unpacked his bag to get his sleeping bag and dry layers out. It was a relief to finally be in shelter and he put dry socks and leggings on and then wrapped himself in his bag. His head was thumping and he took a swig of water from his flask. There were definitely moments when his father's bullet proof positivity and almost endless energy levels was something to be grateful for, and this was one of those.

James eventually came back having filled their collapsible water container and set about preparing some food for them to eat. Jonno huddled in the back of the tent still trying to get warm. The flare and whooshing noise of the stove leant a familiar comfort to the alien, rarefied environment they had arrived in. There is something about the sound of cooking that can make almost anywhere feel homely. He watched his father work quickly and skilfully, boiling water and preparing the drinks and food they were to eat. He couldn't help but be impressed at his seemingly endless energy levels. All Jonno wanted to do was nestle in his bag and try and get warm. His father seemed to revel in each new challenge, there was a genuine vitality about him that shone out.

"Thanks Dad."

"Hey Jonno, how are you getting on back there?"

"I feel pretty cold and knackered, if I had to be honest." Jonno said with a faint smile.

"Ha! You're doing really well, that wasn't that easy. Not ideal conditions but we got through it, that's the important thing."

"True, though do you think it will be OK for tomorrow. Will we see anything?"

"I think we just need to see. After this I am going to go and just make sure I know the path to the snow and familiarise myself with that, and then we can go through kit checks later. I don't feel like it is going to rain all afternoon, when I was out there just then the sky seemed to be clearing a little."

"Sounds good."

"But for now, just rest and get yourself warm again. Keep drinking loads of water and just try and relax. You've really pushed yourself these last few days."

"Thanks Dad, so have you."

"Ha! This was my idea; I have no choice!" James laughed as the water began to boil.

"I think you love this stuff don't you?"

"You know; I was pondering that same question earlier this morning. I think I do, even though it is hard. I find that there is something exhilarating about pushing yourself to the edge of who you think you are. I think as humans, we are capable of so much, but we can never know unless we try, unless we go for it."

"How do you mean?"

"I mean, Jonno, and maybe you'll see this more as you get older. Life is a constant choice, of sticking with what you know or seeing if you can go further. For me it doesn't stop, the exploration of my boundaries. I see so many people, especially through my work, who have given up and settled for the particular story they have told to themselves who they are. And often they are bored and unhappy, waiting for the world to come and find them. I don't want this in my life."

"Fair enough." Jonno added, unsure whether his father was being patronising or simply sharing something important with him.

"I feel life is short Jonny, perhaps even shorter than we are aware. And we have to make use of the time given to us. I meet people at work all the time whose lives have suddenly changed and they have lost the good health that they never even realised they had, that they took for granted. And they are left with regret and resentment about never taking any of the opportunities they never even knew they had. I want to keep climbing mountains while I still can, I don't want to wait for tomorrow, I don't believe in that."

Jonno paused, having never heard his father speak so honestly before. He didn't really have anything to say, but he wanted to hear more.

"Not only that Jonny, but this is special for me to do this with you. To have this experience. I wasn't able to do these sort of things with my father. He worked so hard, which provided a very good roof for us to live under and food on the table. But I didn't see him that often as he was so busy. I promised myself that when I was a father, I wouldn't be like that."

Jonno took a deep breath and looked at his father. His crouched back to him stirring the pot on the stove, unsure what to make of what he just heard. The last thing he wanted to do was get into a row up here and something in him boiled as he heard these words.

"Look Jonny, this is why I wanted this trip. Amongst many things, it was to share something amazing with you. I have realised recently we haven't spent as much time together I would have liked. And I don't know about you, but I am loving the adventure of it. Here we are, father and son, out here in the wilderness, pushing ourselves, climbing mountains. For me, it doesn't get much better."

"Yeah Dad, it is pretty awesome, I must admit that. Even if I do have a thumping headache."

"Ha, yes, it is tough. But that is what makes it such a valuable experience. Not many people have the drive to do this, to take themselves out of their comfortable and easy lifestyles and really push themselves. They want the glory and intensity of life without getting their hands dirty, and then they sit around complaining unendingly, watching their box sets and eating fast food, that life is boring. I believe we grow as people when we choose the hard option, not the easy option. This is what we are doing now and these are the memories we will revel in later. I know it."

"You have an amazing drive Dad; I'll give you that." Jonno let the words fall from his mouth, even though part of him found they tasted a little bitter in his dry mouth. He took another swig of water.

"Haha, that's kind of you Jonny."

"No... I don't mean that..."

"Ha, it's OK," James interrupted, handing Jonno a bowl of hot tea, "I know you mean well. It's good to share this with you, honestly. Cheers!" And he motioned his own mug towards Jonno's and they gently clinked before taking the warm fluids deep inside their cold bodies. The tea, black and dark, tasted superb, one of the best Jonno had had for some time. The warmth of the plastic mug in his hand and the steam rising up onto his face was soothing and reassuring. Both men let the conversation drop, letting the tent fall quiet as they drank. For a brief yet lingering moment, Jonno had a sense that there was nowhere any better than this he could possibly hope to be. He clutched the mug firmly so as to feel and absorb all the heat and tried to savour each sip, he felt a gentle dampness in the corner of his eyes. This was a cup of tea he did not want to rush.

Once they had eaten James left the tent to go and check the route to the snowline. So far his extensive research seemed to be paying off. The trail to the campsite had been as he hoped and it matched all the reading and images he had found when he was preparing back in the UK and also when they were in Huaraz. This trip had reminded him of one of his many medical exams, the endless gathering of information, the pouring over of different sources and viewpoints. He had enjoyed the build-up and it was satisfying that it seemed as though it was coming together. Although he hadn't been in the mountains for quite some time, the old habits and tricks seemed to be coming back to him without too much extra effort. He had been quite experienced when he was climbing regularly and he felt that a lot of this had been returning over the last few days. Occasionally there had been a nagging thought about whether a guide might have been sensible, but he had found various ways to shut this thought out. Independence had been the baseline for all his success in his life so far he mused, so there was no need to change that now.

The snowline was under hour away and he found it fairly easily, following the well-trodden path that seemed to have cairns regularly dotted along it showing the way. It felt as though this was all coming together nicely, that his preparation had been correct and that Jonno was coping well. The sky was heavy and the mountains all blocked from view but thankfully the rain had stopped. Hopefully it would clear tomorrow and they would have a decent enough conditions to attempt the summit. Once he reached the snowline he saw a path of footprints cut into the snow where others must have walked this season. Casharaju was a popular mountain and he knew that they should be able to use this to trace their way to the top. As he inspected them, while still on the rocks, he saw there had been some recent snowfall and they were not as deep as he was expecting. They were still visible but a bit softer than he was expecting. Walking through them was going to take a little more effort than he was hoping for, but he decided not to dwell on this. They were here now and tomorrow was the day. He moved quickly without the pack on his back and returned to the tent to find Jonno fast asleep.

The afternoon was spent preparing for the next day. James quickly returned to his previous intensity, meticulously going through all the kit, making sure everything worked and fitted correctly. Jonno felt exhausted and just wanted to rest but James would not let him and until he was satisfied with what they had and they knew how to use it. Everything was laid out, tried on, clipped in and tested to make sure it was working. Then they spent a good period of time practicing rope work and making sure they knew how to tie in together properly. James found the old dexterity with the knots and the ropes was still there, his fingers seemed to instinctively remember what they had to do. Casharaju was not going to demand anything more than a long day walking to the top. He had begrudgingly made an agreement with his wife before they left that they would turn back if any ice climbing and abseiling was involved. At the time he felt irritated by this but now, with the reality of the mountain physically looming above him even though he could not see it, he felt this was the right approach. He was here for the summit, but not, as he had promised many times, at the risk of his son.

Chapter Nineteen – Mountain

"Right Jonno, the day is here" A voice came from the cold dark in the tent.

"Errr...wha...ah...yes...morning Dad."

"Did you get some sleep?" the voice continued

"Not really to be honest, it was hard to switch off, and I needed the loo a few times as well."

"Well at least you're hydrated."

"True, I shouldn't complain I suppose."

"Right let's get on with this, the day is here!"

Jonno opened his eyes and felt the cold bite into his face despite being in the tent. His body felt warm and snug in his sleeping bag, and a voice in him was pleading not to leave its cosy safety. James eased himself out of his bag and was quickly dressed. In almost no time at all he had the stove fired up in the porch and busy boiling water for breakfast. I bet his patients love him Jonno thought, and then laughed quietly to himself, wondering what must have happened to him on this trip to be thinking so positively about his father, especially in such an early and dark morning.

Outside the tent was still black, they had planned to rise just before the dawn and get to the snow as the sun was rising. James didn't want to walk on the snow in the dark, even though it might make the walking easier, that was one risk he didn't want to take. Normally the snow is more compact at night and makes for easier walking with crampons. When the sun comes up it begins to melt and makes for a softer footfall, meaning spending more energy. Jonno shuffled out his bag and into his trousers for the day. He was bursting for the loo again and squeezed his way past his father and the hissing stove into the early morning air. He looked up and saw a clear sky strewn with a litter of stars in all directions. It was a new moon making the night feel even darker which allowed their light to really burn uninterruptedly. Without his torch it was very dark, the sort of darkness that you could not see your own hand in. Jonno turned his torch off as an experiment and found the sensation of himself disappearing into the night. As his light extinguished itself, all there was left was twinkling stars in the night's sky and a deep and unfathomable blackness. For a brief moment he found himself existing as simply a disembodied observing presence, surrounded by an ocean of sparkling suns. The loss of his familiar body unnerved him and he quickly turned his torch back on, it was strangely comforting to see his hands again.

James finished preparing breakfast and they had a fine meal of porridge and tea with snickers bars. James was clearly excited, and his body seemed to bristle and twitch with energy. Jonno could see he was doing his best not to champ at the bit and get on with the day. With their snow clothes on and warm down jackets, they were able to sit outside the tent on a nearby rock. Neither said much, which allowed each of them to be lost in his own thoughts with the silent backdrop of an exquisite stillness. They were the only ones in this rock field, on the side of this mountain but they were together. This shared solidarity accompanied by the silence served to only intensify a mutual respect for each-others strength and perseverance to have made it to this place. There were words that were almost impossible to say but deeply felt by both. Both had their doubts, similar yet different, yet again these too went unsaid. Both found themselves drawing courage from the fact they were with the other.

With breakfast finished, they stacked the bowls and went through the last checks of kit. Everything was in order and they were ready. James was carrying the bulk of the load and ropes, which he noticed was somewhat heavier than he would have liked. They both had their snow boots on which, like ski boots, made walking a slightly clumsy affair.

They followed the trail through the dark moraine to the where the snow began. It was steep and awkward in places as they moved through the winding array of rock and boulder and then onto more switch backs as they climber ever higher. The lack of light made for a disconcerting experience for Jonno as he was unable to see any further ahead than the light of his torch. This meant that he could never gauge where they were or how far they had to go. With the air being thin he carried doubt as well as his kit in his bag. He walked slowly, wondering if he could make it. When he forgot himself and let his mind wander to other things, the steps came easily. But then every now and again the boots made him stumble and he had to come back to the exhausting concentration of paying total attention to where his feet were going. Having nothing to distract his eye made the walk feel long and arduous. Being with his father was probably what kept him going, even if he found himself cycling through some of his many frustrations with him, especially following each new stumble. Having a torch on was curiously blinding as well as illuminating. With it on meant that he could see a few meters ahead to where he was going and nowhere else. Yet on the occasions that they both stopped to catch their breath they would sit and turn them off. Then they would, as Jonno found at the tent earlier, seem to disappear while the light of the stars would re-emerge as their eyes adjusted. So would return the surreal sensation of floating in space with and endless canopy of stars above and deep nothingness below.

Finally, after what seemed an eternity, Jonno saw a faint silvery glow further ahead. The blackness of the sky was beginning to soften as sunrise approached. Shapes and outlines were beginning to appear on the edges of his vision and he was needing to rely on the torch less and less. The clear sky meant that he could see the contours of land reveal themselves from far away, and other jagged peaks that had been hidden began to rise up. The sunrise was taking them both from a shadowy and unformed sense of anticipation to a now solid reality and challenge. With sight came a serenity. Seeing the mountain ahead was infinitely easier than trying to imagine it.

As they walked, scrambled and climbed on, the dim white ghostly spectre of Casharaju loomed up more and more to his right, where it must have been hidden by the blanket of grey cloud the day before. He couldn't see the top but suddenly it was there looking back at him, a shiver of excitement ran through him. It looked magnificent. Its vast white, smooth, triangular shoulders sloping inwards. Jonno felt as though he was in the presence of a god, looking calmly down at him, utterly confident in its own power. *No wonder people worship these things.*

They stopped to put their crampons on and rope up. The other mountains were coming into view, some looking like ragged teeth with their points facing skywards. The land was stirring with gentle colour. Jonno sat on a small rock catching his breath and clipping his crampons on. He was used to be being almost permanently out of breath now at this altitude and had learnt to just try and not panic from it. Whether resting or moving it never felt like there was enough oxygen.

James busied himself with getting the roped ready. Intense, serious, he looked as focussed as Jonno had ever seen him. Despite this, he fumbled his crampons initially. James, with a mechanical but authoritative voice, went through the do's and don'ts of how they were to approach the ascent. Mountains were ruthless and utterly dangerous he kept repeating. He seemed to end every almost sentence with: "My word is final on the snow."

Jonno had never been up to anywhere close to 6000m's before. And Casharaju stood at just below this. They had another 1000m's to go in height before they got there and today was going to be a tough slog. He thought of what his friends in Spain might be doing right now on their holiday. "This is cool" he thought, "I bet they'd love to be here."

There were clear footprints on the snow where others had walked, but they didn't appear as defined as he was expecting. The recent bad weather must have caused some snowfall up here, James had said, which was going to make the conditions a little harder. As they began to crunch their way onto the snow, roped about 10 meters from each other, Jonno felt his feet sink into the tracks on each step. It was not the familiar bite of crampons on snow he had experienced when they walked together in the Cairngorms a few winters ago, but instead a gentle giving way of the feet as they sunk on movement. Within a few steps Jonno was already realising that this was going to be even more effort that he had hoped for.

James led the way, following the tracks that were still visible. It was slow moving due to the lack of certainty under-foot but they began to make good progress. The route was initially switch-backs to get up to the enormous white shoulder of the mountain, which was directly above them. Clear zig-zags marked the way but it was hard going even from the offset. Occasionally a cold gust of wind would blow through and take all the heat from his hands, despite wearing the best gloves they could find, Jonno felt the beginnings of numbness in his fingers. He always suffered from bad circulation and had experienced painful hands before, this was one part of the climbing he never enjoyed.

However, the sky was now opening out and sun appeared close to arrival. The stars had faded away and serrated lines of mountains to the east initially blocked its light. An orange hue materialised as the first edges of the sun touched the horizon, then slowly and steadily it began to creep into sight, showering all it touched with its light and warmth. Over to the west were the four peaks of Huandoy rising up out of the gloomy earth beneath. As the sun came up over the horizon Jonno gasped as he saw the upper parts of the summits explode with yellow light as though it were a golden crown on fire. All the other peaks of the other mountains that could receive the light had a similar effect, as though they were ignited, blazing away in the early morning light. The early daylight gave the snow a deep blue quality while it was still in shadow. The colours were vibrant and concentrated in a way that was not possible to appreciate from down below.

Lost in the wonder of what he was seeing he felt a sharp tug on the rope almost knocking him off his feet.

"Jonny, what are you doing? Are you OK?"

"Sorry Dad, I was just taking in the view. It's incredible." He half-yelled and half-gasped.

"Isn't it something?" his father appeared to be grinning under all his protective gear and safety helmet. "We've been very lucky to see this; I think there are clouds on the way. We need to keep a steady pace I'm afraid."

Jonno looked around and saw the beginnings of some grey clouds float their way. The clear skies were not going to last long and so he did his best to take in what he was seeing as much as he could do. The deeper snow meant that his feet were resting inside the snow which had the effect of making them lose heat quickly. Similar to his hands he felt the beginnings of numbness creep in.

They followed the soft tracks slowly and steadily and arrived after a few hours to a flatter plateau where more of a 360-degree view was possible. To the right was where they had just come from, they could see down into the valley and the moraine camp. Interspersed amongst the rocky landscape were lakes that looked like they were jewels studded into the landscape. Emerald greens and turquoise blues greeted their eyes, the uniformity and vibrancy of their colours along with their calm and flat surface was completely at odds with the rugged and rocky surroundings. The landscape was one of total contrast with the smooth and curvaceous snow of the mountains against the hard, rough rock that it had settled on. To the left seemed an unsettling sheer drop, down into a similar looking valley floor but with a vastly steeper gradient. Jonno was glad that the path they were on did not go too close. The white had a purity to it in contrast to the relative dark and almost dirtiness that the rock seemed to possess. Above the snow line seemed another world, one of grace and beauty, high above the dust and chaos of all that lay below. It appeared clean and without angle, all smooth curves and no solid edges.

Occasionally as they walked Jonno was reminded of the danger of where they were as they passed in close proximity to the edge of a yawning crevasse which appeared to have no bottom to it. Fangs of icicles seemed to surround its mouth, giving a sense of vertigo if he stood looking for too long. Jonno was finding that he was having to stop and recoup energy much more than he wanted to. James seemed a little impatient with this, reminding Jonno that they were in for long day and they needed to keep momentum. Jonno trudged on, oscillating between awe at what he was seeing and fatigue from his body. He found it easiest to walk in the exact footsteps that his father had made ahead of him. He chuckled to himself at the irony of this as he had only recently made a pact with himself in the last year to be nothing like his father. Yet whenever he experimented and tried walking off the beaten path, he found that his feet sunk further and he had to spend far too much energy to move.

They stopped to take some mid-morning food and catch up with each other. The clouds had begun to thicken and lot of the surrounding landscape had been lost to view. Casharaju was still in sight, but a lot of its fellow mountains were hidden again behind a foggy veil. Occasionally they would part and give a glimpse of what lay behind, but then they would shut again and the climbers would be left with only the mountain they were on. Jonno noticed that his father was breathing heavily when he sat next to him.

"You OK Dad?"

"Yeah…. I'm fine. Just hard work getting through this snow that's all."

"Still feeling confident we'll get to the top?"

"Jonno… I have no doubt. If I sign up to anything then it is not going to beat me. Not before now and certainly not now." His eyes remaining fixed on the direction they were heading.

"You climbed this before didn't you? Has it changed much?"

"Funny you should mention that, but it feels very different. I remember the route and approach as very different. But it was a long time ago. What is amazing is how little snow there seems on the mountains around us. When I was here 20 years ago, the whole area seemed covered in it. I'd heard that global warming might be affecting these mountains and they have certainly changed in this short time. I wonder if one day these might be mainly rock climbing rather than trekking on snow."

"Do you think we have far to go still?" Jonno asked not sure if he wanted to hear the answer.

"At least another 4 hours I would say, if the going is good and the weather holds. It's hard to make quick progress with the snow the way it is."

"Yeah, it's so hard to make easy steps. What's it like at the front?"

"It's OK, I'm managing. Its…" James paused, "it's a good challenge."

"Well I really appreciate it, thanks Dad." Jonno suddenly said, aware that perhaps this was the first time on the trip he had directly thanked his father for anything.

"Ha! You're welcome son. I can't tell you how special this is to me to have you here." James grinned broadly from behind his reflective goggles. "I never did anything like this with my father and I didn't want to miss out on that with you."

"It's incredible dad, honestly. I'll never forget this morning's sunrise."

"No, it was quite something wasn't it? Right…let's saddle up and go, time is ticking and I don't want us to be on the snow after dark. It's going to be a close-run thing."

"Fine." Jonno muttered, "Onwards."

After another hour or so on the plateau they arrived at a part where the snow and ice began to steepen again. Looking upwards was an ungainly but achingly smooth mound that rose up ahead of them. Behind it was only clouded sky and it stood alone lifted up from the plateau. James pointed his ice axe in the direction of its top, "there she blows!" he yelled.

They walked on following the tracks and began to snake up higher and higher from the floor of the long plateau they had been on. The clouds were now fully around them and there was nothing else to see but the mountain they were on. The summit was finally in view but as they were to discover over the next few hours, it would keep playing with them. Appearing to be over the next horizon, over the next crest, only for another set of ridges to appear and make them feel like they had to start all over again.

The final few hours to the summit proved to be utterly mentally exhausting. Both men silently convincing themselves that they were almost there only to have to see their hopes dashed yet again and muster up the strength and resolve to go again. Added to this for James was a nagging sense of time that he did not want to be spending so long exposed above the snow. He was feeling much more tired than he was hoping from the last few days and the extra kit he had been carrying. He hadn't wanted to mention it to Jonno but it was playing on his mind. The low clouds unsettled him. He was aware that the weather could close in in such conditions but he didn't want to miss out on the summit despite whatever assurances he had made to his wife. He felt he was walking on a tightrope of expectation against reality that was becoming ever more finely balanced. Part of him wanted to play safe and turn back, but another voice boomed back from deep within him demanding he continue. He looked back to see his tall and angular son making his way through the snow, he looked like he was still strong, James thought. "We can do this" he told himself out loud, "we can do this."

And then, just when both men were really starting to wonder if there was an actual summit to this fabled peak, it appeared. They arrived within 100 meters of it. No more false summits, no more ridges or elevations. The steepness of the mound had levelled out again and they saw a small flag blowing in the wind ahead of them.

"Almost there" yelled James, trying to stay calm and focussed, but his body throbbed with excitement, washing away some of the deep doubt he had spent the last few hours keeping at bay.

Each step by now was hard won as the altitude and deep snow took its toll. But finally they, father and son, unsupported, had arrived. James reached the flag first raising his hands triumphantly above his head, holding his ice axe to the sky. Then Jonno arrived soon after and slumped to his knees. James spontaneously leant forward to give him a hug, the first he could remember giving his son in many years. He knelt down on held his son tightly, surprised at how exhausted and fragile his body was.

No longer protected from the wind, he felt himself buffeted by strong gusts and so decided it was wise to keep low. "We did it!" he roared in his son's ear, "congratulations Jonny, you did it! Fantastic!"

"Wow...thanks Dad, I feel broken, that was so hard." Jonno did his best to speak loudly back. "I just need to lie down a minute."

"Are you OK?" James asked.

"I'm fine. I just feel fucked," Jonno said facing the snowy floor. Normally James was very strict about his language, telling him that swearing was sign of a lack of intelligence. But he just didn't care at this moment, he was too tired and that word seemed to sum up everything he needed to say.

"Ha!" James laughed loudly, holding him even tighter. "Me too!"

Jonno held his father equally tightly, not wanting to let go. He closed his eyes and felt tears form behind his goggles. He let them fall until they misted his lenses knowing that his father wouldn't see them. He hadn't even looked at the view yet, but he didn't care. He was just so happy and relieved to be there.

James held his son, revelling in the purity of his own moment before common sense came and found him and he remembered to dig an ice anchor that they could clip into. He helped Jonno to lie down on the ice and quickly got the equipment from his pack and put one together, clipping them in so that they could relax on the summit without fear of slipping off. He then put his bag down as a mat and sat, taking it all in. The months of planning, the intense preparation and detail, the constant research, the gamble of going unsupported, the doubts of those back at home, his own doubts and the success of his own son in making it. The image of his own father briefly popped into his mind, but James quickly shoed it away not wanting that to impinge on what was happening now. He had thought about his father a lot on the way up, especially the last hours before the summit and used the frustration and pain that seemed to bubble up from his memory to keep going through the deep snow. James did not want this to be a poignant moment, but one of celebration. All he wanted to was look at his own son, slowly sitting up and taking in the scenery.

The clouds briefly parted and he saw snow-capped mountain upon snow-capped mountain laid out in front of them. All of different sizes, shapes and swirls of snow and rock, the view was spell-binding. Both men on top of the world and needing to be nowhere else. The exhaustion and fatigue only made it feel all the more deserved.

Jonno slowly rose cautiously to his feet, taking in where they were. James could see he looked unsteady but did not want to crowd his moment and watched him stand unaided. After turning around in a full circle he raised his arms to the sky and let out a deep guttural roar that immediately was carried away to silence by the howling wind.

"Yeaaaaaahhhhhhh! Come on! We did it! Yeaaaaahhhhhhhh! He could see the lips move on his son's face. James stood up and went to give him another hug. Jonno flung his arms around his father, embracing him with strength and purpose.

"This is incredible Dad! Thank you so much for believing in this."

"Thank you for coming," James replied mischievously.

"You're incredible for getting us up here, Dad!"

"Haha, I am so proud of you Jonny," James yelled into his son's ear.

Both men looked directly at each other through their snow goggles, but it was hard to see through the impenetrable reflection of their own image that appeared in the others' lens. The words "I love you" were on the tips of both men's tongues, but for some reason didn't come, as though perhaps one was waiting for the other to say it first. Yet it didn't spoil the moment, as they embraced again and both roared in unison into the unflinching and wild wind.

They sat and ate some chocolate bars and take in the changing view, that morphed from being cloud to endless landscape and back to cloud again. It was now past 3'o clock and James knew they had to get going soon. Sitting still after all the effort of getting there, they had begun to cool down and James felt himself shiver.

"Time to go?" James put his arm around Jonno's slim shoulders.

"Yep, I'm getting cold. I'm looking forward to dinner!" Jonno bellowed.

"Vamos!" James exclaimed and pointed his ice axe theatrically back to their footsteps where they had come from. It was now very overcast and difficult to see too far ahead, but as both men were feeling so elated, the external view was no longer of any importance.

The descent proved to be not as straight forward as they both had hoped. Jonno was a lot more fatigued than he had realised and found that his legs kept giving way under him. He regularly needed to sit and rest, saying that he was fine but feeling exhausted. James wondered whether the adrenaline of the moment had worn off and he had forgotten that getting to the summit was only half-way there. They had a lot of ground to cover and he felt worried that they would still be on the snow until after dark. James noticed he was finding regular resistance on his rope as he tried to move forwards. He didn't want to lose the happiness of the joy they had shared together but he also knew that they still had hard work ahead of them to get home. By 6 o'clock they were still well above the snow line meaning that they would be needing their torches again. By 7 o'clock it was almost dark as they sat and rested again for the umpteenth time. The sun had set unannounced behind the blanket of cloud and their world began to retreat back into snowy shadows.

"Come on Jonny," James said trying to hide his irritation at how slow they were being.

"I know Dad, I'm sorry. I just feel so wrecked."

"It's OK, you're doing well. But it's getting late. You need to try and push through this."

"I'm doing my best Dad," Jonno mildly slurred.

"Are you drinking and eating enough?"

"I'm trying Dad, I'm trying."

James reached into his pack and gave his son two of his own chocolate bars and a packet of glucose tablets he had for an emergency. "Eat these and take a good slug of water. We need to get moving, it's not good to be here after dark when we're both tired."

"I know Dad, I know. It's just tough to pick yourself up again after all the effort to get to the top." ·

"The top is only half-way, Jonny" James said sternly.

"Now you tell me!" Jonno attempted to make a joke but his fatigue he ended up sounding surly and sarcastic, he saw his father flinch.

"Come on, eat up and let's get going" James responded, doing his best not to lose his temper.

"OK, OK," Jonno devoured both chocolate bars in almost one mouthful.

The light began to fade as they trudged on. The yielding snow and Jonno's fatigue made for a tortuous descent. In moving slowly and not as fast as he wanted, along with the low cloud and reduced view, it gave James time to think. Leading them home he had planned to do this quickly and what was now happening was not going to plan. As a rule, in life, he liked to move fast and decisively. He too was feeling weariness and hunger having not eaten as much today as he would have liked. He had imagined they would be back in the tent by nightfall having one of the add-boiling-water ready meals that he had brought. There was a spicy sausage and rice one that was making him salivate.

Time to think made him feel uncomfortable. He had spent a life built on not waiting, but getting on with things. He could feel the heavy weight of his son on end of the rope that was behind. Jonno was clearly shattered and he didn't want such a wonderful day to boil over into frustration and argument but he was finding himself increasingly irritable. He let his mind wander to mind at home and what awaited them at the end of the trip, he felt a pang of sadness that this great trip might be coming to an end soon. It had taken over most of his spare time and thinking since he had thought of it and he felt the potential of a void opening up once they were home. His tired mind wondered what he might organise next but it was hard to focus. He thought of Macie and how he would love to do something amazing with her, maybe a safari or something. She would be feeling quite left out from this trip. He thought of the patient and supportive Emma, who had always encouraged him to follow his ideas and dreams in their marriage. This adventure had happened as much thanks to her as him. James thought he must call her as soon as they are back to Huaraz in a few days' time; he had warned her that they would be offline during this week.

The light soon faded gently and without fanfare. Dense cloud meant there was no spectacular end to the day, but more a slow shuffling away of the peripheries. Ever since the summit, visibility had been confined to only where they were walking. Dropped down onto the plateau of the great shoulder of the mountain they had arrived on in such high spirits and continued walking. James was finding his own legs were not as accurate and responsive as he would have liked. He too just wanted to be back in the tent. His body was still here on the mountain but his mind had been elsewhere for some time. He had an awareness that this was a precarious place to be in and did his best to bring himself back to the yellow torch light and line of footsteps they were retracing. The snow sparkled in the light like the stars had done at the beginning of the day, glinting and catching the beam of his head torch. It was quiet as the wind had dropped and there was not much else to hear but his and his son's stumbling footsteps and laboured breathing.

They came off the shoulder to the initial switch back descent where they and started. It was steep but the crampons held well and they eventually made their way off the snow to the edge of the moraine. Psychologically this was a great victory, feeling the crampons clink on the hard rock was a sound that he had been longing to hear. Jonno slid off the snow and sat, visibly shrunken at his father's feet.

"Dad, I'm sorry. But I am just done," he whimpered.

"You're doing really good Jonny," James said with a distinct lack of emotion to his voice.

"I wish you would stop calling me Jonny" Jonno snapped.

"It's your name, the one we gave you when you were born," James bit back, as he helped the crampons off his boots and unclipped him from the rope.

"But you know I prefer Jonno, Dad." He replied. James looked at him but couldn't see his eyes as his head torch dazzled him making his face a dark silhouette.

"I am not calling my son by a nickname." James said coldly. "Anyway this is not the time to talk about this. We just need to get home. Give me your bag, I'll carry it."

"Dad, I can……I can do it. I want to do it."

"You're too tired. Just give it to me."

"But….."

"No buts. It's been a long day. I just want us to get back in one piece."

"OK….sorry Dad."

"Don't apologise, it's just how it is." James heard a small voice in his mind asking why he couldn't have been a bit more compassionate in that moment but by then his mouth had shut. The priority was getting back now, he could afford to be warm and nice when that was achieved.

Having been freed from the bondage of uncertain ground and the ropes and crampons, they followed the rocky path they had taken earlier in the morning. It proved harder that James had anticipated and not quite as obvious as it had been this morning. His tired mind was struggling to make sense of the way, the evening darkness meant he couldn't see that far ahead and occasionally it was not obvious which way to go. The snow boots they were in made it hard to walk comfortably and he could sense that Jonno was stumbling and struggling with the co-ordination.

They snaked down the path that had been so laced with excitement and expectation earlier in the day. Taking regular breaks, they eventually got into a good rhythm and James began to feel they were close. The small rocks on the path occasionally led to a lack of grip and both men had a couple of near escapes when their feet almost flew out from beneath them. James' legs felt heavy, especially now with the extra weight. It was taking every ounce of mental strength he had to keep himself sharp and alert.

The main difficulty was that this rocky terrain looked so similar, and he didn't feel entirely confident in the direction they were going. There cairns littered along the way but he couldn't remember any particular landmarks. It felt correct, but he couldn't be one hundred percent sure. There were a couple of potential junctions where he wasn't entirely sure whether they should go right or left and so followed his intuition rather than any actual knowledge. Given that they were walking downhill but they were moving slowly he had expected them to be back in definitely less than two hours, yet when he checked his watch he saw that it had been two hours since they left the snow and he didn't feel like they were anywhere near their tent. He looked up and could only the dark night sky and a sea of rocks. The tent was a dark blue dome, and the same shape as any of the big boulders they were surrounded by. James wasn't sure if it had reflectors on it or not, he clenched down on his jaw in annoyance.

"Dad, are we nearly back yet?" Jonno arrived next to his father and sat down on a rock next to him.

"I think so." James said not wanting to look at his son lest he betray the fact he didn't actually know.

"I don't remember any of this." Jonno added, trying to be helpful.

"We must be close," James continued. "It's just difficult as it all looks the same. "

"Do you mean you don't actually now where we are?" Jonno asked.

"No….it's just…"

"Great. Well that's great. What hope have we got of finding our tent in this lot. Talk about needle in a haystack!" Jonno huffed.

"This is not the time Jonny, hold yourself together please."

"I am shattered Dad. I don't think I have much left."

"Well tough," James said unfeelingly.

"Humpphh" was all Jonno could muster, letting the breath force its way through his nostrils.

Both men sat on the small rock they were on. The night was still and they were surrounded by thick nightfall apart from the outline of the grey and slate coloured rocks that were in the beam of torchlight.

"This is not good," Jonno said again

"Stop it please Jonny." His father said, "now is not the time."

"Will we sleep out here if we can't find the tent?"

"We will find the tent."

Then silence again.

James was at a loss, he didn't know where the tent was and he was unsure if they had come back on the same path. It all looked so similar and he had had no obvious landmarks to triangulate himself by. It crossed his mind that they might not find the tent until it was light again and that worst-case scenario, they might have to stay out overnight. This was not how he wanted this special day to end.

After ten minutes of sitting in silence, he stood up again.

"Ok we have to find it, simple as that. Come on."

"Dad I am not going on some wild goose chase in this rock field. I am knackered."

"Well what do you want to do then? Just sit here?"

"I just want to sleep."

"Well that is just not helpful. Come on. We must be close."

James stood up quickly, trying to summon some energy and aggression needed to begin the search. He tugged at his son's shoulder trying to rouse him but Jonno resisted, letting his body act as a dead weight.

"Come on please," James said gritting his teeth and pulling a bit harder. Suddenly his grip slipped on the smooth fabric of Jonno's jacket and he took a step back, the weight of his rucksack which was still on pulling him backwards. His legs were not strong enough to maintain his balance and his right foot shot back. It found no purchase and kept skidding. Then as thought the momentum of the situation took on its own energy he felt himself begin to fall backwards, the weight of the top half of his body caught mercilessly by gravity and being thrust backwards. He felt his snow boot stop against a small stone which then tipped and gave way, trapping his foot in a set position. The weight of his rucksack continued but against the way his leg was facing. His trapped foot did not release and he tumbled sideways, twisting as he went down.

James heard the crack first before he felt the pain. Like the sound of a gunshot going off in his ankle he heard something snap. Then as he fell he felt his knee twist violently as this right ankle stayed held by the rocks it had fallen into. Red hot pain seared up from his leg into his body, so violently that he was almost sick. He collapsed in a heap with his leg still jammed, head torch shining up to the night sky.

"Dad?!" Jonno yelled suddenly aware that something had happened.

"Shit!" James yelled. "Shit!" he did his best not to scream.

"Dad, oh God, Dad, are you OK?"

James lay there stuck, knife-like pain coursing through his body. "Jonny, get my ankle out of this rock, quickly."

Jonno jumped up to find his father only a few meters from him crumpled in an awkward heap. "Oh Dad, oh God!" he shrieked.

"It's OK, stay calm." James gritted his teeth, wanting to vomit, "just release my leg please."

"OK, OK," Jonno pushed away the rock that had secured his snow boot and ankle in place and set his fixed limb free.

"Ooof, thank you." James breathed out loudly.

"Dad, what's happened?" Jonno said with real panic in his voice.

"It's broken, I heard it crack. I fell and twisted. I think my knee is in bad shape as well. Shit." James could hardly speak.

"Oh God, Dad." Was all Jonno could say. He looked at his father's leg and saw his foot facing in a direction that it shouldn't be. The sight of it made his stomach turn.

"What does it look like?" James said forcefully.

"It's all twisted. It doesn't look right."

"Twisted which way? Medial or lateral?"

"Sorry? What?"

"Twisted left or right?" James snapped.

"Oh... twisted right, about 90 degrees."

"Shit. OK. I need you to turn it back."

"What?!"

"Jonno, listen. You have to... what we call reduce the fracture. Otherwise my foot is going to lose its blood supply. I'll tell you what to do."

"Really? This can't be happening!"

"Please, it is happening. OK take my boot off, that's it. And then take my ankle in your hands."

Jonno took his gloves off and undid the laces of his father's boot. He could hear his father's shallow and quick breathing. He felt queasy again. With the boot off he saw how mangled his ankle was. Facing 90 degrees to the right. It looked sickening.

"OK, now I need.... I need you to twist it back to the right direction."

"Are you sure?"

"Yes, just be quick and purposeful. Both hands, take a good grip. Hands on either side of my foot"

"I have never done this."

"That's fine. You'll be fine."

"OK, what next?"

"On 3, I want you to twist my ankle and foot back so it faces where it should."

"Ok... "

"1...2....." James took a deep breath, " 3....."

"Argghhhhhhhhhhhhhhhhh!" James screamed deep into the night.

The last thing James thought in the split second before he passed out was what a good job his son had done. Jonno turned and wretched as he felt the bones crunch below his fingers. His whole body felt repulsed at what he had just done. He looked back and saw his father looking like he was peacefully asleep, surrounded by a bed of rocks. In that moment he did his best not to be consumed by total panic. What were they going to do? He had no idea. He could feel himself beginning to hyperventilate. Jonno suddenly felt very alone.

After a few minutes feeling completely at a loss he decided to try and wake his father.

"Dad, Dad, wake up!"

James felt himself being shook and came to, initially confused as to what was going on but then the electricity of the pain that surged though him quickly reminding him what had happened.

"Well done Jonny, you did that well," he said his whole face grimacing.

"What now Dad? What do we do now?"

"I don't know." James said quietly.

Jonno looked nervously at his father, this was a phrase he had never heard him say.

"This is not good." Was all Jonno could think to say.

After what seemed an eternity James spoke again.

"OK here's what I do know. I can't walk, my leg is a mess. I think you have sorted my ankle out but....it's agony. I don't know where the tent is. I don't want you to go looking for it. I think we need to sit this out. Then in the morning, find the tent and work something out from there."

"Can we ring someone?"

"What are we going to say?"

"Can they not come and find us?"

"What do you think?"

"Shit!"

"It's OK, we have just got to stay warm through the night, then after sunrise we can reassess. Thankfully it's not so cold."

"What time is it?" Jonno asked, not wanting to know.

James looked at his watch and saw that the face had cracked which meant he couldn't read the display. "Hmm... I don't know, but probably late. We'll get through this."

"What do we have to do?" Jonno asked again feeling his chest tighten.

"Nothing." Said James, "We do nothing until the light. We just need to keep warm. I have a medical kit in my bag, in the side pocket, it has space blankets in it, get it out can you?"

Jonno scrambled around and found them, he jerked them out and ripped their packaging open. He covered his father in one and wrapped himself in the other.

"Come sit close Jonny" James said, we need to share body heat."

"Are you serious?" Jonno asked.

"This is not the time to mess around son," James said firmly, his eyes scrunched closed.

Jonno came and huddled next to his father who was now slumped against a rock. He pulled up the hood on his jacket and put his arm around his shoulders. He felt the strength and solidity of his father's body next to his. James kept his eyes shut as though locked in deep concentration.

"It's OK Jonny, we'll get through this." He said over and over again.

The night passed agonisingly slowly, with no sense of time or certainty, both men sat there holding on to what warmth they could. Jonno put his body as close to his fathers who seemed to dip in and out of consciousness. He held him tightly and did his best not to think about anything but getting to sunrise. He found himself saying "it's going to be OK Dad; it's going to be OK. I'm going to get this sorted in the morning," even though he had no idea what he was going to do. Every now he had to get up and stretch his legs and he put his blanket over James. His down jacket was surprisingly warm and he found he could maintain his warmth with a little movement. James said little when he was awake, it seemed he was just concentrating on letting himself not be overwhelmed by the pain. When they were sitting huddled next to each other, Jonno turned their torches off and the two them would be lost again to the darkness, only knowing the other was alive by the sound of breathing and the heat from their respective bodies.

Eventually cracks in the night sky began to appear. To the east a small blue light crept stealthily through, as it had done the day before. The sky still had cloud obscuring the peaks around them but gradually and imperceptibly the rock field began to emerge from the blackness. From the murk came shapes and form and a greater sense of where they were. The moraine camp slowly materialised around them. It looked familiar but also so alien and hostile, this was not a place for the living. Jonno stood up and stretched his limbs. He shivered as he moved, his tired muscles having been chilled by the night's vigil. Out of the corner of his eye he saw something that wasn't rock, it looked soft and material like sticking out from behind a large boulder.

Leaving his father who had drifted off to sleep again, he set out to go and see what it was. As he got there, no more than 30 meters away he couldn't believe it. It was their tent. They had been so close, all night. The nausea returned, his exhausted body shuddered. He scampered back to his father and shook him awake.

"Dad, Dad! The tent, it's literally right here, I've found it!"

"Whaaaat? Really, you're kidding?!" James said drowsily.

"Come on, let's get to the sleeping bags. Can you move?"

"I'll try. I'll try."

Jonno helped his father tentatively to his feet removing his arms from the straps of his rucksack, each movement and adjustment causing him clear agony. Then step by step, with James, holding onto his son, dragging his injured right leg and making small, intensely excruciating movements with his left leg. Each step required facing inexorable pain over and over again.

Then they were there and Jonno unzipped the door, he lowered his father and helped him inside. James crawled to his sleeping bag and passed out again. Jonno went back and brought down the heavy bags to the door of the tent. His mind was a mixture of exhaustion and confusion. They were finally back in the tent, but what next. There was no clear answer, only chaos. He re-entered the tent and lay down next to his father who was asleep again wrapped in his sleeping bag. Jonno reached into his bag to find his phone but as he pulled it out he saw it was turned off which was strange. He tried turning it on, but nothing. He then looked for his father's phone in his bag where normally kept it under the hood. Again it was off and would not turn on.

At a loss of what to do, Jonno lay back next to his father. His eyes were heavy and his body on the verge of breaking. Give me rest he felt his body asking, and without any resistance he slipped into a sudden deep and overwhelming sleep.

Chapter Twenty – Leaving

Jonno pulled the zip of the tent, seeing his father's strained and lined face disappear behind the yellow zip and blue canvas. His eyes were locked on him as the flap was closing. The air was still fresh and the sun was early in the sky, meaning that he wanted to keep precious warmth in. Last night had been an ordeal; their bodies had been close through much of the night, which felt both natural and uncomfortable. James had been in and out of consciousness for the most part, groaning in pain and mildly shivering. Jonno too had been cold but had an overpowering sense that he couldn't afford to give into his own needs.

The following morning, they had both had come to they had agreed on a plan. Not much of one, but the best one available. Jonno was to go and find help. It was as simple as that.

He headed off from the tent not really knowing what he was going to do. He remembered there was a village about half a day's walk away. He just needed to follow the path and it should be fairly straightforward. What he really needed was some sort of working phone to ring for help. He felt confident he could make some sort of gesture to say what he needed and that he was willing to pay. He had money on him and his Dad's bank card. He smiled at the irony of how often he wished he had had his father's credit cards to buy the latest Xbox game, or get some new clothes to add to his wardrobe. He knew he needed to stay calm and not do anything stupid. How would he explain to Mum and Macie if only one of them came back, or if neither of them did? The thought made him feel tight and unhappy so he tried to block it from his mind. Although he allowed himself a small guilty smile when it crossed his mind that if neither of them came back then they would be saved from having to explain anything.

He turned back one more time to see the tent hidden amongst the large boulders in the moraine. No wonder they couldn't find it the night before; it was blue, well tucked in and its dome looked very boulder shaped. There was something both brave and pathetic looking at it, how small and insignificant it looked compared to the vast scenery that it was pitched in. Behind it stood the vast and sharp white enormity of Casharaju rising up into the deepening blue sky. It looked magnificent this early in the morning, its peak alone in the sky and not surrounded by clouds. It was hard to believe that they were both there almost twenty-four hours ago, gasping their way to the summit and falling to their knees in wonder, solidarity and exhaustion at the top. High up amongst the gods of the white jagged peaks, he had felt himself both loved and immortal in that broken moment.

But things had changed and this all seemed an increasingly distant memory. For all the joy of yesterday, what would it mean if they didn't both come back? Jonno felt tears in his eyes as he started to move. He took one last look at the peak that yesterday he thought was going to define him and change his life. He had been certain that something amazing had happened and things would be so different because of this. And now he stood at the precipice of disaster. A voice within urged him to move.

He started to wind his way amongst the boulders, following the dusty path and occasional pile of stones that had been placed by others who had made their pilgrimage here. These cairns gave him good landmarks and a sense of security as to where to head. Occasionally there were loose rocks that he put his foot on like his Dad had done the night before. A couple of times he almost lost his balance on them and went hurtling into a large rock nearby, putting his hands out to save himself. "Come on Jonno" he muttered to himself, "pay attention."

It felt good not to be carrying so much in his pack, his shoulders and back had felt really sore over the last few days. He thought of the stories his Dad had told him of Everest and some of the weights the porters had carried there, that they got paid by the kilogram and pushed themselves to the limit to make money for their families. *How easy life is back at home, how much we are given, how different our challenges are.* Having less weight gave him a freedom but also meant that he had to find help fairly soon, he had left the majority of the food and water with Dad in the tent, so he had a few snacks, some liquid and purifying tablets. They had both hoped it would be enough for Jonno to get to the village.

The landscape began to open up in front of him, to his back the mountains and to his front was the valley he needed to descend into. The plateau of the moraine was beginning to come to its end and the steep descent that they had struggled against only few days ago was appearing. This was a first major hurdle complete, to make it this far. The sky felt so vast and uninhabited. Despite the track there was a deep sense of wilderness about where he was, a sense that these places were not for human habitation. There was nothing here but the rocks and rivers that worked their ways through. It was a place that asked to be visited but not one that wanted anyone to stay for too long. Jonno stopped to catch his breath. Looking out over the drop into the valley he was heading into, he had a strong awareness of being very alone.

He turned around doing a 360 degrees to try and take it all in, the enormity of the peaks amongst which Casharaju was nestled, how calm and patient they looked in direct contrast to his own mind which was spinning and felt like it was going at one hundred miles an hour. How little wildlife he could see; apart from what was growing from the earth, this was a silent place. An eeriness began to creep, a sense that he did not belong here and he was out of his depth. The space and freedom that he had felt here only a few days ago was long gone. He now felt small and insignificant, the vastness felt like it had the power to crush and obliterate as much as it did to set one free. Jonno drew in his breath while bent double next to a dark boulder that was bigger than their family car.

The sun was beginning to strengthen and so he took out some sun-cream, his face had taken a battering in the snow yesterday and had a hardness to it. They had really pushed themselves on that mountain and being on the face all day had meant his skin had taken a lot of the intensity of the sun and wind. His face felt slightly numb and tight, his lips dry and taut.

He got out some water and took a swig. The coolness of it seemed to momentarily light up his insides and he felt he could almost trace out his gullet to his stomach before disappearing again as an awareness of his own thumping heart took over. One thing he realised from trekking at altitude was that no matter how much you tried, you never really got your breath back; your body was under strain the whole time. He imagined how he must look from the sky right now, would a plane or helicopter even see them if it did fly over?

With the bottle back in the bag he clipped up again to continue. Despite the adrenaline there was a deadening fatigue in his legs that made him nervous. He noticed that time and time again his muscles were sluggish in responding to the questions asked of them by the uneven and unpredictable footing. Every now and again he would stumble just regaining his balance in time. "Be careful man" Jonno scolded himself out loud on one occasion, "don't mess this up."

Chapter Twenty-One - James, Morning

James watched the zip of his tent close through half shut eyes. Huddled in his bag he watched both his son and the outside morning light disappear from his gaze. As though a curtain falling on the stage, he was now left alone behind the screen as the audience had begun to depart. In many ways much of his life had felt like an act, moving from grand performance to grand performance. Enjoying the role he was playing and lifting himself over and over again to meet the expectations of the crowd.

Normally this gave him great pleasure, and the feedback from those he had involved himself with had given him a buzz, a sense of purpose and meaning. It sustained him and allowed him to cope with the quiet times until he was called to action again. Only now this was different, very different. In the almost seamless blink of an eye, he had gone from capable mountain leader, surgeon, and father to an immobilised, cold, wounded middle aged man stuck in a tent in an empty moraine camp. His ankle was agony; he knew the break was bad. Then there was his knee, badly twisted, he was unsure if the Anterior Cruciate ligament had gone, but his foot had planted as the stone dislodged. There was no point even trying to walk on his leg, it would just compound it, he would have to trust the plan that they had agreed upon.

The pain throbbed deep inside both ankle and knee. The exposure of last night had chilled him deeply. Thankfully he had spent money on good down jackets and Jonny had done his best to keep him talking and warm but he was cold. He thought of his son, how brave and remarkable he had been under pressure. He thought of him as a little boy and how he grown so quickly into this almost-man. He tried to remember the various steps of how he had grown but struggled, there were blanks and bits missing. He felt a tightness of despair in his chest as he realised he could remember more of his own life and achievements in the last ten years than he could of Jonno's. Nausea overwhelmed him and he lay back with his head on the small makeshift pillow from his rucksack and Jonno's roll mat. He closed his eyes, *I just need to wait it out* he thought, *it'll all be OK. It'll all be OK.*

They had organised his supplies well before Jonno had left. Plenty of water in the tent and there was enough food to last for a while. Ready-made packet meals that he could just pour hot water into and eat. He wouldn't starve but he wasn't looking forward to the challenge of needing the toilet. There was a peculiar silence around the tent, no wind to ruffle the synthetic material, just calm. He strangely thought of Coleridge's Ancient Mariner and the *"water, water everywhere, but not enough to drink."* He had never liked English Literature particularly, he had found it by-and-large pointless, but there had been something about this line that had always stuck with him. He had never really understood it but there was something in that poem that spoke to him, so he secretly carried that line with him as though it might make sense one day.

He loved the mountains; they had been the first place in his life that had ever given him a sense of confidence. All those years ago, the same age as Jonno roughly, he came travelling on a year of adventure. Somehow he had been persuaded to try trekking and he loved it, loved the adventure and the need to be self-supported. There was a purity and simplicity of action and control that made so much sense to him. It reflected how he wanted to live his own life, making his own decisions, working it out for himself, physical and psychological heroism to endure the elements, to endure the heavy pack, to endure the tough times. The trekking turned to climbing and he used his university holidays to pursue mountain after mountain. They become goals to be ticked off, each completed one adding to his sense of confidence and sense of self. It complimented his medical life, an intense physical hobby away from the rigorous intellectual demands of the knowledge he was expected to acquire. He had wanted to share this with his own father, or at least want him to notice. But no matter how much he pushed himself there was always the same response, *"that's great James, but what next?"* He had used this as motivation to be the best at many things, but there remained a nagging suspicion that whatever he did was never enough.

James sat up, a large surge of pain ripped through his right leg causing him to cry out. These thoughts were unsettling and he didn't like them. He would rather have pain right now than to let the mind wander. Yet movement was too painful; he could shuffle, with little lightning bolts of pain, but he could not move. This is what he always did when he felt difficult thoughts approach, he would outrun them, outmanoeuvre them, use being busy and important to skilfully evade them. But now he was stuck, his main way of coping had been brutally removed. For the first time in a long while in his life, he had to wait. There was just him and his increasingly loud thoughts. A sense of feeling alone entered the tent with him, he flinched and another jag of pain ripped up his leg. He felt his mind race, his breathing quickened and his heart began to thump. "Just get a grip" he whispered to himself, "you're better than this, only weak people can't cope." He thought of his own father and how he had never seen him cry, this was a sign of strength in his eyes, the man who could endure all and never let anyone know. These were the type of men the British Empire were built on; stories of stoic, hard and dedicated men who were able to transcend whatever they were doing without so much as a flicker of expression on their faces. These were his own heroes growing up, these were the men his father had respected and talked in admiration of. This was the type of man he had wanted to be.

Another unwelcome thought entered his fraying mind, *"where has this got you now?"* it asked almost tauntingly. *"Here you are, badly injured, lying groaning in a small tent on the side of a mountain in Peru, how is that heroic? They'll all be laughing at you at your funeral."* He clenched his teeth and slapped himself around the face, "Come on. Stop that" he snapped loudly. "Think of surviving this; think of the stories you might tell of how you made it through. I might even be able to write a book on this." His ankle caught in a fold in his sleeping bag, "Arrrrghhhhhh" he yelled. "Arghhhhhhhhhh" he yelled again and again. But there was no response, only the sound of his own breathing and the soft ripples of the gentle morning breeze against the wall of his tent.

* * *

Chapter Twenty-Two - Searching

Jonno finished what he was eating. He had been walking for almost three hours and had come to a standstill. He had found a small clearing by a river and made a space for himself in the shade. He refilled his water and dropped some of the purifiers in, before lowering himself onto the ground and resting his weary body. The walking had been intense, so much time in his own mind with the endless spinning of his thoughts. He had felt so small and insignificant in this vast world of rock, wide open horizon and snow. In the UK hardly a day went by without bumping into another human or other. There were so many in such a seemingly small space. Whilst it added intensity to life, it also added a feeling of safety, that others were there too.

But here, by the gently flowing river, that provided the murmuring soundtrack to his brief break from the walking, Jonno felt a deep outer silence. There was sense of stillness and calm, despite the racing of his own head. Everything was just existing, carrying on, flowing in its own way. The trees and their branches gently swayed in the breeze, the rock and boulders in the river let the clear water wash over them. There was no stress, just space combining slow and patient movement. Such a contrast to the hectic concrete environments of London or other such cities that Jonno had visited before. While he felt deeply worried about what was happening, there was a deeper sense of calm that infiltrated the air around him. He closed his eyes and felt himself breathe. The air was thin and his heart was beating hard against the wall of his chest.

The peacefulness of the place began to lull him to sleep and he felt his thoughts begin to detach from the incessant whirring of his father and what he needed to do into a dream space where he was with Macie filling water balloons from a running tap. They were smiling, giggling and splashing the water at each other. His mother entered the room they were in, smiling also; he could hear his father rustling away in another room but couldn't see him. He wanted his Dad to come in and fill balloons with them, but he wouldn't. Jonno left the tap and went looking for him; he walked through the door into a sterile and brightly lit room. He saw a metal upright chair in the middle of the room with his father's bag left on it. He ran over hoping to find his father inside but instead found nothing but a picture of his grandfather holding his own father as a child. There were words written on the back of the photo, but he couldn't decipher them. The older man in the photo was smiling towards his son, while the young boy was looking sternly into the camera.

The room then began to fade and shake as the walls started to fall away. Jonno could hear water on the outside flowing towards him and there was heat on his face as he looked at the light bulb that was glowing. The temperature on his face was heating up and he brought his hands to his face, in doing so waking himself from sleep. Comfortable on the soft grass it took him a moment to remember where he was and why he was there. He opened his eyes looking into the overarching electric blue sky with the sun overhead bearing down on him, he heard the flow of the river dancing gently by and he caught sight of the mountains in the distance. "Dad!" He suddenly yelled, "Shit, I need to get going!"

Cross at himself for drifting off, he quickly stuffed everything back in the bag. His face felt hot and tight from the sun again and so he smeared on some more sun cream and took another swig of water. His stomach growled, protesting against the thought of more exercise without decent fuel, he felt a gnawing sensation underneath his breastbone. He jumped to his feet but felt disturbed by a lack of bounce in his legs as he came to land. As he stood up fast he felt a dizziness pass through him, momentarily making him sway. A dark veil descended over his eyes causing him a momentary loss of vision and nausea. He widened his feet to gain a bit more balance and held the branch of the tree he had been sitting under. The tree held strong as his body went through the process of rebooting itself. Jonno closed his eyes and took a deep breath, steadying himself.

He rejoined the path and started moving again. The way was clear but he did not feel as powerful or in control as he would have liked. There was an uncertainty and slight jerkiness in his movement that had not been there before. He was also starting to feel the beginnings of pressure in the front of his head. He had left all the pain-killers with Dad and so had no way of making it go away. He took another swig of water and took out his Camelbak and pressed the bag of it against his head. The coolness of it felt good against his heated brow and he replaced it again within his pack. His stomach however hadn't enjoyed the water as much and a wave of nausea passed through him. "*This is not ideal*," he thought. "*Come on, time is ticking.*"

As he struggled on, he thought of his father back in the tent and began to feel angry towards him. Why had this happened, why were we here, without guides, climbing on our own? Of course it was going to be dangerous, why did Dad have to be so insistent? He felt a frustration for not having voiced his own misgivings at the idea of how to climb the mountain and how they were going to do it themselves. Everyone had warned them that it was going to be bad idea but Dad had almost taken pride in this. There had been such a drive in him to get this trip right, to be the boss, to be independent. Jonno had felt this had been bordering on unhealthy at times, his Dad seemed to have made this trip and mountain into an obsession. The way he had kept going to the top in the deep snow, there was an unnerving relentlessness to him. Jonno thought of Grandpa and how Dad just didn't want to talk about him, to open up. However, since his death he had not been the same man, so much quieter and even more driven about everything that he did. There had been an intensity in him and his actions that had become difficult to be around. This trip had become everything, all they talked about. It had been lovely to begin with, as it meant they could spend time together and get excited, but it had become so much more than that. Jonno loved being in the mountains but climbing them wasn't everything. He loved the adventure but he had learned on this trip that he was just as happy to look and take them in as he was to interact with them.

But Dad seemed to always need to win, to achieve, to stand at the top of something. He had this drive to always do well, to go further. But it never seemed to make him any happier. Instead he would quickly start talking about the next thing he was going to do. It was as though he couldn't stay still and

Jonno felt he had been sucked into this world by wanting to spend quality time with him. Why couldn't they have come here and gone to Machu Picchu like everyone else? Why be so different, why make life more dangerous than it had to be? And now where had it left them? Dad was broken and in pain in a tent hours away and Jonno feeling increasingly weak and light-headed looking for help in a place where he knew no one, knew where nothing was and had no idea how to speak Spanish let alone Quechua. Rage swelled deep within him at the ridiculousness of this situation, how unnecessary it all was. Jonno promised himself that he was never going to get swept up in any of father's schemes or ideas like this in the future. He was going to make his own decisions and not go along with anything that didn't feel right. He was going to be honest with his father when he found him again and tell him his feelings, about what he thought of him, the way he lived his life and put work and personal success over everything else.

An intense energy of resentment flooded through him and galvanised his steps, he saw his mission in a new way: not just to save his Dad but also that he could finally be honest with him. That once they were through this he would let his father know what he really thought, how selfish he thought he was. Jonno had had enough, he had been passive for too long and this is where it had led him. He had watched the increasing sadness and distance between his father and mother and the impact this was having on their home. This was his moment, Jonno thought, to let Dad know the impact of who he is. I just need to save him first.

Not looking, Jonno missed the rock in front of him and went sprawling, putting his hands out to save himself. He felt his palms skid over the rough track and his knee bang another rock. "Argghh!" he yelled, "Arrgghhhhhhh" he yelled again, not wanting the sound or feeling of expression to stop. He felt held in the noise of his own pain. Eventually he ran out of air and was reduced to panting silence. There was no one about, no one coming to sort this out, no one who was going to make this go away. Kneeling on the path, he lifted his head; he still could see no village or any signs of anyone else. He felt the mountains at his back looking at him, reminding him that they wouldn't be able to care for his father for long. He gingerly got to his feet, knee throbbing and hands smarting at the fall. "Pay attention" he scolded himself, cross that he had both fallen and, then as an afterthought, that he had just uttered a phrase his father always used.

Chapter Twenty-Three - James, Early Afternoon

James opened his eyes and looked up at the domed roof of tent. For a brief moment he couldn't quite remember where he was or why he was there. He had been dreaming of sitting in the garden with his wife and young children, watching them tearing around and play with endless energy. They laughed and giggled, occasionally looking over in their direction, before heading off again back into whatever imaginary world they had invented. His own father had been there too, but for some reason he was not in the garden, he was in the house. They were waiting for him to come out and join them but he had something very important to do, he would be out shortly. James had felt a sense of not knowing whether he should be in the sunshine with his family or inside with his father. Eventually he gave in to his curiosity and went inside to find him, but he was nowhere to be found.

In the half-world of being awake and asleep, these images played on his mind. It was a dream he was beginning to have quite frequently since his father had died. Not always the same in terms of action but always with an unsettling ending. He would look for his father but could never find him. These dreams left him feeling disorientated and confused; James had prided himself on the strong road map of his life so far. He had worked hard on creating a sense of order and place in his world; science and hard-won knowledge had given him answers and security. He worked in a profession that valued control and this accumulation of knowledge. These were all aspects of life he aspired to, to know as much as possible and to use that to create order. But these dreams left him with little more than chaos. The scene in the garden felt as it should be, and it shouldn't have been too hard to find his father as he knew he was in the house. Yet he was unable to, leaving him unsure as to where he should be. It bothered him that this theme of not knowing where he should be kept reoccurring, he had felt so secure of his place in life only a year ago. He had just published a well-respected academic paper on a complicated but potentially hugely advantageous approach to knee surgery. He was being asked to come and speak, to share his knowledge across the UK and write for various other publications. He felt he was on the top of his professional game, even though he had the odd awareness that it meant he was not at home as much as his family would have liked. He justified this by saying he was working hard for their future. While they might not see this now, one day they would appreciate it.

He rubbed his eyes and took a deep inhale, slightly longer than normal as he was still not fully used to the thin air. He expanded his lungs to the fullest they could be and let out a long and drawn exhale allowing the air to rub against his lips making a small vibrational humming sound. He repeated this a few times, as much out of curiosity as anything else. He thought again about where he was, images of the day began to flow through his mind. The waking up early and excitement for the day ahead, the deeper snow that took so much more energy to navigate. The extraordinary moment at the summit with Jonny, that would probably have made him weep for joy had he been able to do so privately. The exhausting descent and uncertainty of the route to take. The increasing fatigue and frustration of not finding the tent. And then the injury, yes of course, the injury. The connecting of the dots brought his awareness back to his right leg. He felt his knee and ankle throbbing, like a rumbling engine that had been left on. They both felt swollen, and he had a deep primal sense that he should move his leg as little as possible. Of course in having that thought, he twitched and his leg sent spasms of razor sharp pain cascading into his consciousness. He winced, clenching his jaw and closing his eyes. This was a long way from the original plan, far from the imagined glory of the trip. Hopefully Jonny wouldn't be long he thought. There is village not too far away. *He's a smart lad, I've just got to sit tight.*

James felt the small murmurings of a filling bladder. He knew that at this altitude he needed to keep some fluids coming in otherwise he was going to add dehydration and a crushing altitude headache to his already growing list of problems. There was a bottle in the tent that him and Jonno had worked out would be good to use should he need to. There was no way he wanted to try and crawl out of the tent to even attempt anything different. He hoped that the recent constipation he had been experiencing would continue just a little longer. Even though it had been intensely bothering him over the last few months he thanked his lucky stars that it was now this way, rather than the opposite. *Amazing what we can become grateful for in life,* he mused, half smiling and half grimacing.

He lay there staring up at the tented ceiling. His active and energetic mind spinning through the various possibilities of what could be happening. It was now four hours since Jonno left, from the wrist watch he had on. The tent had heated up from the midday sun and he was feeling warm, if not slightly sweaty. The mountains had a way of requiring one's entire wardrobe. Roasting hot in the sunshine and then perishing cold once the sun has dropped behind the flank to jagged mountains to the west. Water that was lukewarm could go to almost frozen in the space of a few hours. He wasn't complaining however; he had been so cold last night. It had been such a disaster, the crack in his ankle felt so loud and the pain so searing. He felt stupid, such an idiot for switching off for just that one second. Why was he wearing such a heavy pack he wondered, couldn't I have taken it off or shared some of the load. *What does any of this mean, if I don't make it back?*

"Of course I'll make it back," he snorted, causing him to tighten and encourage another shot of pain up his wounded leg. *Why am I really here?* danced lightly and uninvited across his addled mind, and he was lost for an immediate answer. He cycled through the responses he had been telling anyone willing to listen since this trip had been conceived, that it will be a wonderful trip to share with his son, he had been longing to go back to Peru, he fancied a bit of an adventure in the mountains but these all felt slightly hollow. There was truth in them, but not all the truth. His father's face in hospital flashed across his mind, the image of seeing him there had been awful, he could not forget it. The limp eyes, the lack of expression, the staring. It had been so haunting. James thought how many bedsides of his patients he had stood at, confidently talking to family members about diagnosis and occasionally prognosis, but then walking away. Yes, it affected him occasionally, especially when surgery had not gone well, or the patients had become sick afterwards due to being frail and already vulnerable, but he had always been able to walk away confident he had done all that was asked of him and his skill set. That allowed an assuaging of any guilt that might have tried to take up residence in his thoughts. But then the horror and impotence of being a relative, the suffering of being a spectator and the profound lack of control in what was happening. He felt his eyes soften and become damp.

Yet people die, he countered, they die all the time. *Why should my father be any different? I've seen so much death, so much tragedy in my time on the wards, how dare I feel like this is different for me? We live, we die, loved ones live, loved ones die. It happens every day, all the time. I will die, if anything being a surgeon and a doctor teaches me these simple truths every day.* Yet despite all protestations, he couldn't make the inexorable sadness go away that was beginning to creep into his bones and overflow into his blood.

Here he was, alone and stuck on the side of a mountain in the Andes, with a potentially life-changing injury. His son had gone to seek help and he had nothing better to do now than to think and be with his thoughts. No matter how hard he tried to think of other things he couldn't hold on to them for long; the great moments, the happy times, the recognition, the applause, but he couldn't sustain any of them. Instead the sadness kept coming, kept knocking, and kept rattling his increasingly fragile mind. It began to dawn on James that it was not just his body in pain, but that there existed another aching inside of him, and if anything, this was making the gnawing throbbing of his ankle and knee even more intense.

"No more!" he yelled, "Please no more! I am strong and I will be fine. These thoughts are just me going mad! I am perfectly sane, I have had a great life and I will be fine. I will be fine." Outside the tent was still deafeningly silent upon finishing his outburst, even the wind had completely died down. There was only him, his thoughts and the rocks for company. For the first time in a long while, James felt an icy feeling flood through his being. A feeling he had known long, long ago but had built a life successfully avoiding. It was back and felt as brutal as before, only this time, there was no possibility of doing anything to outrun it.

* * *

Chapter Twenty-Four - Finding

Jonno was still moving. He felt like he had been walking much farther than he was meant to. He hadn't taken his eyes off the path and felt he could remember the scenery from when they walked here before. Passing through the same dense forest that had captured his imagination on the way up now meant nothing to him. How stupid was this whole expedition! He thought of his boyhood heroes like Mallory on Everest whose story he had read countless times. The way he was last seen heading for the summit before the clouds rolled in. He never returned but his death had been used as something noble and glorious, despite the fact he had a loyal wife and children waiting for him back home. Not to mention that it was his third attempt. Perhaps to Mallory it was glorious; after all the chaos and devastation of the First World War he had survived, maybe his meaning in life had gone and he had died inside before he even attempted Everest, so physically dying on its broad white shoulders meant little to him. The British Empire, which he had utterly believed in to his core, had been shown to be just as inhumane as anything else in those trenches, the way the men were sent to their deaths by detached generals too far behind the front line for the incessant bomb blasts to shake their glass of port. But still, he had a wife and family; did that not count for anything? What was their story, what did it really mean to them? Why was that part of the story never told?

But as he stumbled, weaving and winding his way down the path, Jonno still couldn't totally concede it was all unimportant. There was genuinely something as heroic as there was pointless about what they had been doing. The struggle they had gone through the day before had pushed both father and son to their limits. Hilary's quote, *"it's not the mountain we conquer, but ourselves,"* had made several appearances in his mind during the climb. It had been hard, so hard. They could have given up at any moment, cut their losses and descended. But they didn't, they pushed on despite themselves. They had entered the forbidden and unforgiving world of snow and ice and fought their way through. The view on all sides when the clouds parted was beyond words, with the world laid out as far as the eye could see in all directions. Other white peaks jostling side by side, the emerald coloured lakes, the distinct lack of other human beings. It was other-worldly. This was something that could not be matched by simply sitting still or reading books. This was raw experience with its unique intensity of highs and lows; there was an exploration of one's own existence that cannot be done sitting watching TV or cradling a smartphone. But at the same time, standing there on the peak was as though they stood right in the middle of a cross, at the perfect intersection of meaningful and meaningless. If they returned, then it was to be celebrated, if they didn't then they would be mourned and, perhaps, even cursed.

What would Macie and Mum say if Jonno returned without his father? Of course they would not blame him, even if he was to blame himself. But how would they move on? How would he move on, knowing that he had not fully made his peace with him, having harboured such building and confusing resentment for so long? Sure, his father was not the father he wanted, but he was still a good man who had had such a positive influence on the world around him. He had helped countless people and transformed the lives of so many. He wasn't a bad person; he just hadn't been there for Jonno like he wanted him too.

Jonno's head swirled. No matter which direction he went in with his thoughts he could find no clarity. There was no clear truth or answer in anything, everything just felt incomplete and ragged. He wanted to talk to Magdalena, ask her advice, to share and explore the endless thoughts that could find no home. Nothing seemed simple; nothing seemed black and white anymore.

His head began to thump; a slow and deep pressure was rising up from within. One thing was clear at least: he needed to keep going and find help.

As he cleared around the bend in the track he saw something ahead in the distance. He craned his neck and squinted his eyes. It looked like smoke drifting into the afternoon sky. There were small shapes with their familiar hats moving. Jonno slipped again with his eyes transfixed on the horizon. A surge of fatigue flooded his legs, "come on, so close" he said through clenched teeth, his head pounding harder and harder.

The smell of smoke became stronger as he approached. The familiar faded brown adobe bricks with tins roofs. Adults in the village looked up from their doors as he approached but then smiled and turned away again. A mother and daughter were sitting by a stack of freshly cut wood. The child looked over but the mother kept her eyes on her child. She looked up briefly, smiled shyly mouthing the words "*hola gringo*" before putting all her attention back into her child. They looked almost identical for what they wore, the big hats and the thick skirts and cardigans. Jonno hoped that she might look back up again, but she did not.

There were some children playing further down the path, others sitting watching. Then came the inevitable armada of local dogs, Jonno was too tired to outrun then, so he just stood his ground looking at them in the eye which said, *please not now, this isn't the time.* Initially they surrounded him, bearing their teeth and barking aggressively. Jonno remained where he was, not from courage but that he just did not have the energy.

The children stopped their playing and saw the stranger having entered their midst surrounded by the dogs. They ran over to him, shooing the dogs with stones and sticks as they went. Upon reaching him, as though an unconscious reflex, one locked his eyes on Jonno and said "*hola gringo!*" then others joined in the chorus and surrounded him. "*Hola gringo. Un caramello por favor. You give me one pencil. How are you? Dame un sol. Un solcito por favor.*" The stock phrases came thick and fast, Jonno found his mouth dry and unable to speak. *Gringo, gringo gringo....*

He began to feel faint, looking at these little mountain people he began to feel his legs go weak. But they didn't stop, smiling, laughing, tapping on his leg.

"Please," he mumbled, "por favor, help me."

"Un caramello gringo!"

"I don't have, please, my father......."

"Gringo, how are you?"

"No...my father, he is hurt..."

"one sol, gringo...."

Jonno's world began to spin. Round and round, faster and faster. The smiles and the enthusiasm, the relentlessness. He was finally here but still felt so far away. The faces and the noise begun to blur, "mon padre, mon padre" he tried to say but his tongue was parched, the saliva all dried up. He looked right at the tallest of the children who had his hand held out in front of him. The child looked back deep into his eyes. "Help me" he said, *"please....I need help."* And with that his legs finally gave way, and in front of his new found audience, Jonno collapsed.

* * *

Chapter Twenty-Five – James, Night Time

James awoke in a start; he opened his eyes but couldn't see. He couldn't remember where he was and for a split-second panicked, feeling lost in the darkness. He put his hands in front of him and saw their outline, then touched his face with his palms the way his mother used to do when she told him that he was safe and that she loved him. He looked for his watch on his wrist but it was not there, he couldn't remember where he had left it. What time was it? Why was he here? Where was everyone else? His mind began to slowly switch on, trying to work out where he was, why he was in a sleeping bag and why he felt so cold. He felt a pressing sensation in his bladder, it wasn't going to be long before he wouldn't be able to hold it in any longer.

Driven by the urge to pee, he made a quick and jerky movement to get out of his sleeping bag. In doing so he caught his ankle against something at the bottom of the tent and a shard of pain ripped through his leg all the way up his spine, *"arrghhhhhh"* he cried out, the sensation bringing tears to his cold face. Then it came back to him again why he was here. The events, the mistakes, the departure of Jonny. But it was dark, why had he not returned yet? Surely it couldn't take that long to get help? What if something had happened to him? The pressing on his bladder was too strong however for him to dwell just yet on these more important questions and there was no choice but to haul himself out of the tent. The bottles he had been using during the day were now full, if he wet the sleeping bag it would be a disaster.

Lying on his left side, James began to swivel to bring his head to the front of the tent to open the door. Once round, he then began to agonisingly inch his way out of the protective cocoon of his sleeping bag, trying to immobilise his right leg and minimise his ankle catching any more than it had to. Each movement jarred and his body pulsed with deep and searing pain, intense lightning flashes that felt like his entire inner world disappeared in a blinding whiteness. Gritting his teeth and breathing heavily he finally made it out of the bag and reached for the tent zip to open the flap. Once done he then had to continue this left sided crawl, drag and shuffle to get to the porch door. Every movement had to be carefully and thoughtfully made, lest it result in more torture.

The porch door opened in a fumble of cold fingers and a blast of cold air poured in from the outside. In his rush James had forgotten to put his jacket on, there hadn't been the time. His beaten body shuddered. The bladder pressed harder. Crawling on his elbows and left knee, holding his right leg up at an angle that protected the ankle but made the knee ache, James started to make his way out of his synthetic nest. He had a flashback of being at a recent conference and how he had agonised over what suit to wear, how to look, how best to present himself to speak to his fellow colleagues. What would they make of this now he wondered? The great surgeon and wannabe mountain climber about to wet himself all alone in the middle of the Peruvian nowhere. Where were their claps and well-wishes now? How did any of that help? Where was anyone?

Out of the tent and onto the cold shale ground he crawled as far as he could manage to make sure that he wouldn't go right next to the tent. He luckily found a slight gradient and used that so it would flow away from him. In a last second flurry of anxiety and movement, he pulled himself up onto his left knee, pulled his trousers down as far he could and relaxed. Hot and warm it flowed away from him, its stream seemingly sparkling catching something from the sky. Relief flooded in as liquid decanted out.

Everything done he put himself back together but the effort of crouching and bending on one knee holding his right leg so attentively had exhausted him. He let himself topple gently to the left side and lay on his back catching his breath. He could feel the liquid heat from a few feet away hovering in the air where he had gone. The smell reminded him of the wards in the hospital and he had a flashback of when he put his first catheter in and how grateful the patient had been. He hadn't really understood why at the time, that gratitude had felt a bit over the top, *it was just a catheter* he had scoffed.

James lay back, his back finding a space to make itself comfortable against the uneven pebble and shale of where he had found himself. For the first time since he had awoken he became aware of what was around him, of the fact he was alive and was breathing. He saw the shadows and silhouettes of the boulders nearby, there was a dark mass rising up beyond them that had a hint of white to it which must have been the mountain. The sky was dark and as his eyes became more accustomed, he began to see small pinpricks of light, and then more and then more. As he lay there, the sky began to reveal itself to him, layer by layer of star after star. Before long, what he saw was an inversion of the original image, dazzling light but with just a hint of black, such was their number. He looked up transfixed, the pain in his right leg made him not want to move and so gave him the opportunity just to stare. There was light as far as the eye could see, like someone had thrown a bag of small diamonds over a dark velvet cloth and then switched on the spotlight.

Stuck there as he was under this endless canopy, James was at a loss of what to think. Despite the fact that his body was shivering and he knew the cold was starting to go deeper into him, he found himself lost in the awe and majesty of where he was. He had seen amazing stars before and had thought about the bigger questions that they posed, but it had never been for long. There had always been a warm house or tent to easily return to. There had been conversations and distractions to take him away from anything too serious. But now, there was simply nowhere else to be.

He looked up and out and wondered what was going on. Why was he here? Why were any of us here? What a miracle that life existed at all. What were the chances? Yet in and amongst his noble and profound musings came a sudden shoal of dark and deeply uncomfortable thoughts, *how can I be here and not share this? What if this is the last thing I ever see? What does it even mean if I am just witnessing this on my own? What of my family, why am I not with them seeing this? What if I don't return, what has this all been for?*

He thought of Jonny and a pang of guilt coursed through him, what if something has happened to him, what if he doesn't come back? *Why did I put him in this situation?* Macie and his Emma appeared in his mind, *where are they? Why have I not spent more time on this precious planet with them? Why am I here, what if I die here? What have I actually done with my life?*

Looking out into the abyss James felt himself lose balance and began to float into the void his own mind had kept him from for as long as he could remember. Questions that he had built a lifetime of protection from began to emerge from the deep. Being marooned on this rocky island of nowhere, his life and decisions began to take on new and more troubling meaning. He had spent most of his fatherhood telling Jonny to take the consequences of his decisions without ever perhaps applying that to himself. Yet here he was now precariously shivering under the ethereal magnificence of the universe, utterly as a result of his own choices.

James thought of how he had spent a lifetime pushing himself, going further, wanting more. When he applied himself to something he wanted to be the best, he could never cope with average. He had wanted a life of epic heroism, to be outstanding, to make others feel inspired in his presence. He had done some amazing things, of that he knew, but at what cost? What did any of it mean if the net result was for him to die freezing to death in a stony graveyard? He didn't have the mental strength this time to stop these thoughts, and let them wash over him.

He felt an icy quake of insight rumble through him, that he had no one else to blame but himself. He had led himself here. The desire for a grand holiday, to be an amazing father, to tell his colleagues more adventures, to make his family proud, to prove to his own father that he was special.

James stopped, that last thought hadn't been part of the usual narrative that came when he thought of his life. He was self-aware enough to know that not all his motivations were purely altruistic but his own father had never entered into the analysis. *"To prove to his father that he was special."* He let the words hang in the air above where his breath was solidifying as he was breathing out, in the distance he heard the sound of rocks and snow falling.

James put his hands to his face again and pushed his palms into his cheeks. He felt a warm moisture in his fingertips of both hands. As he brought his hands away he felt another warm stream leave his body, channelling from the centres of his eyes over his cheekbones to his ears, before pooling in his ears and then dripping to the ground. James couldn't remember the last time he had cried, maybe it was Macie being born, but not since. Too tired to try and take control of the situation, he just lay there, the warm tears highlighting how cold his face had become. For the first time in years he wept, letting out small pathetic high-pitched whimpers as he did so.

The tears had the strange effect of blurring the stars meaning that the border of their light became hazy and began to mix with each other. The sky was losing its clarity but gaining in luminosity. At the same time his thoughts were racing; is this what this is all about? Is this why I am here, has it all been for him?

James saw a picture of his father's face, stern but with kindness. He had been a great man, someone that James had really looked up to, someone he wanted to emulate, someone he wanted the attention and affirmation from. He loved his father but he had never quite felt certain that he had been loved back. So much of his own life perhaps had been seeking that love, seeking that approval. James thought of all his achievements and things that had made the world sit up and pay attention to him, and how hollow so much of it had felt. How in receiving the adulation and recognition, he had always quickly wanted to move to the next summit, the next challenge. How meaningless so much of it had felt once he had received it. How his father had always said "well done, but what's next?" He both loved and hated that response, as it was the closest he ever had to his father paying him the attention he so desperately craved.

And then his death, the horror of the stroke, cut down from life just like that. James realised that he had spent his whole life wanting for his father to simply say "well done, I love you" without having to do anything to impress him but it had never come. It was always as though there was yet another challenge for him to overcome to get there. And then the opportunity was over, his father reduced to a half man lying there, writhing in his hospital bed, speechless, half-paralysed, and half groaning and flailing.

The silence, becoming withdrawn, the extra work and operations, the planning of this trip; it had all been to distance himself from the original failure that had dominated his life that he had never overcome. He had told his father that he loved him while he lay there, eyes staring at the ceiling. He had no idea if his father had heard, but he knew he had to tell him. Yet the real suffering for James was that the moment had gone for these words to be said back to him. Even though his mother, when she was alive, would tell him how proud he was of his son, he had never heard those words for himself. As a man of science, he would tell himself over and over again, I cannot believe anything without proof.

James thought of Jonny. When was the last time he had told Jonny he loved him? In fact, when was the last time he had told anyone he loved them and really meant the words he was saying? The torrent of tears grew in strength and warmth. What have I been doing all this time? He gasped.

He thought of his life and how he had lived, the various passions and pursuits that he had occupied himself with. His desire to be someone, someone great and important. But where had that led him? He had been ambitious and been congratulated for this by his profession, but where were any of them now? His craving to be approved of and looked up to had ultimately led him to this point. Alone, crying, shivering and in pain on the side of an indifferent mountain. Was this heroic? Would it even have been heroic had disaster not befallen them and they made it home full of great stories? If once again he had managed to side-step the true motivation of his life, just more bluster and padding to protect himself from the haunting truth that he had never felt truly loved by his father.

"And now?" James found himself speaking out loud, "To maybe die here, maybe my son will die too, I don't know where he is. To freeze to death here thanks to my ignorance. And of my family, have I not done to them what was done to me? If I die now, have I not just passed on the same pain, and even multiplied it, of that which was passed to me!?"

In that moment a deeper part of James suddenly took over. A new wave of thoughts stormed the building and began to take control. "OK enough of all this," they said, "this won't mean anything anyway unless you get yourself back into your tent and get warm. You are still alive and you have to fulfil your side of the bargain if you want anyone to save you. Get back in the tent. Now."

James came to, rolled onto his side and made the same pitiful drag back to his tent. He was trembling hard and had no idea how long he had been outside for. Scraping his knee and hands on the dirt he finally made it back. The pain was as excruciating as he had known but he didn't feel the need to cry out. Entering the tent was a calmness that had overtaken his body despite the uncertainties that were raging in his mind. "Get warm" it commanded, "do your bit. If no one comes so be it, but at least give yourself a chance."

Chapter Twenty-Six – Village

The acrid taste of smoke brought Jonno to a coughing fit, eyes streaming and throat dry and burning, he came to. He felt hot, sweaty and disorientated. There was something big, heavy and made of rough material pressing down on him and he was lying flat. He had no idea where he was, there was dampness in the air despite the smoke and a faint earthy smell that seemed to be present. His head was pounding and his eyes felt sore, and he struggled to make any sense of what was happening. Looking straight upwards from where he found himself he saw wooden rafters creating a roof. There was a faint orange glow to the room and what light there was seemed to dance and flicker over the walls. He heard a gentle crackling and smelt fire.

He didn't feel strong enough to push the heavy weight off of him and just lay there. His mind was blank, *where am I?* he thought, his confused mind trying to cycle through the various options. *This isn't home,* he thought, *I know that. What have I been doing to find myself in a place like this?* Jonno felt a cold streak of realisation run through his blood, "Dad!" he suddenly yelled, "Dad!"

In that moment a door appeared to open, Jonno sat bolt upright fighting off the covers. He quickly took in his surroundings, he was in a makeshift bed made of thick, colourful woollen blankets, the walls were made of earth and there were wooden rafters in the roof. The room had a strong smell of smoke to it that was coming from a simple stove in the corner, there was a big charred looking kettle made of metal giving off steam. There were other pots and pans next to the stove, all blackened beyond any indication that they were once metallic. The floor was made of simple wooden boards placed next to each other. Despite not having a clue where he was, his initial impressions were that this was a friendly place and his shoulders dropped a little as he exhaled some of the smoky air.

He looked to the door that he had heard open. A simple darkened wooden rectangle that opened inwards. He watched as a figure entered, whose features he couldn't quite make out hidden under shadow of the brim of the wide hat that they had on. The figure was small, but powerful looking, wearing what seemed like leggings and a thick skirt. A thick ponytail of jet black hair draped over the shoulder of this person. Jonno sat transfixed as this other human being entered the house.

The wearer of the hat looked up, and with kind and sparkling eyes he heard in a friendly and female voice,

"Gringo!"

She then, in that moment, turned around and walked out of the room as quickly as she had come. Jonno then heard a rustle and whispers of excitement from outside the door. It then opened again and this time came in four smaller versions of the lady who had just come in. Some dressed in wide brimmed hats, with pigtails and thick skirts, others in tracksuit bottoms and jumpers, they flooded in with a lightness in their step.

"Hola Gringo!"

They all yelled in chorus, smiling at him as he sat there confused beyond words. He was struck by the simplicity in their expression yet the toughness in their faces, open eyes yet hardened cheeks. They ran up to him and then continued to stare, poking and prodding each other, giggling and laughing amongst each other.

Jonno was completely unsure how to act but he knew that he had to do something for his father. The door opened again and this time entered a man with broad shoulders, thick jumper and another wide brimmed hat. He barked something at the children and they dispersed as quickly as they had arrived, like a flock of pigeons having spotted a lurking cat. The man walked towards Jonno, the gentle light of the room catching his face and revealing its deep lines and tough skin. His wrinkles bore the expression of a gentle smile despite his otherwise lack of expression.

"Hola gringo!" he beamed, "how are you?"

"Whe … whe…where am I?" stuttered Jonno, scarcely able to take it all in.

"Como….whaaat? I no speak much eeeglish gringo,"

"Please….er…. por favor," Jonno reached deep inside his limited internal Spanish dictionary. "My father…. Mi padre….is hurt….very bad….err…. muy malo……. In mountains……arriba!" the words fell from his tongue like lead weights. His head was pounding.

"Eh… tu padre…. Como? You no come solo gringo? You muy inferno, very hot!"

"No…. please….por favor no…. mi padre …. Arriba!" Jonno cursed himself for having never paid any attention in class at school, languages had always seemed so pointless and boringly taught, just another exam to pass.

"Arriba… como… tu padre…donde?" the smiling man asked, the lines of face beginning to crease slightly.

"Si….si… he ….very hurt….very malo…..need help, rapido!" Jonno looked pleadingly at this strange man who he wasn't sure had any idea of what he was talking about. His deep and dark eyes looked piercingly at him, staring out of a tough and leathery face. Jonno was sure he could feel them exploring and crawling over the back of his mind. Jonno could feel tears forming in the corners of his eyes, the frustration of not being able to express himself now of all times was enough to make him explode.

The man's expression began to change as though the words Jonno had said were beginning to make some sort of impact. "Gringo....you no come solo? Padre? Arriba?" his face began to harden.

"Si....arriba" Jonno exclaimed gesticulating with his arms as though pointing towards the mountains.

"You.... No guide, no guia?"

"No, stupidos, solo. Mi padre y mi"

"Crayzeee gringos....arriba muy peligroso,"

"Si.....si..." Jonno tailed. He suddenly felt he had no more words he could say. Tears began to fall, pouring out of his tired and confused eyes. However, he kept his gaze on this curious mountain man, wanting him to see his pain and sense of bewilderment. If he couldn't communicate properly through language, then he was going to have to just use raw emotion.

"But Gringo... padre is muerto, he die?"

"No....no, maybe..." Jonno looked at him, shrugging his shoulders. "In tent... leg....very painful" he said pointing to his right leg. "No can walk," he added making a snapping motion of a piece of wood with his hands.

The local man looked at him with widening eyes.

"OK...gringo....espera...you wait."

And with that he turned around and left the room, leaving Jonno back to silence and the orange glow that flickered from the small stove in the corner casting shadows over the room.

Jonno lay back again as a wave of nausea and exhaustion exploded through him. He felt cold and shaky, the weight of the blanket pressed against him and he closed his eyes hoping somehow that all this might just go away when he reopened them.

This, of course, didn't happen and Jonno opened them again to find himself alone in this small earth bricked room. He could hear a commotion outside the door, as though some sort of public meeting was going on. There were raised voices and what felt like some exchanges of opinions, there were multiple voices and it appeared as though they were not necessarily agreeing on what they were talking about.

The door flung open again and this time another man walked in, wearing almost identical type of clothes to the last man, similar stature and another kindly and calm face. He was holding a mobile phone in his right hand and passed it Jonno, the light on it was green and the screen lit up. Jonno took the phone half wondering who knew he was here to ring him, feeling things couldn't get any weirder, he put it to his ear and said, "Hola... hello....?"

"Gringo..." a voice barked from the speaker, "Gringo, this is Morales from Huaraz, my brother, you in his house. Why you in village? I speak English, tell me what happens?"

"err....hi...my father, hurt his leg, he is in tent near the snow."

"You don't have guide?" The voice asked

"No..no guide, we go solo...." Jonno crimsoned.

"Ok....and your padre...which mountain?"

"We went to Casharaju, he fell and hurt his leg, no can walk"

"And now, he in tent, solo?"

"Yes, he cannot walk, I come down to find help."

"He is bleeding?"

"No...but very cold, we spend all night out of the tent after he fell."

"He has cell phone?"

"yes... but no battery..."

"Ok Gringo, but now is night time. We cannot go now, it is too far, too cold. We cannot carry him to village in night. Tomorrow we go."

"But I am worried for him, he is very cold and in much pain."

"I am sorry Gringo, tomorrow we go. I tell Morales."

"Ok... thank you... but....."

"Now I talk to Morales, you can pass me?" the voice interrupted him.

Jonno looked up and saw that the other man was still in the room watching him intently. He passed back the phone and the man put it to his ear and immediately broke into a language that Jonno had never heard before. The two spoke quickly, initially seriously before breaking into laughter. Jonno felt so powerless watching the fate of his father decided by a man he had never met, another man he was unable to communicate with and a group of villagers from a place he didn't even know the name of.

The man turned the phone off and again left the house. Outside the din of conversation and opinions seemed to rise up again. The tone seemed to oscillate from seriousness to laughter and back again. The shadows of the room he was in flickered and danced on the walls. Jonno waited. He thought how he had taken pictures of these people as he had walked through the village the first time as they were trekking up, feeling as though they belonged to another time and place. They seemed so strange and alien to him at the time, incredible in their own way but so far removed from anything he had ever known. But now he was in one of their houses waiting for them to help him find and recover his injured father.

The group chat seemed to die down outside as though some sort of consensus had been agreed. The door opened again and this time the first man who had come in entered, he walked slowly and purposefully to Jonno's bed,

"Grinngooo….mañana, we go. Now you rest, my daughter she bring food. Mañana we go when sun come, ok?"

"OK…gracias…" garbled Jonno, wanting to say so much more but with no idea how.

"now you rest, OK?"

"OK…"

And with that, the man turned his back and left the room, leaving Jonno once more to the flickering shadows.

* * *

Chapter Twenty-Seven – Sunrise

The door thudded with the knocking from outside. Jonno came to, having been dozing. He hadn't really slept last night but just drifted in and out of his thoughts. No matter how hard he tried, he couldn't make any sense of what was going on nor let go of it enough to rest. He had been largely left alone, in what must have been a small kitchen, overnight with the occasional lined face putting their head around the door to either stare at him or check he was OK. One of the children, possibly a young teenager not much older than Macie who had face both impossibly young and old at the same time, had come with some broth for him. Awkwardly in her wide hat, colourful cardigan and numerous skirts she had tiptoed in. She gave him the broth and her wide dark eyes met his and she blushed and smiled. "Gracias," croaked Jonno before she swung around, almost clobbering him with her heavily plaited pigtail and hurrying for the door.

The soup had been the first proper thing that Jonno had eaten for about 24 hours and he set about it with great appetite. It seemed full of grain with a hint of chicken. "Delicious" he thought to himself as his spoon hit something solid at the bottom. Hoping for a chunk of chicken, Jonno put his spoon under this object and brought it out to the top. In his haste and hunger he put it straight into his mouth without looking and bit down. It didn't feel anything like chicken but more like a twig with three branches coming off of it. He put his hands to his mouth to have a look at it and he almost dropped his bowl in shock, as it came into view. It was a chicken foot! In his soup! The ribbed aspect of the leg merging into its three toes and claws at the end. Jonno looked in horror at what had just been in his mouth and what he had been chewing. *Where am I and what is going on?* He repeated this, as though some sort of soothing mantra, over and over again.

Jonno had been mainly warm during the night, despite a cold face, once the stove in corner had simmered down. He was surprised how warm the blankets were, but try as he might he couldn't get comfortable. He looked around at how simple his room was while there was still some light. The bricks made of earth, simple wooden beams holding up a roof of what looked like thatch. He saw the stove and the blackened pots and pans that sat by it, reminding him of his kitchen back at home. It seemed that despite the location not much was different, people all needed somewhere solid to sleep and some way of cooking. While he might have been used to modern comforts back home, it was essentially the same here just without electric ovens. People were obviously able to survive here just as well as people back at home, but in more sparse conditions.

The knocking of the door brought him back to the present and he startled,

"Hola?" he called out.

"Gringo!" a voice boomed from the other side.

"Si....?"

"Gringo... vamos eh!? »

"Vamos?...OK... si....I come.."

Jonno pulled back the heavy covers and found his shoes next to where he had been sleeping. It was still dark but his eyes had adjusted and he was able to get himself ready. His bag was also by his bed. He took out his jacket and hat and put them on, it was still going to be cold outside and then he slung the bag on his back.

He opened the door and as he squinted in the light, he needed a double-take. There in front of him were about ten of the men from the village dressed and ready. There was also a horse waiting patiently, being stroked by one of them. They broke off from their conversations and laughter to look at the young dishevelled gringo who had just arrived in their midst.

The same man who passed him the phone the night before came up to him and slapped him heartily on the back, smiling a toothy grin with his dark eyes ablaze. He put his thumbs up and said something that Jonno had no idea what it meant. The first man who he had spoken to then came up to him and said,

"OK gringo, we ready, we find tu padre."

"OK, gracias amigos" Jonno responded.

"Casharaju?" The man asked.

"Si!" Jonno confirmed, the name making him feel sick.

"OK, vamos!" roared the man and the others all joined in with great gusto. "Vamos amigos" he heard them say before coming over to Jonno and slapping him gently on the back.

The man with the horse gave it a small slap on its behind and shouted "*ooosshhhhh*" and they were off, heading back onto the path that only yesterday Jonno had been staggering down. The darkness of the night was just beginning to lift and there was a blue haze hugging the horizon. The sun was on its way.

***

James too hadn't slept. The uncertainty and the cold keeping him awake. He had spent much of the night cycling through his thoughts, thinking of all the new revelations he had had the day before. He felt a profound sense of anger and irony at the combination of insight and helplessness. He had also realised that he had much to do upon returning to the world to sort out, so much to put right. Whether he could or not would be up to Jonno, there was little chance of him dragging himself down the mountain but he still had this as a final option if Jonno just didn't come back.

The unwelcome desire to pee came back again, aching in his bladder. James looked in vain for something to go into in the tent. Yet he was met with the same lack of options as before.

He swivelled again, his leg had markedly stiffened overnight and it meant handling it and moving it was impossible without pain. He loudly grunted and groaned his way out of the tent again. Shuffling and crawling on his forearms, he dragged his unhappy right leg behind him. The pain was constant and so he gave up trying to avoid it. This time he did bring his jacket with him just in case he got stuck out there again.

Once out he made his way over to the same place that he had found the night before and using the same tactics managed to relieve himself without too much extra difficulty. As he finished he turned to look at the skyline. Where had been shadowy mountain hulks and bright stars was now beginning to reverse itself. A strong cerulean hue was beginning to line the edges of the peaks and the white of their snow was coming increasingly into focus. The stars seemed to be retreating back into the depths of space and the light from the sun began to take over, extinguishing everything that was not of the planet.

The outlines of the mountains made James shiver. Despite the situation he was in, he couldn't help but be lost in admiration for their size and power. Given the injuries he now had, there was no way of imagining himself successfully striding up one of these majestic summits, so instead he could only look in admiration. The peaks all soared into a sky that was deepening in colour. The air was cold but so was James, so he was happy to just sit and watch. There was nowhere else he needed to be right now.

He saw the sky begin to change, as night began to withdraw and colours emerge in the land around him. The boulders he was sitting amongst lost their dark and shadowy complexion, beginning to become three-dimensional again. The skyline to the east began to develop an orange tint, outlining the jagged teeth of the peaks of the mountains. Rock and snow, as though on a negative in a photographic print room, began to emerge from the side of these beasts tinted with a blue tinge. The world of shadows was falling away and the clarity of a new day was returning. In this uncloaking of what was around him he noticed a deep stillness, a peacefulness that could not be disturbed. Creation was beginning again, new hope and potential accompanying its first light.

The sun peaked its way above the horizon and he felt subtle heat on his face for the first time that day and felt held by it. Despite loving and knowing all about the way the earth moved around the sun, and various physics involved in gravity and how it happened, James could not explain the beauty of this moment, the overwhelming sense of calm and grandeur in the mountains that only sunrise can bring. In witnessing this moment in a way that he couldn't move from it, the wonder of simply being alive took on new significance. So much of his life had been spent accumulating and acquiring. He had chased a life of recognition and wanting to be seen, to be heard and listened to, he had wanted to be someone of importance. Yet here now, all of that seemed to fade away as he found himself dissolved in creation's morning dance of light, heat, cold and shadow.

Water came to his chilled eyes; its warmth awoke parts of his face that had also felt numb from sitting outside for so long. He felt a deep yearning to experience more of this wonder, to have the chance to get home and look again at the life he had built for himself. To work out whether his priorities were correct and re-examine exactly what it was he was chasing. He could not recall a moment as moving as this at least since Macie was born, the wonder of seeing new life in the outside world for the first time and the sense of limitless potential that came with looking at a new-born. He realised that his life had been one of constructing safety; so many actions had been done in order to protect himself from actually living and feeling life. Shielding himself from feeling the fleeting beauty of life, feeling its joys and sadness as he passed through it. He had deadened himself with seductive narratives of needing to be in control. The sun lifted its head above the range on the east of him and flooded the valley floor with light. James didn't want to move, he wanted this moment to go for as long as he could suffer it.

Leg stretched out in front of him, he smiled at the deep irony that he would know exactly what to do to fix himself. He would reduce the fracture and take it to theatre for pinning; it would be a tricky procedure as the fracture was likely to be complicated. Then there might need to be a cruciate ligament repair as well, depending on the results of the tests. But what did it all matter now, the knowledge and skill he had accumulated, how did it help in this moment? He thought of a Buddhist story he had casually read once in one of his wife's self-help books that were often left on the kitchen table. It was about an educated man on a boat who spent most the voyage chiding the less educated crew on not knowing what they should. However, when the ship came to sink, the same crew told him he was going to have to swim in order to survive to which he said he did not know how. Then, they said, maybe this is what you should have spent your life learning.

For the first time since the accident, James laughed, loud and long until tears again came to his eyes. He saw himself sitting there, small and broken surrounded by the expansive unity of vast sky, land and mountains. He saw how tiny and minute he was in comparison to the universe he was in. He saw how a blind and misunderstood slavery to ego was possibly the most dangerous disease to mankind and how he too had been infected by it. Its fever had brought him here, and its outcome might not bring him back. James relaxed, working his back into an aspect of the boulder he was sitting by to become comfy, he didn't want to move for now, he just wanted to sit and be with this sunrise. A sunrise that was feeling like his first true sunrise, but also one that might be one of his last.

***

They were making good progress despite Jonno being the slowest in the group. The men seemed to move so lightly and gracefully over the path that it looked like they were pirouetting and dancing at times. There was an elegance in their steps as they moved up the gradually ascending trail. Jonno could not get over how often they laughed with each other, despite their clear strength and age; they seemed to not be able to resist having fun or a joke. They were both serious and light-hearted at the same time which Jonno had not experienced much of with the so-called adults in his own country. They gestured to offer Jonno to ride on the horse every now and again when they felt that he might have been struggling, but Jonno refused. He wanted to be their equal, he wanted to arrive to his father on his own two feet. He wanted his father to see him having done it properly. For all his desire to get there as quickly as possible, a part of him made sure he was getting there in the right way.

The sun was now just about to climb above the horizon, the light had strengthened as they were walking and he was able to see his feet clearly. Still chilly, the walking was warming him up, partly why he refused to go on the horse. His legs ached however and his lower back felt sore. He encouraged himself by saying that he wouldn't be trekking for quite some time after this, just one more day.

They passed thought the forest and up onto the high plains. Jonno saw the mountains come into view, gaining in height all the time as they approached. When he had first made this journey with his father only a few days ago he had seen them so differently. They were magnificent, welcoming and the gateway to glory. Yes, they had looked enormous and imposing but he had embraced this. He had seen great meaning entering this arena with his father, a chance to prove to him who he was and what he was made of. He knew how much his father prized a challenge and he wanted to be a part of that.

Now as the sky deepened, the blue becoming more vivid and alive, the peaks of the mountains became more prominent. Jutting out into the endless ocean of sky, as though someone had ripped a piece of paper and held it in front of a still sea. There were a few clouds providing the froth in the sky, but otherwise the day was clear. Jonno felt a sense of foreboding, as he realised he had no idea what to expect, let alone how they would help bring his father down again. The horse was a great idea but would he be able to cope with the pain.

The same mountains and scenery now began to appear hostile and threatening. There was a sense that these were not places for humans to come and expect to achieve and conquer certain things. Instead they were in fact arenas of great danger that brought humans to their limits and perhaps even tragically beyond them. There were no guarantees in an environment like this, only the arm-wrestle between risk and ego. They had the power to humble or destroy with very little in between. He thought how easy it had been to imagine himself standing at the top of the mountain in his mind and how horrendously difficult it had been to physically achieve it, how much separation there was in imagination and reality. How the drive for success and experience had pushed them on. How momentarily glorious it all was, to how futile it all seemed with his father badly injured. Why climb these things, what was it all for?

He looked at his fellow travellers on the path, men of all ages who he had never met but were willing to come and help him. He felt frustrated that they could not communicate as he had so much he wanted to ask. While they were clearly human like him he could not have felt any more different from them and their lives. There was no way of telling how old any of them were as they had such tough and old faces, lined by years of hard sun and hard mountain living. Yet their bodies seemed young, strong and supple. Their faces had an innocence and goodness in them that shined out; there was an uncomplicatedness of word and deed. They wore simple clothes, dark trousers and thick jumpers; some had shoes, others had bare calloused feet and sandals. They all had their wide brimmed hats on, putting their faces in shadow. They seemed to enjoy each other's company, and the journey was lit up with whoops and shrieks of laughter. Occasionally one would say something to Jonno which he couldn't understand and they would all fall about laughing. It was as though this was both serious and not serious at all, they were able to flit and fly between the two at any moment.

Jonno wished he could talk more with them, understand more about their lives. What did they think of the mountains, did they want to climb them? Did they like their lives, did they have ambitions to leave the village and make a life for themselves anywhere? Did they use the internet, did they want to travel, what did they think of foreigners? There was so much and more he could have asked. He imagined trying to paint this scene, using the iconic dark silhouette of them with their hats on in front of the tower mass of rock, snow and sky in the background. Do these people still notice the mountains, Jonno wondered, if they live alongside them every day?

They wound their way along the trail and Jonno saw where it began to steepen to head into the moraine. This bit had been breathless when they had their packs, it had been tough going, yet with a lighter bag and with the easy-footed villagers they made good progress. He felt them close to his father, it wouldn't be long now. Jonno just had to remember where the tent was but he figured that in the day it shouldn't be too hard to locate it. He felt the sun on his face and a strange mix of pride and fear rise up in his chest, they were close and somehow he had managed to find a help party to come and rescue his father. Yet he also didn't know who or what they were going to find. The air suddenly felt very thin.

They ascended into the moraine following the dusty trail that wound through the various boulders. There were the familiar cairns guiding the way that Jonno could remember from before. And then, in the distance, tucked in amongst some of the larger rocks he saw a flash of blue, the tent! Not knowing what else to say he just yelled "Dad!" as loud as possible, the others turned and looked at him and he started pointing. They followed his outstretched finger to where the tent lay. But then to Jonno's horror, they saw something else. Something that appeared like the body of the man slumped against a rock about ten meters from the tent, and he was not moving. "Dad! Dad!" Jonno screamed as he broke into a run, but there was no answer. The body appeared to be still. Peaceful, yet deathly still.

***

James felt the arrival of the group before he saw them, he felt something change, a sense of his own skin becoming on edge as though he was no longer alone. From sitting there lost in his own thoughts, attempting to make sense of all he had been through in the last thirty-six hours, he had the abnormal sensation that something living was nearby. Part of him had stopped resisting where he was and what was happening to him, there was a level of acknowledgement that he must accept his fate and what it brought. With that came a deeper connection with where he was, the less he fought to be somewhere else the more he felt he began to connect with the environment he was in. The pain throbbed but meaning was providing a potent analgesic.

He heard voices in between the rocks, but not his son's. He felt the deep pang of wanting to see Jonny again, to look at his face and to say the things that he had neglected to recently. He wanted his son to come and give him a hug in his strong arms and take him home where he could start again. He went to shout but found his mouth dry and without power.

Hurried footsteps approached closer. There was a delicate crunch of shale and almost inaudible breathing as though this person coming was almost floating his way. Then from around one of the boulders appeared a young, dark skinned and smiling face. "Señor Gringo!" its wearer beamed "how are you?"

"Hola," croaked James, "bien…mas o menos" he smiled, wanting to say so much more.

The face then disappeared from view and James heard a shrill yell, like something from a Wild West movie when the Indians were jubilant. This was then accompanied by more whoops and yells from the near distance.

"Dad! Dad!" James heard in the distance,

"Jonny!" James yelled back,

"Dad, we're here, we're coming!"

"I'm OK!" James yelled back.

"I knew you would be," Jonno's voice shouted back.

The face of the first young man, who had found James, returned and fixed his deep and piercing eyes on him. Smiling the young man said,

"Crayzeee gringo, no guide, no guia, you are loco…."

"I know," James replied, "Ya lo sé, tontos, silly gringos!"

"But all OK now, we find you."

"Thank you, thank you, muchas gracias amigo," James responded with his voice quivering. Even this briefest of human exchange was enough to show him how spent he was and how alone he had been. He had been strong enough to keep himself together but no more, now the emotion and exhaustion begun to pump its way through him. The young man with his old face looked at him with a mixture of curiosity and compassion. Not taking his dark brown eyes off of him for a second.

"It's OK Señor Gringo, esta bien tio" he said smiling.

James just looked at him, unable to speak. If he did he knew the tears would fall and perhaps never stop. The pain he had accessed over the last thirty-six hours of a life that he was only beginning to understand could make him weep for a long time; he suddenly became aware of this. Not wanting to let his son down he gritted his teeth, crying was one thing, a great breakthrough. But to cry in front of others, men and his own son, he refused to embarrass himself.

He then saw the face of his son coming hurtling around the boulder. Jonno's face looked gaunt and he had deep bags under his eyes yet he was grinning madly. As their two faces met there was a brief moment of silence before either of them spoke, both transiently transfixed upon the image of the other. Jonno saw his father's tired and crumpled face, his wet eyes and tense body. He saw a man who had wanted the best for himself and had been driven by his needs to be seen and recognised. For the first time in his life he saw a good man trapped in a world of pain of his own making and felt nothing but love for him.

James looked back at his son, initially unable to bring words to his mouth. He saw an open face that had been beaten by both weather and exhaustion. He saw his own father in the wide eyed curiosity but also the early lines of sadness forming from his eyes where uncertain thought was beginning to etch its workings. He saw youth and all its glorious potential and for a split second he wondered if he was gazing back in time at an earlier version of himself. He was transported to his own younger times when he had summited his first mountain and gained an insatiable hunger for more. How he had been bewitched by the meaning and identity he had derived from it. In Jonno's glassy eyes he also saw his own reflection in the shadow of the great surrounding cordillera and how wretched and beaten he looked. *What sort of man am I, where have I been?*

Both men stared not knowing what to say or how to greet each other. There was so much to say and seemingly so few ways of saying it.

"Dad," blurted out Jonno, "I'm so glad you're OK. Sorry we've been so long."

"Well... you took your time." Smiled his father, his lips cracking from the cold.

"I tried...." Jonno stuttered, catching his foot on a loose stone.

"Come here," James gestured with his open arms yet unable to physically move towards his son.

Jonno hesitated a little before lowering himself into his father's awkward embrace. Gently bending down   so as not to add to his pain he rested his head on his father's shoulders and put his arms around his quietly shaking body. For a moment time seemed to stand still as the two men embraced, the great peaks of the nearby white mountains simply held the space as their bodies held each other. James gripped him tightly. Despite the physical awkwardness of their embrace, Jonno was leaning over and his body too was tired and back sore, he did not want it to end, this hug had a different quality to the one they had shared at the top of Casharaju. He felt his father soften and collapse into this one, not stay strong and rigid as he had done at the top of the summit. He wondered who needed this hug the most, him or his father.

James crumpled into the strong figure of his son; he had no power left to try and pretend to be anything but the broken man he was. His son's robust and youthful frame held him tight. He thought of his own father and how he had never hugged him, never known the quality of his physical strength and body, that he had only ever known him from an abstract and intellectual distance. He felt confused as he wanted to be the tough one for his son. Yet his wonderful son had come back and found him, forgiven him and was here to bring him home. But he still wasn't ready to fully break and found some inner reserve to hold yet more tears back. Aware of the group of local men that Jonny had brilliantly found and recruited, he still couldn't let go. Something deep inside still wouldn't let him.

"I love you Dad," the words fell from Jonno's lips, tumbling out, gone and picking up speed before he could shut his mouth and stop them.

"I love you too Jonny, thank you," whispered his father, scrunching his eyes shut.

"Please stop calling me Jonny, Dad, you know I prefer Jonno these days, Jonny reminds me of being a child." This time the words were delivered gently and with care.

"Sorry... sorry.... Jonno," James feeling too exhausted to think of any possible reason against this.

"Thank you."

There was a silence and stillness that seemed to last an eternity, there was nothing else in the universe of any significance but this moment. The two men, lost in and among the rocky terrain underneath the bright and broad canvas of blue infinite sky, held and were held.

"Gringos!" the words punctured like gunshots, "Gringos, vamos eh!?"

Jonno and his father looked up having completely forgotten where they were. The band of local men stood looking impatiently at them.

"Si...si....we go, vamos amigos" James offered, without having any idea how.

"OK Dad, I'll sort your tent, you just stay here."

"I wasn't planning on being anywhere else," James smiled, painfully cracking his dry lips again.

"Well, just in case you were, I know you can be a busy man."

"Haha, Jonno, this is no time to score points."

"Haha, we've lots of time for that later." Jonno flashed a warm smile at his father.

James felt himself relax for the first time since the accident; he watched his son head towards the tent and then leant back and looked up at the sky and let out a deep sigh. He saw the peaks of the nearby mountains touching the heavens and felt a pang that he was about to be leaving them. These were sacred places for James. He felt he had become a man in his own eyes when he summited his first peak, had coped with the danger, the physical endurance of it, the needing to be resilient and mentally strong to make it. He had come down that first mountain a man to the adolescent boy who had climbed it. That had given him the spring board to begin to believe in himself, to chase the parts of life that were seemingly out of reach, to go beyond what he thought was possible. It was the first summit of many, in terms of actual mountains and also subsequent career. But he was also now acutely aware that the summits had become an addiction, something he had chased relentlessly, wanting to add more and more to help himself feel good about himself. It was no surprise, in hindsight, that he had chosen to go mountaineering after the death of his father. It was no surprise that he had wanted to do it with himself as the leader, taking his son to the top of his first Andean peak. And it was no surprise, after all that had happened, that his drive, intensity and focus had led to his injury and harrowing night alone on the mountain.

It was not lost on James that here he was now being helped off the mountain by his son and a group of men he had never met. It dawned on him that the same mountain which had made him all those years ago had now broken him and taken him into a brand new space of understanding. He knew, somewhere deep in his being, that he would be coming down this mountain a changed man, just like he had been all those years ago. He had no idea what this meant or how it would play out over time; something had been irretrievably lost but also something precious had been gained.

"Señor gringo?" One of the young men had come over to him breaking his thought, dressed in unassuming clothes and with the charismatic hat of the mountains, hardy yet soft face. James half wondered whether he was one of the spirits of the place rather than an actual person.

"Si?"

"We go now? You like horse?" James immediately felt safe in his company despite him being half his age.

"You have horse?"

"Oh si... caballo bonito, very strong for Señor gringo."

"Perfecto."

He pointed over his right shoulder and James saw a medium sized dark horse patiently waiting about ten meters away. It looked sturdy but calm. He hadn't ridden a horse for many years and was aware that this was likely to be a painful trip, but he had no choice. Once at the village they could ring for help and get in contact with the insurance company who could arrange a helicopter when they were a bit lower down. He mentally congratulated himself for having taken out decent insurance and double-checked the medical aspects of it. While he had been headstrong in trying to climb the mountain he had at least been sensible in not taking any chances with their cover.

One of the lads went to get the horse and took him over. Jonno and some of the others had sorted the tent and packed away everything and it looked like they were ready to go. Everyone was helping to take something so as to lighten the load and James felt mildly shocked at how much there was, how did they not rent porters or guides to help them, what was he thinking? He saw Jonno laughing with a younger man similar in age to him about packing something away and felt a glow of pride. He had a flashback to when Jonno was a small child and he would put him in a backpack high on Exmoor and go walking with him and how they loved that together, now the tables had turned and his son was carrying him home.

The men came over and with great strength yet gentleness hoisted James up onto the horse. His right leg screamed in pain as he straddled the animal but this was tempered by the fact he knew there was no choice, he breathed in sharply and out forcefully as a way of coping with the initial sharpness of the movement. The horse seemed to intuit the fragility of its rider and as it moved appeared to take extra care in each of its steps. James boggled at the accuracy of the way its four hooves were able to pick a path through the rock fields and keep balance. Each step sent small shocks though his damaged ankle and knee but he gritted his teeth and tried not to think about the nausea in the pit of his stomach. Sitting upright was the only real way of keeping his balance which meant his legs had to hang, he managed to hook his right foot into the stirrup for some support but it was still agonising.

"Dad? You OK?" Asked Jonno, sensing his father's discomfort through his slightly exaggerated huffing and puffing

"It's just my leg, it's so painful. There's no way of putting it anywhere without it being agony."

"Hmmm…. I'm not sure what we can do."

"Me neither, did it take you long to get here today?"

"About three or four hours, think you'll cope?"

"I guess I've got no choice."

"Not really…." Jonno tailed off.

"OK, well don't worry, this is just part of my penance for putting myself in this mess in the first place," James said grimacing.

"How do you mean?"

"Well I have brought this upon myself."

"Really? You've just been unlucky haven't you?" Jonno asked, slightly disarmed by his father's sudden personal candour.

"Well perhaps, but it's funny, a lot of time alone gives you a good chance to think about life."

"Tell me about it," added Jonno, "these last few days have been tortuous."

"You know, I can't thank you enough for what you've done," James said whilst trying not to let the pain of his leg overcome him.

"I had no choice, I suppose. I mean what else was I going to do?"

"Haha, OK true, but still. I think you are heroic, honestly."

"But Dad, I'm not the one who has just survived two nights up mountains with a smashed up leg, that's ridiculous. One night exposed and the other on your own, I don't know how you did it."

"I'm not sure I did," James grimaced.

"What do you mean?" asked Jonno finding his father to suddenly be a little mysterious.

"So much to talk about, we will in time." James added, gently but firmly. "But put it this way, pain and isolation are good interrogators, and the results are not always pretty."

"I don't follow."

"Jonno....being alone out there for the last twenty-four hours without any guarantees and in the sort of pain I have only seen in others and not myself has been quite an experience."

"Pain of your leg?"

"Yes, but there has been other pain too."

"Like Grandpa?"

"Yes...like Grandpa..." James tailed off as a familiar tension filled his body that he wasn't sure he wanted his son to see.

"Were you close?"

"That's a very good question and one I am now not so sure about."

"How come?" Jonno asked tentatively.

"It's complicated and I need some more time to think to be honest. But I have also seen that I want to make sure I don't repeat his mistakes with you."

"Mistakes?" Jonno couldn't quite believe what he was hearing, what did Grandpa have to do with all of this?

"Maybe *mistakes* is too harsh a word, arrghhh" as they went over a bump, "not mistakes implies something else. I guess....." James paused, weighing up whether he wanted to say what was about to come out of his mouth, " I guess...I mean... well, I never felt good enough for him, never felt liked he cared, never felt like what I did was enough. I have spent a life trying to impress him and be noticed and he never seemed to. Then... and then he just died, just like that. Gone, and no time to ever have those conversations, no time to be honest, no time to tell him what I thought, what I wanted, what I needed."

Jonno didn't know what to say. Where was the great Mr James Cooper who was unstoppable, the powerful and strong father who was unbreakable? The man who never had any problems or found anything difficult.

"Dad...I don't know what to say."

"I suppose time in that tent on my own has made this all very real to me. I thought I might die up there when you didn't come back. I haven't had that feeling before. I have seen plenty of death and known it must come my way at some point, but I had never felt it. In many ways I have spent a life trying to avoid it."

"Go on...."

"I have just realised some painful things about myself Jonno, that's all." James started to rein himself in, realising that this might be too much for his exhausted and addled son to take in all at once. "And one of those is that I want to see more of you, Macie and Mum. I have let work and all that goes with it become too much in my life, and I don't feel I have been there for you all enough."

"Dad.. you've always provided for us though." Jonno butted in, feeling he had to defend the old version of father he was used to.

"No...I know, I've done my best, but I think.... Well I think this has given me a bit of shake up. And I'd like to start being more in your lives again. If you'll have me back?"

Jonno looked up at this man on the horse whom he recognised but also felt like he'd never met before. He was caught off guard by this; he hadn't been expecting it even though a part of him had longed for this. It was almost too much, he felt unnerved by it all even though he wanted to hear more. He looked up and saw his father's tired but strong face, his eyes looked moist and there was an almost permanent twisting etched into his features. He had never seen his father in pain, either physically or emotionally until the last few days and it was scrambling his own neural circuits. He too had so much to say but it was still deep inside of him and he lacked the language to prise it out.

"Dad, please, what are you saying? It's amazing having you as a father, you do so many amazing things in the world and everyone thinks you're incredible. But... yes I would love to hang out more. I think we all would. I know Macie loves you so much and as for Mum..." Jonno felt he was moving into dangerous territory and so held back a little.

"Yes... I know Jonno, I have work to do when I get home."

"Work?"

"Sorry... things to sort out."

"Haha, sorry Dad, the last thing I want to do is get on your case after all that's happened. All I know is that leaving you and going down to find help was one of the scariest things I've ever done and I am just so glad to have found you in one piece. When we came over the rise into the moraine camp and we saw your body against the rock I almost collapsed from fear. I'm not sure what Mum and Macie are going to make of all of this, whether they are going to welcome us back as heroes or give us a massive telling off!"

"Ha! Shall we tell them?"

"Haha, well. Do you think we can cover it up?"

"Hmmm, might be tough unless we extend the trip until my leg is better?"

"Might be a tough one to swing, but worth a try?"

"Your mother has always questioned whether climbing mountains are worth it."

"And now?"

"Well she is sort of right and sort of wrong. You can't learn this stuff reading books I suppose."

"But books don't kill you."

"Well they could do if you had enough and the shelf broke!"

Jonno rolled his eyes, "Good to see you haven't changed too much Dad!"

They walked on, father and son and the men of the nearby village. Passing through the immense open foothills of the Andes back to the village. Despite the lack of language between the two there was a shared sense of spirit, every now and again they would catch each other eyes and smile. No doubt there would be stories to tell of these crazy headstrong gringos who had tried to beat the mountain themselves and who themselves had taken a beating. The local men had all learnt these lessons years ago in their own lives, growing up in this fierce and brutal environment, where any action that doesn't involve respecting how small one is compared to the vastness and power of Pachamamma might involve a hasty homecoming, to being returned deep into her soil. They had a mixture of admiration and suspicion for the gringos who made their way through their villages into the highlands, although they could never understand the desire to risk their lives for anything as odd as climbing a mountain.

Chapter Twenty-Eight – Return

Eventually the familiar sight of the village came into view. It was the smoke from the chimneys and the fires that first gave it away from the hillside. The smell of burning drifted through the thin air and caught Jonno's nose. His father had become increasingly silent for the last two hours and he felt somewhat alienated from the Peruvians who had accompanied them on the rescue mission. He found himself at a loss to understand them after a while. On the one hand feeling deeply grateful to them for what they had done, but on the other he was beginning to find their manner hard to be comfortable with. This was not helped by the inability to speak Spanish, let alone Q'echua, but also by how loud and boisterous they could be. They seemed to be really enjoying themselves, spending time together and this put into stark contrast the fact that conversation between him and his father had gone quiet. Jonno found the silence hard and harder still the fact that the Andean group would occasionally roar with laughter looking right at them both. He couldn't tell whether he was the butt of a joke, whether they were or whether they had nothing to do with what they were talking about. Jonno was starting to want this experience over as soon as possible.

He wondered how this would affect his father and their relationship, whether anything would change. What would this do to his father, would his leg be OK? He wondered about his mother and how he was going to be able to tell her about this, what would she say, would she be angry at the risks they took? And then of Macie, would she understand or even find it that interesting? Would she tease him when she found out he had slept by the river or collapsed in the village? Did he even want to tell that bit of the story? It was hardly heroic and to be honest it was not him that rescued his father, it was the local men and their generosity of time and energy. What was the story of what had happened; would both he and his father even tell the same one?

His father had seemed different since they had found him, it was as though he had deflated slightly and he had less to say. Jonno knew he was shattered and he was in severe discomfort, but this was something else. He wondered what had happened to him while he was on his own up there in the tent. That couldn't have been easy, thought Jonno, I have no idea what I would have done. Deep down Jonno felt a pang of sympathy for his father, for all he had been through. He had never really thought about his father's relationship with Grandpa, he just thought that's how men got on. That's what he was coming to expect from his own father. Stability yet distance. But then his Dad had opened up like that after being hoisted upon the horse and this had taken Jonno by surprise. *Since when did Dad talk about things like that?* There was something that Jonno had really connected with in his words even though he didn't really understand what they meant, an honesty and openness that resonated with him even if he didn't fully know why. Jonno had never really questioned *why* his father was the person he was, he always thought that was just *how* he was, *how* he was made. The revelation that he too had struggled with his own father was game-changing. Jonno thought how much he had struggled with his father but was beginning to accept that this is how these type of relationships are meant to be. Other friends of his at school with hardworking and successful fathers had noted similar things, a combination of wanting to impress and stand out but also resentment at the seemingly futile effort they had to put in to be noticed. But there had never been any talk of what made their fathers the men they are, it had only ever been about the effect they had on their sons.

As they approached the edge of the village Jonno saw lots of people standing looking out. There were women, children and the other men of the village. There was music blaring out and what looked like some sort of party being prepared. Huge steaming vats were being stirred by women in big hats and multiple colourful skirts. Everyone looked bright, clean and colourful, as though wearing their best outfits. Children were running up and down the rough path with ragged footballs and chasing each other, screaming and laughing. There was a celebratory atmosphere; *this couldn't be for them, could it?*

They entered the village and everyone seemed happy to see them, patting Jonno on the back with smiley sparkling eyes and toothy grins. There was a distinct smell of alcohol on the breath of some of the older men, but there was nothing troubling about them or sinister, they just seemed to be having a good time. James was more alert now and doing his best to interact with the multitude of well-wishers and those who were smiling his way.

"Gringo! How are you?" came the cry over and over again.

Thumbs up, James roused himself and grinned, riding in on his horse as though some sort of triumphant war hero, "Bien! Gracias," he revelled in his homecoming. Jonno, on the other hand, felt bashful for all the hassle they had caused and slightly confused that they might be throwing a party in their honour for returning.

The men and the horse stopped off at the same small building Jonno had slept the night in.

"OK Señores, llegamos, we arrive now" smiled the thin yet sturdy young man who had been leading the horse.

"Gracias, muchas gracias," James and Jonno replied almost in unison.

"Ahora a descansar, mañana a Huaraz", the young mountain man continued.

"Tomorrow to Huaraz?"

"Pero esta noche, fiesta!"

"What's he saying Dad?" asked Jonno.

"Tomorrow we go to Huaraz but tonight there is a party!"

"A party?! For us?"

"He didn't say, hang on..."

"Amigo, la fiesta? Porque?"

"Ah" beamed their new friend, "Hoy dia fiesta de la Virgen de las Montañas, today beeeg fiesta!"

"Some sort of religious day fiesta, amazing!" James added.

The man they were with then made the universal signs and gestures for having a drink and party, moving his arms and legs with almost joyous exuberance. He then made an aggressive whistling sound calling over some of his friends who had stopped to chat and laugh with some of the women who were out helping prepare the fiesta. They looked around as though they didn't want to be disturbed as this was a lot more fun than hanging out with the broken and silent gringos. They seemed to be much rather teasing and flirting with the ladies who were all dressed up for the day in their bright colours and best hats.

They came over and helped James off his horse, his leg was now beyond feeling painful, just stiff and numb but there was no way he could put any weight onto it. They helped him, one man taking one shoulder and another taking the other and laid him down on the same bed Jonno had slept in the night before. James looked so grateful to be lying somewhere comfortable he almost fell asleep straight away, pulling one of the blankets over him.

"There was me thinking they had prepared that all for us," remarked Jonno.

"Haha, me too," added his father wearily. "But I need some rest, I feel pretty broken right now."

"Sure, how's the leg?"

"Just a mess, it needs seeing to sooner rather than later. I need to reduce the fracture properly as soon as possible. I'm not sure I can handle another horse ride back down tomorrow though, I think the best thing to do is call the insurance company and get myself helicoptered down."

"Helicopter?"

"Yeah, I've been thinking about it, it'll be the best way."

"Ok, but how do we do that?"

"Well I imagine getting a phone here will be difficult as they all use credit and an international call will use all of theirs, but I think we have a phone charger with us? We can get that charged up and I can ring. I also think this might be a late one for these guys here tonight and they might not be so enthusiastic about helping us tomorrow!"

"Fair enough,"

"Could you have a look, I'm about to pass out and not sure what use I can be I'm afraid."

"Haha Dad, you just relax, I'll sort it."

There was no response; he was already snoring, wrapped in the warm and heavy blankets of the village. Jonno rummaged in the bags and found the charger and the phone. Again, he had no real idea how he was going to sort this out but experiences in the last twenty-four hours had taught him that if he just gave it a go, something was likely to happen.

Jonno shut the rickety wooden door softly and headed out of the house clutching the phone and charger. It must have been late in the day and the light was beginning to change. A softness had fallen on the hillsides and the greens and browns of the fields were giving off an added golden colour. The tall trees were lit up with late evening glow and seemed almost regal as they presided over the end of the day. The mountainside felt inviting again, as it had done when they had first walked through and there felt a protective quality to where he was. Everywhere he could see, there were people milling around. There was excitement in the air and a sense of celebration to proceedings. Groups of men and women were scattered around the village locked in great conversation with the occasional roar of laughter. A group of women were still by the huge vats he had seen earlier, stirring something that was giving off intense steam. They all had what must have been their daughters with them, standing alongside, learning the time-honoured ropes of what had to be done.

In a grassy flat patch of land just down from where his house was another group of women were playing volleyball on a makeshift net. The game was played in their traditional clothing, all bright and colourful skirts and cardigans of pinks, turquoises and purples. Not to mention they were still wearing their broad brimmed hats! It was as competitive as any he had seen back home and the women were giving each other no quarter, jumping and competing as though they were not just there to play. The huge dark plaits that ran down their back leapt as enthusiastically as they did into the air when challenging for the ball. Children dressed identically to their mothers sat watching or entertaining themselves, occasionally one would run on to the pitch only to be clucked at and gently scolded by what must have been their mother or sister. This normally accompanied some comment from another followed by more laughter from everyone. Jonno decided to sit for a brief minute, aware of how unique this was to simply witness, a far cry from the rushed and awkward fending off of local children who asked for money and sweets when they had walked through the village before. He felt privy to another way of life that existed for these people and these people alone, away from the endless blogs and guide books. These strange but curiously similar people were living to the best of their abilities and enjoying life when it happened to give them a natural pause. Despite the punishing conditions that they must have to live in, he thought, they not only build a life on hard work but also colour, laughter and play. It was the same as the men who accompanied him to find his father that day, they were a fluid mixture of both serious and light-hearted. They did what they had to do but then seemed intent on enjoying the rest of their time with each other.

Jonno thought of how this must compare to life back at home, where for many was the cramped mass of suburban malaise, everyone out working so hard to be able afford their houses and their cars. The community days at home always seemed somewhat forced, with only a few people believing in them and others just showing their faces so as not to be badly thought of. How little people actually knew of their neighbours but how much they believed themselves to understand celebrities in the media and their friends on Facebook and WhatsApp. Jonno felt the laughter in the air again and let its polyphony of notes and vibrations linger in his mind for a moment, it seemed as natural here as the birdsong. There was a vitality about these people that he wasn't sure he had encountered back at home. If he was to compare the comfort of what he had in the UK to what these people had here then *I must be a millionaire* Jonno thought, *but I definitely don't laugh as much as they do. I'm not sure many of us do.* For all the intensity and focus of climbing this mountain perhaps he and his father had forgotten to properly look and appreciate the real view on the way up.

"Gringo!" a warm voice appeared out of the late evening sunshine that was falling on his shoulder and face. Jonno recognised the face of this man and it had been bugging him as he didn't know from where. But there was something incredibly familiar about him.

"Hola!" Jonno looked up and saw one of the older men who had helped with the rescue,

"Tu padre, que tal?"

"Ah...OK... mucho pain." Jonno scrunched up his face and pointed to his leg, "...but... ahora... sleeping," again making the gesture by softening his face and putting his hands in a pillow shape.

"Ah...OK... mañana vamos a Huaraz no?"

"Si...gracias...but... make telefono call?" Jonno said making the sign of telephone with his hands. "But... no electricidad...can charge?" He showed the charger with its adaptor.

"Por supuesto amigo." The man said with great exuberance, his eyes looked straight at Jonno. His wide bright eyes beaming out from under his dark hat. "Venga" he said standing up.

They walked together to a small house nearby that was near an electricity pylon. Spilling down from it was a spaghetti-type mess of thick dark wires that entered the roof of the house. Not sure what Health and Safety would make of this, he thought as they passed through a metal door into what must have been a small shop. At one end of the room was a small television on a table by the wall. Behind were large cartoon representations of what must have been Jesus and Mary, along with some old yellowing newspaper clippings of pictures of footballers. There was a grubby plastic table and chairs and then on the other side a collection of shelves packed with small items to sell. Biscuits, noodles and local versions of Coca Cola seemed to be mainstay, some vegetables and some grimy containers of sweets also stood on the counter ready to be added to the shopping basket.

They walked through to the television and the man showed Jonno a dusty looking multi-plug,

"Esta bien?" he asked gently.

"Ah... I try," and Jonno somewhat nervously put the plug towards the socket, not quite sure whether he really trusted what was happening.

"Like theeees," the man said, seeing his alien companion's hesitation and grabbing the plug. It popped into the adaptor with a pleasing click and then a small flashing light appeared on the screen of the phone.

"Perfecto!" exclaimed Jonno, smiling as he did.

"OK!" roared the man as though it was one of the most significant moments in mankind's history.

"I come back later?" Jonno motioned with his hands pointing in the direction of where he was staying and making a circular motion with his hands.

"No pasa nada amigo... coca cola?" he said pointing to the shelves.

"Ah....OK, si...por favor..."

He grabbed one the grey looking bottles and dusted it off, before grabbing two plastic cups and walking back to Jonno. He pointed to one of the plastic chairs as though to sit and Jonno did so gratefully, feeling the tiredness in his body creep back in again. With a crackle, hiss and fizz the man opened the bottle, Jonno could almost taste the sugar as the top came away and it sent his mouth into a salivary frenzy. The black fizzing contents were poured into the cups.

"Brindis amigo!" the man said holding his cup out to Jonno's.

"Ah....si...cheers!" Jonno replied, holding his cup back out to chink plastic. They both smiled and took a sip. The coolness of the liquid and the sharpness of the sugar and bubbles flooded into Jonno as though some sort of drug. The two sat quietly for a moment both looking towards each other but also elsewhere, into the other unseen spaces of their lives. Jonno noted that while this didn't taste anything like Coke it was possibly one of the best fizzy drinks he'd ever had.

***

Back in the small house, Jonno found his father awake munching into a bowl of soup, similar to the one that had caused him such surprise a few days ago.

"How is it?" Asked Jonno with a wry smile on his face.

"Well. As Seneca likes to say, "*hunger makes for the best sauce*"" his father answered with small laugh.

"You always have a line for every occasion, don't you Dad?" Jonno responded, the majority of him amused by the answer but a small part remaining cross at his father's incapacity to never just be normal and give a simple response.

"But no, a lovely older woman brought it in for me, all smiles and laughter. I couldn't understand a word she said but she seemed like she had lots to say. There were some shy younger women with her, practically hiding behind her many skirts. If my leg wasn't hurting so much then I might have had more to say, but instead I played the meek and hopeless gringo lost in the mountains act and let them carry on! Speaking of which, how did you get on with the phone?"

"Fine actually, one of the older men who helped come and rescue you took me to his shop and he had some sort of electricity set up that I could plug it into. Should be ready in a few hours hopefully."

"Great. Then I'll call the insurance company and get things rolling."

"How's the leg now?"

"Just numb to be honest, I think we did a good job of reducing the fracture on the mountain but I'm not totally convinced we did it completely. If I don't move it then it is more or less manageable, if not, it is pretty grim."

"OK, and if we can't get the insurance sorted?"

"We'll cross that bridge when we come to it I think. Worse case, back on the horse to the road and then hire a car home."

"OK, fine. Sounds like we have a plan."

"Yes, it should work out OK. What's happening outside, looks like they're prepping for a good night?"

"Yeah... the village all seem to milling around, preparing food, playing games, hanging out, having a few beers, there's some music being set up. It's pretty amazing to get to see it to be honest."

"Will you go and take part a bit later?"

"I'd like to, but it's a bit awkward being the idiot gringo who can't speak to anyone and who went up the mountain without a guide and then needed help to come down."

"Don't start... please..." His father's voice quivered.

"Oh no, sorry Dad, I wasn't having a go, I was actually making fun of myself!"

"OK, sorry." James said wincing slightly as he spoke, "I just feel really bad about this whole mess. I really do."

"Dad..." Jonno paused trying to make sure that he said the best words for what he wanted to say, "not sure how to say this without sounding like you, but don't worry. It's happened, we're OK, we have a plan and we can move on. I'm just so glad that you are OK, it was awful coming down the mountain without you, really. But what is there to say now? We're here, it seems like we've gotten away with it and that's that."

"Haha, great wisdom Jonny, you're right to keep it simple. Still, I'm proud of you, I really am. My father never used to tell me he was proud of me, he always asked what I was aiming my sights on next. I hope I haven't been like this with you?"

Jonno stopped and looked at the crumbly adobe wall above his father's head, wondering what he really wanted to say. Part of him was angry at the man his father had been and he wanted to say this, another part of him was just too tired to be cross and cause more friction than was needed. Seeing his father looking so beaten up, he didn't really have the inclination to further kick a man who was already down. "Dad, all I know is that you've always given your best to life and people love you for it. You've had a phenomenal impact on the world around you and it is impossible not to be proud of you. But, I would like to see more of you, if you know what I mean?"

He watched the words wing their way to James and the expression on his face as they settled and then went about becoming part of him. "Got it, I agree, I will try... " he responded "...try to be there more. I have thought a lot about things while I was up there Jonny. This isn't me trying to confess my sins to you, as like you say I have done lots of things to be proud of in my life, but there are some priorities I would like to work on when I get back."

"Dad, please, don't worry..." Jonno was feeling himself becoming out of his depth in this conversation. There was so much to say and perhaps this was the time to say it, but at the same time Jonno wondered if it was worth it. His main concern was protecting his father and getting him down safely, the other stuff suddenly didn't feel as important. His overriding feeling was one of love and compassion for his father, not because he was his father, but because he was able to clearly see a wounded human being in front of him. Someone who, at this moment in time, had suffered enough for now and just needed support.

James saw and felt the silence from his son and instinctively knew what was going on in his mind, he too saw the pain and conflict of this young man but also the desire to care and protect, to be bigger than the situation.

"Thank you, Jonny."

"Jonno!"

James found it hard to tell if this really did annoy him right now but decided to play it safe nonetheless. "Sorry. Thank you, Jonno."

"Now just eat your soup." Jonno grinned, "and be grateful for any surprises!"

"Haha, Si Señor!"

***

With his father again sleeping, Jonno headed out a little later to retrieve the phone. The villagers had seemed remarkably respectful of their new arrivals and had let them more or less rest in peace. Apart from a few bumps and giggles coming from outside of the door, they were left to their own devices.

Now night had quietly fallen and Jonno needed a torch. The village didn't have street lights or anything else to show him the way, but he could hear the noise of what must be the party in full swing. The paths were more or less deserted and he was able to make his way through the rocky, uneven path back to the shop where he had left their phone. There was light and noise coming from where the school was slightly up the track. The utter quiet of being in the mountains allowed the sound to be louder than it was and he could hear music and chatter. It was now so much colder than in the day, one of the things Jonno still hadn't adjusted to was how quick the temperature dropped once the sun had headed west. One of the reasons their rucksacks had been so full was the need for warm clothes as well as the ones they were trekking in. It was mad, Jonno thought, that you could get viciously sunburnt during the day and then freeze from cold at night. He was glad that Dad had made him get some proper kit before leaving. Jonno zipped up his jacket, put his beanie on and headed onto the path.

The stars were once again burning bright in the sky, something that he felt deep inside of him that he would miss when getting back to the ambient orange light-filled evenings of where they lived at home. Jonno thought of the app he had recently downloaded before leaving about where the moon was and how big it was going to be. He loved the idea of the moon and had a quiet interest in astronomy without ever wanting to admit it in case of being seen as weird or geeky. But since they had been in the mountains he had seen the moon most nights and just knew where it was in its cycle. Jonno couldn't help but wonder whether all the electricity and lighting that was taken for granted back at home actually had the effect of blinding everyone from the bigger picture of where the earth was in the universe. He loved the sense of how small it made him when he could see it so clearly, it was almost comforting that he was reminded that he was only a tiny piece of a much bigger puzzle. How frantic and ambitious the world back at home seemed. In a world where the night sky is consistently washed out, how can you see, feel or have any appreciation of what else is out there?

Jonno arrived at the shop but there was no one there. The wooden doors seemed bolted shut and there appeared to be no signs of life. He knocked tentatively a couple of times and then a bit louder, but nothing. He heard again the sound of music and laughter drifting through the stillness and realised that if he wanted the phone now he would have to be brave and head up to the party. He knew his father wanted to get on with this tonight so try and tee it all up for tomorrow. Another trip on the horse and then by bumpy car back to Huaraz would be torture, probably for both of them. His father had been very brave up until this point but Jonno could see that he didn't have much left in the tank. Taking a deep breath of the ever thin fresh mountain air, Jonno blew his cheeks out watching the air condense in the cold air as though he was exhaling a cigarette. He did it again, partly out of curiosity to see it again, partly out of nerves to delay what he had to do. Although he was curious he also felt anxious of heading into the unknown. He wished he could speak the language better and that they were here only having climbed the mountain, not being rescued from it. Part of him was worried he might turn up and just be laughed at.

With a lack of choice came action, and Jonno re-joined the track and headed toward the revelry. There was no moon tonight and so he needed his torch to help himself avoid the large pebbles and rocks on the way. The climb was a little steep and he found his legs quickly burning and that he began to breath heavily again. *Nothing about living in the mountains is easy*, he thought, passing the small, dark earth brick houses on his way up. *They must be so tough these people.* He laughed imagining Macie and her hatred of being cold. *She wouldn't last ten minutes* he smirked.

Jonno arrived at the gates of the school and saw the party in full swing. There was a small band playing in the far end with a young woman in a colourful hat and a bright red sequinned skirt and jacket singing passionately. With her was a man with a triangular type of harp that look like it was once a guitar in a former life and also another man on keyboard doing an impressive job of playing and dancing at the same time. The three were utterly lost in the music they were playing. Jonno heard a combination of humour and sadness in the music, a combination of desperation but also happiness as the higher notes jostled their way into the night air. The words felt staccato and the rhythm harsh but it seemed to work. In front of her was a crowd of swaying people, all similarly dressed, seeming lost in the words and music she was creating. Away from the impromptu dancefloor Jonno could see other people sitting and huddling in groups, all wrapped in thick and vibrant blankets. There was a huge fire crackling in the near corner of the school yard and the smell of meat being cooked somewhere. Jonno saw the kind man who had helped over by the fire and so summoned up the courage to go and ask him for the phone.

Passing through the throng Jonno felt many pairs of eyes on him. Rather than feeling any hostility there was sense of gentle curiosity for the stranger in their midst. He walked past a group of older women all sitting in a group, wrapped in their heavy blue and striped mountain shawls, thick leggings and small children asleep in their laps. One of them yelled out something that ended with "Gringo" and they all collapsed in fits of giggles. One of them jumped up and seemed to motion to Jonno to go and join the makeshift dancefloor that had sprung up in front of the band.

At full height her hat only just about reached Jonno's nose and he had to crouch in order to see below the brim. Her seated friends howled with delight as she placed herself directly in front of Jonno, clearly not going to allow any form of "no" from him. Jonno could tell she had been drinking as the smell was strong and fresh on her breath as she put her face near his, eyes wide and smiling. Yet there was also a serenity about her, not the wild sort of drinking that Jonno had begun to experience back home, but a gentler, carefree spirited approach. She had an expression that both radiated hardiness but also grace. It was impossible to tell how old she was as her skin was dark and beaten by the sun, she moved surprisingly daintily, jigging from one foot to the other as she begun to feel the music. "Venga gringo" she said insistently pressing her rough hand into his delicate one, she then spun on her foot and with surprising force pulled her powerless victim into the melee. Jonno cringed as he was dragged through the assembled throng as he has neither idea how to dance to this music nor how to blend into a crowd that he was literally head and shoulders above. The crowd seemed to part easily as they passed through before he found himself at the front right next to the band.

The lady singing smiled widely and again said something with "gringo" in it which made the dancing mass first laugh and then roar with approval. Before he knew it he was surrounded by smiling faces, people putting their thumbs up and many hands patting him on the back. Jonno, at loss of what to do and simply too tired to resist, just surrendered to the moment and smiled back, mouthing the words "gracias" to everyone whose eyes he met and reciprocating with a return of the thumbs up. The band seemed to intensify their output and the singer managed to find even more oomph to her already straining voice. Jonno began to move his feet, following the example set by his enthusiastic dance partner. He started to move from side to side and place one foot down and then another. The energy and good will of the dancefloor began to find him as he let the music guide his body. He had no idea what he was doing but he stopped thinking and just let his body move as it seemed to want to. As he danced with these people, who could have been from another planet only a few days ago, he began to lose a sense that he was so different to them. Yes, their language and dress was different, but otherwise, what else? As he watched them move it struck him how human they all were. Everyone making the best of where life had placed them, and all wanting to create ways to creatively escape from the day-to-day stresses and strains that being alive put on them. While Jonno realised that he might never understand this world and what it was like to live this unforgiving life on the side a mountain high up in the Andes, for a split second something in him saw beyond this and simply saw a group of people (himself included) all celebrating the fact they were alive and taking a break from daily struggle and routine.

Jonno let himself fall into the music and let his feet move as they chose. He looked up and met the many eyes that looked at him with a smile and expression of relaxation. Every now and again his mind would click back into action and try and make sense of what was going on. In these moments his movements would become jerky and self-conscious. Thoughts of finding a reason to leave and ask for the phone so he no longer had to operate this far outside his comfort zone, but then the rhythm would catch him again and he would lose himself once more in the moment.

The songs came and went and before long his dance partner was replaced by another and he found himself holding a bottle of beer. Jonno took a long swig and the bubbles tingled against the back of his throat. The dancefloor was a swirl of colour, material and movement. For the first time in his recent life Jonno didn't feel like a stranger, despite not knowing these people, this land, this continent. He felt a deep sense of belonging that went beyond the here and now. As he danced and moved he felt that it was good to simply be alive and he had as much right as anyone else to be on this planet. The claustrophobic awkwardness and sense of feeling separate that had for so long clouded his teenage years seemed to momentarily lift, and he was aware that he was part of something wonderful, something unexplainable and something so much greater and vaster than he could imagine.

***

Eventually, as it must, the music came to an end with the band members exhausted from the efforts. Jonno had no idea how long he had been dancing and suddenly had a sense of being back in his body, people were again clapping him on the back and saying things that he had no idea what they meant. One chap, who perhaps had had one beer too many, came over and gave Jonno an enormous bear hug, almost crushing all the air out of him. This man was about the size of Macie but had a vice-like grip, full of love but bordering on lethal at the same time. This man then proceeded to excitedly talk to Jonno about something that seemed incredibly important but that which Jonno hadn't the foggiest what he might be saying.

He was eventually saved by the man who Jonno had come to originally see. Feeling a tap on his shoulder he spun around to see the man who had taken him to his shop earlier. He too seemed a little merry but also holding it together. He gestured to Jonno putting his hand to his face as though it were a phone, stretching his little finger and thumb from ear to mouth. Jonno smiled, nodded and put his thumb up. The man then grabbed Jonno by the hand and led him from the makeshift dancefloor and out of the school gates. Passing by the groups who were still seated on the floor, Jonno saw the lady who had dragged him onto the dancefloor originally and waved. She caught his eye, yelled something that had the word "gringo" in it before she and her friends erupted in hilarity.

The cool night air began to restore Jonno's senses and he found himself thinking how far away he was from anything that he knew. Despite the apparent merging of his reality with everyone else's on the dancefloor, he now felt the deep separateness of being fully back in his own body and a pang of loneliness stalked through him. He longed for someone he could share all this with, someone who might be able to understand him and he could open up to. He knew his father had his limits and while they had become closer, it wasn't like they were friends. The people of the village were amazing but all communication came physically rather than with words. He thought of Magdalena back in Huaraz and hoped he would have a chance to talk to her before he left. He had no idea how he was going to make any sense of this trip to people back at home.

They arrived at the man's house and he unlocked the wooden door. It was pitch dark inside but he moved nimbly through as though with perfect vision and found the phone and charger bringing it back from the darkness. Jonno turned it on and the battery showed full, then after a couple of seconds the reception bar filled. Jonno had never been so happy to have coverage on a phone. He patted the man on the shoulder and said "gracias Señor." The man looked at him, with a slightly confused expression and then held out his hand. "*Algo*?" he said, rubbing his thumb and finger together a few times. It took Jonno a minute to realise what he meant before he cottoned on. Slightly disarmed by this as he suddenly realised that he wasn't sure what the cultural protocol was, Jonno mumbled a hesitant "*ah si*...money, *dinero*, si....mañana Señor."

"Por favor," the man said, neither aggressively nor insistent.

"OK, si.... Mañana," replied Jonno again, feeling uncertain of what was expected of him in this moment.

"Gracias amigo gringo" And with that the man was gone, the door locked and he was half way up the hill to rejoin the party. Jonno found his torch in his pocket and followed his way back to where him and his father were staying.

"Jonno?" the voice came from the darkness.

"Oh... Dad?"

"Where have you been?" It said wearily.

"Oh sorry I got caught up in the festivities up by the school, I couldn't leave until they made me dance with them."

"Haha, amazing, good for you."

"Yeah. It was quite something. I went to go look for the owner of the shop who had the phone and so went up to the school, they were all there. Then one of the local women grabbed me and made me dance. I had no choice!"

"A man in demand!" James laughed from the darkness.

"Haha I don't know about that. More of some sort of half-time entertainment perhaps. I don't think I've ever enjoyed having so many people laughing at me," Jonno said with a smile on his face and without any bitterness in the words he was using.

"These people are quite something, aren't they? I mean, how on earth do they not only survive in these conditions, but also then enjoy themselves. There are so many people I'd like to drag here from back home to give them a bit of a wake-up call. Show them what they have, how much they have."

"Yeah, I agree. It makes you think doesn't it Dad?"

"Certainly does. Certainly does" James voice faded briefly. "Speaking of which, any luck with the phone?"

"Ah yes. It looks charged and has coverage"

"Great, I've got the insurance details saved on it, I'll get on with ringing and get us out of here."

Sitting in the darkened room Jonno listened as his father made the calls. Half an hour later after some toing and froing with a very helpful man who seemed more excited that he was talking to some people on the side of a Peruvian mountain than perhaps focussing on the task in hand, James triumphantly put the phone down. They would send a helicopter from Huaraz in the morning to bring him straight to the hospital and get him looked at. Then depending on the outcome they would fly back to Lima a few days later. They were going to miss their original flight and Jonno the start of the school term but that would all be taken care of. James knew he could be a little over the top about some things but part of him still felt extremely satisfied at the fact that he had taken the time in getting really good insurance for this trip. Jonno could feel the satisfaction in his father as he relayed the plan but didn't quite have it in him to openly acknowledge his father's obsessive organising. Despite all that had happened and the closeness he now felt to the man lying in the bed, there were certain aspects of him that were still trying.

The makeshift bed that had been made up was big enough for both of them and Jonno took out his sleeping bag to prepare to settle down. The helicopter had been agreed to arrive just after sunrise the following morning. He considered heading out again to the party but a powerful wave of tiredness swept through and overpowered him; he was asleep the moment his head touched his airline issue pillow.

Chapter Twenty-Nine- Evacuation

The thunder of engines throbbed through the village, Jonno and James were already awake and Jonno was sitting out on the hillside looking out for it. The noise arrived before the sight of a small speck in the distance which grew bigger and bigger from down in the valley. The sky was clear with its blue becoming ever deeper as the sun gained in power. The village was quiet and few people were initially milling about as Jonno had begun to wait, resembling a ghost town after all the festivities the night before. Even the ever threatening and borderline xenophobic dogs were nowhere to be seen; obviously not having the energy to bare their teeth one final time at their odd smelling guests.

Jonno had woken early in the excitement of the day ahead. He had had vivid dreams of Macie and his mother and woke in the half light of the morning. His father still asleep, Jonno crept out to take in the mountain panorama again for one more time. Despite the need to leave, he was sad that this trip might be coming to an end soon. He left the small house with his warm jacket on into the fresh and fragrant mountain air. Perching himself on a small rock he looked back up the valley from where they mountain had been. The shadows were long as the low sun skimmed over tree and rock on its way up to the heavens. There was a warmth and gilded texture to the scenery as the gently morning light began to bring it to life. A kaleidoscope of dusty browns, greens and blues met Jonno's eyes. The terracotta tiles of the house began to glow and the shadows began to shorten. The sky was empty but at the same time had the feeling of being full, there was no one around, but Jonno didn't feel alone. There was something deeply alive in the landscape that he was aware of, a presence and energy that lay beneath the superficial appearances of how it had been farmed or organised. Jonno felt the sun touch his face, warming the skin that had felt chilled from the early morning air and had the experience that he was being held. Too bright to look at directly, he had to squint his eyes and eventually shut them to stay in this moment. The light gave a golden hue to the space behind his closed eyelids. Despite not being able to see, he suddenly felt as though it didn't matter. He knew he was being held by something far beyond what his eyes could make sense of.

The moment was slowly broken up and fragmented by the roar of the engines in the distance. Jonno turned away from the light down the valley to see the enlarging speck making its way towards them. Its vibrations seem to shake the village awake as a few faces began to appear at their doors to see what was happening. Tired faces peering out from the darkness behind rickety doors, all wondering what was this outside commotion to rudely break the still that had descended after the night before.

The helicopter approached louder and louder until it was overhead. They had asked for someone to be visible the night before and had agreed that Jonno would have his red travel towel and be waving it around. He stood and began to swing it around his head. The helicopter seemed to acknowledge this and altered its trajectory accordingly. There was a flat patch about 100 meters from where they had slept and it began its descent, kicking up dust and sending small rocks flying as it did. Jonno had to cover his face as it got closer to the ground. The sound was impressively deafening yet he felt a pang of shame for the utterly indiscrete way they had organised to leave the village. From having felt very close to these people, he and his father were able to leave this world by virtue of a simple phone call.

The metal hulk came closer, drowning out the mountain silence. Jonno and the other villagers who had gathered had to take shelter so as not to have small rocks and dust blown into the faces. Finally, the blades stopped whirring followed by a small whining of the engine shutting down. The doors opened and two smart, lightly coloured skinned men in medical looking jumpsuits and aviator sunglasses jumped out and walked towards the village. Jonno came out of where he had been hiding and waved at them,

"Hi sir!" came a shout from down the path.

"Hi!" Jonno shouted back, relieved that there might be a chance to speak some English to someone other than his father again.

The men came closer, both looked young and fit which helped put Jonno at ease. *There is always something comforting if your doctor looks healthier than you*, he remembered his father saying.

"Hi sir," the man said again as he got closer, "How are you?"

"Morning, thank you so much for coming," Jonno replied, "I am fine but my father is in some pain, he is in the small house over there." He said, pointing behind and letting out a little gasp at the size of the crowd that had formed of the villagers who were naturally curious as to why their mornings had been rudely interrupted by this incredible but thunderously indiscreet piece of modern technology.

"You did well to survive the night here." The first man said, "village life is not always easy. These people can be very different. Most of them are alcoholics!" He smirked.

"No. Everyone was amazing," Jonno replied hesitantly.

"So, where is the main man?" He then said cheerily, almost cockily, Jonno thought.

"Just over here. I'll take you."

The crowd of villagers parted as they walked through them. Jonno noticed how different these Peruvians were from those in the village. He assumed they were Peruvians as they were speaking Spanish to each other and looked very much like some of the people he had seen on the streets in Lima. They were clearly taller, had much paler skin and an air of confidence and sophistication about them that was very much as odds with the earthy, fun loving and humble nature of the men he had spent time with here. Even though they shared the same flag, they could have been from entirely different solar systems.

They arrived at the house and entered. In the dark corner lay his father, eyes open and looking as though he had been waiting. He lay still but he was clearly alert.

"Good morning sir, Dr Cooper!" The first man, who was clearly the senior and thus vocal partner of the team, greeted him.

"Buenos Dias señores!" James responded enthusiastically from the shadows trying to hurriedly sit up but wincing as he caught his ankle.

"You hurt your leg and had some adventures I think?" The pilot said, still with his sunglasses on.

"Si. Long story, but I think a bad break to my right ankle and maybe knee ligaments too."

"OK, I think we just need to take you to Huaraz and there we can make a plan."

"Sounds good, if possible can they not operate here? I want them to just reduce the fracture and send me home. I have good people I know in the UK that can help."

"That's not up to us sir, we are just the mountain ambulance service," at which point they both sniggered, "we just make sure everyone is alive and then take them from A to B, nada más, nada menos."

"Fair enough. Well, thank you for coming."

"Any other problems you have sir?"

"Well, perhaps, but none that I need to tell you both about." James responded with a faint glint in his eyes.

"Sorry sir, how do you mean? You are in pain?"

"No, sorry, I was not being clear. Everything else is OK. I am in pain but I took some strong painkillers this morning and they seem to be working."

"Bueno. OK we go and get the stretcher. Maybe we can give some intra-venous pain relief on the way down, we see how we go."

"Great, thank you, I appreciate you coming so much."

"No pasa nada Señor Doctor, like you say in your country, *just doing our job"* and they both grinned again. Then with a great flourish they turned and headed back to the helicopter.

Five minutes later they were back with a variety of bags and a stretcher. They entered the room and did some basic tests on James before moving him onto the stretcher. It wasn't easy due to the pain in his numbed leg but eventually they got there after plenty of joke cracking and huffing and puffing. Jonno watched his father clench his jaw and go pale as they stabilised his leg and moved him across.

Once all strapped in, they packed their bags away and brought them back to the helicopter. James in his immobilised state turned to Jonno with a smile and said, "Going to be like bringing out the dead!"

"Haha, tell me about it. I'm feeling pretty tired too, do you think they might carry me next?"

"Cheeky!"

"Are helicopters safe in Peru?" Jonno found himself asking.

"Well it made it here in one piece, so that has to be a good sign I suppose."

"Good point."

The men returned and picked up James with more care and attention than Jonno had been expecting. Jonno followed them with the heavy bags that he had packed the night before. He found he could only manage one of them at a time and so he first took his fathers to the helicopter. They walked through the crowd of villagers who were clearly enjoying their morning's entertainment. Plenty of laughter and mirth seemed to be had as they passed through them. Lots of children were standing playing near the helicopter and the pilots seemed to actively shoo them away as they got closer. James seemed to be enjoying being stretched off, waving and saying "*hola*" to anyone who would listen. Jonno wondered if he thought that he was being given the send-off of some sort of hero.

As the men were putting him into the helicopter Jonno turned back to fetch his own bag. As he got to the house, he found it and then made his way for the door. As he left he found himself face to face with the kindly man who had helped lead the rescue party and then charge their phone.

"Hola gringo" the man grinned, with a faint stale smell of alcohol on his breath.

"Hola Señor," Jonno replied, blushing in the embarrassment that he wanted to say more, to express his gratitude for all the help they had received.

The man then said something with a serious expression that Jonno didn't quite understand. It felt important and he tried his best to make sense of it. It was only when he saw the man show his open palm and then rub his thumb and first finger Jonno cottoned on to what he was asking for.

"Ah si... dinero." Jonno responded, and he pointed to the helicopter as he knew his father had some in the bags. Part of him felt uncomfortable that he was being asked so directly but then another part of him couldn't begrudge the request. All the help they had been given and the way the men had given up their time to rescue his father. How could he say no? Although it was one thing wanting to give money and another being asked.

Back to the helicopter with the man in tow and the engines were beginning to whine.

"Dad?" Jonno shouted over the increasing din.

"Yes, Jonno."

"Dad, they're asking for money. Have you got any?"

"Are they?"

"Yes. I think we should, they helped us so much."

"Of course, have a look under the hood of my rucksack, I think there is about $100 there or something, that should be enough."

"OK great."

Jonno jumped in and grabbed the bag, he found the money as his father has said and he jumped out again. Standing face-to-face with the local man, he looked him straight in the eyes.

"Señor, muchas gracias" was the best he could come up with, despite having so much more to say. With that he pressed the notes into his hand, unsure how else to do this. He was acutely aware that many eyes were watching.

"Come on, sir!" yelled the pilot from the cockpit, the engines were really starting to sing now and he could sense the propellers beginning to turn.

The man looked back at him and closed his hand. He didn't offer any emotion to the money that was in his hand. He simply smiled, slightly cocked his hat and nodded at Jonno.

"Sir, now please!" The pilot shouted again.

With that, Jonno lifted both arms and waved at the crowd that had retreated at this point from the noise and the soon-to-come wind, then turned his back on the village and jumped in. The door slid shut and he strapped himself into the small seat next to his father who was lying staring at the ceiling. The helicopter began to shudder as the blades began to turn, the noise deafened out the possibility of any thought. Then jerkily, the machine lifted itself, as though unpeeling itself from the ground and headed skywards. The reds and blues of the villagers became smaller and smaller until Jonno could no longer see their faces. The white mountains then appeared in the background, rising up majestically into the blue heavens.

Chapter Thirty - Justino 2

It is funny seeing them go, off in the loud, clanking flying machine. It makes such din compared to the peacefulness we normally have here. Not only that but all our heads are a bit sore this morning after the party last night, that was great fun and a break from the normal hard work of living up here. I love it when these *fiestas* come about, we don't have enough of them! Life is not easy up here and these give us all a chance to drop everything and just enjoy ourselves, drink some beers and relax. Although there are always a few who take it too far, Morales is still asleep by where the fire pit is and is going to not feel well for a few days! He never knows when to stop, he loves these *fiestas*, a little too much perhaps.

But a new day has started and life carries on again. We have lived here all our lives and wouldn't live anywhere else. I know a lot of the young people in the village find our way of life boring and without hope, they want to head to the city to make a new life for themselves. I suppose I can't blame them, but we do miss them. It leaves us older people having to work much longer in our lives as our children don't come and join us in the fields any more. The city promises so much; different work, a chance to earn better money, new clothes, educations, meeting other people. It must be very exciting but it was never for me. This is my home, this village. My father and his father all worked here. I used to work with my father and that is just what we did. There was never any thought of leaving, this was and is our world. We learned how to look after the land from those who had gone before and carried on. It was simple but not easy, yet we grew up being taught what to do. Now my own children are here but coming to an age where they are wondering what they want to do. Part of me wants them to stay here, another part said they must do what is right so they can look after themselves. If they stay here that will the best for me, they can help and then look after me as I get older. If they go, I am not sure what will happen.

It was interesting to have the two gringos here. We all enjoyed going up to look for his father up in the moraine camp. We were laughing at how crazy they were for going up without a guide, totally *locos*. Maybe they thought they knew the mountains really well, but still! Not to mention they could have paid someone to help them and given someone local a bit of extra money for his time. We can always do with more money. They gave us a small amount of money for finding him which upset a few people, we were waiting right up until they got in the helicopter, but instead they just kept saying thank you and then left. If they can afford a helicopter, then you would have thought they could give us all a few more dollars than that.

This is the difference between us and them, they always seem to have access to money and we do not. They can always leave any place where they are when they want, they have the money and they can go. We must stay, that is our fate. I think they must have many more choices than us. But they can be very tight with their money, seeing as they must have so much!

I remembered them from when they walked up here a few days ago and I remember thinking it was strange seeing them, as no one normally climbs the mountains in this season. I also remembered them because they were alone without a guide and that really shocked me. I am not sure they remembered me though, every time I looked at the young gringo he always seemed to smile but never know who I was. Perhaps he didn't see me as they came up, but he definitely waved and I waved back, I remember. Maybe we all look the same to the gringos, just local *campesinos* who look good in their photos and nothing else.

I did enjoy when I took him to my small shop and we had a Coca Cola together though, he did seem grateful and it was easy to spend time with him. He seems different to his father, more open. His father seems quite unhappy, but then that is likely when you have hurt yourself like him. I wonder if he will walk again. If that happens to one of us here that is it, we will become lame. It is too expensive in the hospitals to have the treatment unless we are lucky. When we are injured it makes our lives very difficult, as it is our bodies that keep us alive. I think the gringos use their brains to earn money in big offices with electricity and computers. Maybe then their bodies become weak and so they have to spend their spare time doing big adventures? Perhaps this is why they come?

His father looked very hurt, he looked very pale and not strong when we found him outside the tent up there. He is lucky that he made it through the night with his injuries and the cold. We hear stories all the time of gringos and guides dying on the mountains. At least five every year, it always seems a bit strange. Why risk your life for going to the top of the mountains, how does getting there change anything? What about your wife and children, what do they say when you don't come back? Who earns the money for them when you are gone? I was lucky my father was alive for a long time and we worked for many years together. Even though he is dead now, I still know he is here, I feel him in the wind and hear his voice in the trees. He looks after me now just like his father did to him.

There they go now, a small dot heading down the valley. I hope they will take good stories of us back to their people. I wish them well and feel some sadness that they go. In some ways it was nice to have them here, in others it is not as they remind our children of the world outside of the village and they might think again to leave us. Who knows? Anyway the sun is up now and a new day has begun. My head is a little foggy but there are things to do. I hope Morales wakes up soon, or his wife will come and give him a piece of her mind!

* * *

Chapter Thirty-One - Last Night in Huaraz

Jonno sat alone in his hotel room, the sun had set and he had only a small sidelight for company. His things lay strewn all around the floor, he knew he had to pack as they were leaving early tomorrow but he couldn't quite bring himself to muster the energy to do so. Part of him was excited to get home, back to see Mum and Macie, see friends again and tell stories of the trip. But it still felt unreal and otherworldly, sitting now in the clean and comfortable hotel room with a large plasma television screen and hot shower, he wondered if any of it had happened. The climb, the accident, the exposed night, the help from the village, the night of dancing, the helicopter ride home. It all felt like something from a movie.

It had been a whirlwind few days since the helicopter had taken off. They had arrived back in Huaraz after one of the most spectacular journeys of Jonno's life. The irony was not lost on him as he was given a bird's eye perspective on the great mountains of the *Cordillera Blanca* and a real sense of how vast and incredible the area they were in was. But this journey came at a price. Had his father not been badly injured he would not have been able to see these things. His heart leapt as the helicopter lifted into the sky and he saw the mountains in another way. From the ground they all looked so towering and impressive, mighty and magnificent. Yet above them in the air he saw how many there were and how their perspective changed, they became more and more stretching as far as the eye could see. It made him wonder how many could be climbed, given that there were so many. Each peak seemed to offer something different, but they seemed endless, how to climb them all? Was one better than another, or were they all just different experiences that ultimately asked the mountaineer to risk his or her life for something that perhaps was not even aware the climber was there? He found the spectacular landscape gave him only questions, very few answers and he had begun to feel nauseous to the point where he needed to shut his eyes.

His father had been taken to a private hospital and they had had a good look at his ankle which was in a real mess. They had done a good job of putting the fracture back in place on the mountainside but it had not completely gone back in place. There was some worry that the blood and nerve supply had been affected. It meant them having to re-break his leg and reset it again. James had been a particularly unhelpful patient not wanting to have any surgery in the hospital. He had contacted some of his friends and surgeons back in the UK and told them the situation and he wanted them to operate on him when he got back. Jonno had felt embarrassed his father hadn't fully respected the local doctors and their technical skills but he also didn't want to get involved. They had all eventually agreed to plaster up the leg and get him home as soon as possible. His knee also looked in bad shape with a very likely diagnosis of cruciate ligament damage, the small cross shaped ligaments that keep the knee in place. This, too, would need surgery back at home. It was likely that James was going to need some time to recover and he might not ever fully get the movement and sensation in his right ankle and foot again. He had taken the news fairly well, suspecting it himself, but he had been very quiet since getting off of the mountain and being in hospital. Jonno had felt some of the same distance from him return. But at least there was a plan and the insurance had sorted everything. They were to fly to Lima the following morning and then back to the UK in the evening.

With his father in hospital Jonno had been left to his own devices for a few days. He had slept a great deal from the sheer exhaustion of the experience, and when he did wake he hadn't really wanted to leave the hotel, valuing the safety and comfort of the familiar walls. This had given him the good fortune to bump into Magdalena once or twice and she had taken great interest in their story. In fact, it turned out most of Huaraz was talking about them which at first seemed quite fun but then became quite irritating. The gringos who tried to climb the mountain without a guide and then needed a helicopter to take them home. Jonno had felt slightly distrustful of the smiles from the hotel staff. His lack of language skills made the experience all the lonelier and he had begun to long for home.

He had spoken to home every day since they were back. His mother was remarkably calm about the whole thing. She had been emotional to begin with, saying over and over again that she knew something was not right, that she could sense it. Macie seemed quite indifferent to it and was wanting to tell Jonno about her experiences down on the beach in Cornwall where her and Mum had gone. But she did say that she was glad that they were OK and Mum had been very worried. She also added, slightly mischievously, that it might be some time before mum lets any trips like this happen again. In his exhausted state, this didn't seem to threaten him, but instead he actually found himself feeling quite grateful that him and his father were so cared about.

A knock at the door broke his daydreaming and brought him back to the here and now. He stretched his arms and called out asking who it was,

"It's me, *soy yo*" a soft voice came from the other side of the door.

"Who, Magdalena?" he responded, trying not to let a sudden flood of excitement give himself away.

"Yes... me, the same. Are you there?"

"Hang on." Jonno stuttered. He looked around at the room and saw what a mess it was.

"Don't worry about the mess, it's normal" said the gentle voice, teasingly from the other side of the door.

"Haha OK, I am coming."

Jonno opened the door to the beaming face of Magdalena. The warmth that came from her smile and dark eyes seemed to go on forever. Her dark straight hair fell to her shoulders over a neat charcoal cardigan, that manged to both show her off but also maintain a conservative appearance. She was wearing a simple pair of light coloured jeans and flat shoes but still managed to give off an unmistakable air of elegance and sophistication. Jonno felt his heart thud in his chest. Yet instead of being the suave and polished man he always thought about trying to be in these situations he was able to do no more than simply stare at her.

"Hey Gringuito, you have woken up now, how's it going?" Magdalena said, appearing not to notice the essentially starstruck fellow teenager standing in front of her.

"Hey, yeah, good thanks. Just packing for tomorrow." Jonno manage to croak something from his dry mouth.

"Si...I heard that you were going *mañana*, very sad."

"I know; I can't believe that we're finally going home. That it's all come and gone."

"So what are you doing tonight?" Magdalena asked,

"Uh... how do you mean?" Jonno's palms moistened.

"Well tonight, it's Saturday. Normally us people in Huaraz go dancing, go find the music. Normally I go with some friends but they are not free today, so sad. So I thought of you, maybe we can go somewhere?"

"That...that would be amazing." Jonno stuttered, "thank you. But I think I have to pack and be ready for tomorrow. We have an early start." A voice in his head exploded, begging him to explain why he had just said this.

"Oh. OK. Well it is up to you." Magdalena replied, her shoulders seeming to drop a little as she spoke despite maintaining her smile. "I think it will be fun though, I heard you like dancing."

"Oh, you did? How?"

"Well it's not every day a gringo dances *Huayno* in the villages. You are quite famous, you know." Magdalena offered teasingly, raising both eyebrows at the same time to give a look of mock surprise.

"What! You know about that? How!?"

"Haha, oh come on. You and your Dad are famous. It is not just that the gringos didn't take a guide, needed a rescue and helicopter, but also the gringo who danced Huayno in the village like he was a natural, a *campesino puro* some were saying. I wish I had seen it!"

"They know that I was dancing? How?" Jonno's eyes doubled in size.

"Oh por favor chico, you think a story like this doesn't get told, it's too good!"

"No. Oh, I feel so embarrassed. I didn't think..."

"Haha, venga, you don't need to feel embarrassed, it's a great story. The local people, it makes them very happy. You know, so often the village people only see the climbers from far away. They feel so different to them. But now they see a *Gringuito* dancing with them and it makes them so happy. This story is good for them, so good everyone hears it very quickly. You are famous!"

Jonno was stunned.

"Haha OK, my secret is out. But you know they gave me no choice, this one lady, I had no option. I don't think I ever met anyone that strong before. She literally dragged me onto the dancefloor."

"Haha tio, these people are incredible. If they want something they will manage. You cannot stop them."

"Tell me about it, I realised I had no say in what was happening. I had to just give in and go for it."

"That is what they say. You dance like a real *campesino*, like you have the music in your blood. The people wonder if maybe you are from the mountains and not a gringo afterwards."

"Haha, I don't know where I am from anymore."

"Ha, then you are now like me."

"Ha!"

"So, venga chico, come on, I know you like dancing, I take you out tonight. And don't worry, I know you have to sleep so we come back in good time. I promise."

"Uh... OK, go on then." Jonno let the words tumble out. "That will be really fun, thank you."

"Haha, you British say *thank you* so often, I wonder if you mean it?"

"Oh. Sorry."

"Haha and you all say *sorry* all the time, again I think the same thing."

"Oh..."

"But better that than you say nothing maybe!" Magdalena chuckled, "But *que bonito* that now you say yes, we will have lots of fun. I know the best places in Huaraz."

"Perfecto".

"And now you speaking Spanish, even better."

"Ha!"

"OK amigo, I have some chores to do for Papi still but then we can go after, what do you say?"

"Sounds great. Thank you. Oh, I mean, gracias!"

"Perfecto, see now you even teach me my language. OK then, maybe I see you in the reception in two hours. We take some dinner and then go find the music."

"Amazing, thank you."

"So polite Gringuito, I think your *mamacita* brought you up very well."

"Ha!"

"OK see you!" and with that Magdalena spun effortlessly in the spot, her dark hair lifting slightly off of her shoulders and almost brushing against Jonno's dazed face and headed soundlessly down the stairs. He was left standing alone and found that his heart was still beating just as hard as it had been at the beginning of the conversation.

***

Jonno spent the next two hours frantically trying to pack, showering, scrubbing and fretting over what to wear. He had cursed himself for leaving his best shirt back in the UK, having to make do with his second best T-shirt which was one of the only ones he had left to wear that wasn't in desperate need of a wash. Walking downstairs with the slightly unfortunately worded 'SWAG' written on his chest below his favourite hoody (which mercifully was clean), he wondered whether Macie had been right about his fashion sense.

Magdalena had kept him waiting long enough for him to wonder whether he had misunderstood her earlier. He had sat in the lobby doing his best to look like he was there for another reason other than waiting for the owner's daughter to take him for a night out. Eventually she breezed in, feet hardly seeming to touch the floor wearing exactly what she had been earlier but still looking like she made an incredible effort to get herself ready to go out. Jonno did his best to retain his composure but his cover was blown as he hit his right shin on the low glass table that he had been sitting next to when he stood up to walk over to her as she walked in. The pain smarted and it took all his strength of character to give away nothing more than a small grimace. As they left the door of the hotel together Jonno was convinced he saw the male receptionist give them both a dirty look but he couldn't be sure as the doors closed quickly so as to keep the heat in.

Magdalena's choice was a million miles away from the restaurants him and his father had eaten in. Rather than the expensive gringo based places that they had been in and enjoyed, she led him off the main street down some back streets to a small place on the corner. "*Polleria Los Angeles*" the loud yellow and blue neon sign boldly yelled into the eyes of anyone choosing to look this way.

"You're taking me to Los Angeles?" Jonno asked,

"Haha, I bring you for a Peruvian delicacy, chicken and chips!"

"Amazing!" said Jonno, "finally some real food!"

They both laughed as Jonno, remembering his Britishness, rushed to grab the door to hold it open.

Inside the place was buzzing, much larger than the outside suggested and full of young Peruvians, all hanging out. The décor was no different to a standard fast food restaurant, open plan with plastic tables and chairs but it was heaving. There wasn't a foreigner in sight. Magdalena breezed in, as she was in habit of doing, and made for the queue to the till. Behind where the cashier stood were spits of and spits of roasting chicken, Jonno felt his stomach purr with anticipation.

Jonno was revelling in the fact that he was somewhere off the beaten track, despite feeling very out of place, he also had the strange sensation of feeling in place. Queuing up no one seemed to pay him much attention, it just seemed they were all here to enjoy the Saturday night in the company of friends, away from the prying eyes of parents and the older generation and just let off steam. The place crackled with conversation and laughter. Although, again, Jonno couldn't help notice that the two of them were subject to the odd narrowed eyed look from those sitting around. It was too subtle to ever catch but he was sure he could feel eyes upon them. But whenever he looked around, everyone appeared lost in their own meals and friends.

Chicken and chips ordered they found a spare small table and sat down with a Coke to wait for it to come. He was impressed at how unflustered Magdalena seemed to make everything, nothing appeared too hard for her. Even ordering chicken and chips she had made appear like an art form.

"So you like it?"

"Yeah, it's perfect, thank you."

"Haha always "thank you," so polite."

"Haha, OK sorry. Oh no, I mean...oh I don't know what I mean" Jonno smiled back.

"I thought I'd bring you to a proper Peruvian place, where Peruvian people actually eat."

"Yeah? I thought you all just ate guinea pig all day long!"

"Ha, this is what all the gringos think. I think they read the guide books and then expect everyone to be like they are in the picture. Sometime I read them in the Hotel and they make me laugh. We are just normal people."

"Haha, yeah I wondered, before you come here you think everyone lives in Machu Picchu and has a llama as a pet!"

"*Verdad*! So true. I am not sure these guide books help so much."

"Well my father loves his, I know that!"

"Just not in the mountain!?"

"Oof, low blow..."

"Low blow, I don't understand this English?"

"Oh you know, like if you punch someone below the belt, where it hurts."

"Ah, I like this!" She smiled.

At this point a young looking man with thick gel in his hair and the beginnings of an unwanted moustache came over holding the order. He arrived at the table in a very perfunctory fashion, and seemed to offer little care in placing the plates down. For Jonno he seemed to make some effort but to Magdalena he appeared as though he practically dropped it in front of her making her startle backwards lest it fall in her lap. With no attempt to offer an apology, he then turned and headed back to the kitchen.

"Cabron!" hissed Magdalena.

"What was that all about?" Jonno whispered.

"They are so jealous, and this is why I am leaving!" she said angrily.

"Leaving? When? Now?" Jonno looked longingly at the chicken and chips that had arrived, not daring to look up.

"No, not now, that would be to let them win. No we ordered the food, it would be a waste. But one day I will go, this place, the people are so small."

"Small, like their height?" Jonno asked, but immediately regretted his stupidity in being so literal.

"No, haha, no, I mean like their minds. They are so narrow; they are only from here these people. They have no knowledge of the world, they are so stuck in their machismo, their stupid traditions, how they want their women to be. I hate it."

"Like the way he was with you then?"

"Si. Yes, it is like this. They are so jealous; they think I am Peruana so they get angry if I am with a gringo. They think I belong to them, that I must live by their rules. But I am not going to, one day I will leave. Then they will see! Cabrones!"

Jonno was stopped in his track. With his mouth half full of roasted chicken, he realised that he liked her even more.

"It makes me so mad," she continued, "the way it is to be a woman in this stupid country. The men, *los tios*, they have it all, we have to fight for everything we get. Things are hard enough with our stupid government and the way they run everything badly, keeping all the money in Lima. But then to be a woman, *una mujer* as well, it is like you have do double to get any respect."

"I hear this said In my country sometimes" Jonno cautiously offered, having made sure that he had swallowed all his chicken. "They get so mad about things. They say they are treated badly too, that they have to fight harder. The problem is as a guy, it is hard to see, as it is not happening to you."

"Maybe then you are part of the problem?" Magdalena shot back, "if you are not looking?"

"Woah. Hang on, don't start attacking me now as well." Jonno replied, feeling his heart race, "what have I done?"

"OK, lo *siento*. Yes, I am sorry." Magdalena paused, breathing out, looking over Jonno's shoulder with a distant look in her eye. "I am sorry. It is just I am fed up of this. We live in a world that people cannot see, and if they cannot see they cannot understand, and if they cannot understand then it cannot change. And men think we are lying when we say these things, but all women here know the truth. But so many do not want to fight, they want the easy life, they put their head down. "*Si Señor, no Señor*" they say, not wanting trouble. But it is not right. You are lucky to live in a more liberated country, or if not you, maybe the women in your country."

"Is it really that bad?"

"Did you not see that, the way he treated me?"

"OK. But..."

"No! Do you not see; it is part of the institutional abuse. Small acts here, small moments there. It is done to keep us

scared, keep us in place, keep us saying "*Si Señor, no Señor*."
There is real violence here, bad things happen to women,
especially behind closed doors. The men, they grow up seeing
how their fathers act, how their mothers are. They feel they
should be the same. To be a woman here, we are not free. We
must be careful. All the time. And when we speak our mind,
when we say the truth, then it is worse."

Jonno saw tears forming in the corners of Magdalena's eyes
as she spoke, one dripped down her cheek into her plate of food
that had been untouched since they arrived, being absorbed by
the bright yellow chips.

"I'm sorry," he said, immediately sensing that this particular
word might not be welcome.

"It's OK, I trust you, I do not think you are like this" she
said. "You have a softness and gentleness to you, I remember I
saw it the first time I saw you. I don't feel like you want to own
the world like so many men do."

"I don't know what I want."

"Yes! But that is part of the problem for so many of these
muchachos. They don't know what they want and in the
confusion they try and control everything, including us. That is
what makes people dangerous, when they feel out of control,
when they don't know what they want. When they don't even
know they are out of control and confused. Then they cause so
much destruction and damage. Women have always suffered for
this."

"You make me think of my father," Jonno added, "he loves
being in control, but I never saw him abuse women. I think he
is a good man in that respect."

"Yes, but then maybe he takes his desire to be in control
elsewhere, no?"

"How do you mean?"

"Well, why are you here? Why do you come to the
mountains? Why are your mother and sister not here? Why do
they not climb?"

"Well, Macie is too young, and Mum is not interested, never
has been."

"This is it, men have to conquer things, they have to win. I
see it in their eyes all the time when they come to Huaraz, to
the *Cordillera.* They are here for themselves, not the mountains.
They don't come to be *with* the mountains, but to beat them, to
show that they are the *el gran jefe,* the big boss."

"You think this is why we are here?" Jonno felt his shoulders
tense.

"Pues, well, this is why I see you are different. Your eyes did
not have the same lust in them when I first saw you. For so
many, they look at the mountains and they see only
themselves. They see the awe, the power and the danger and

they believe that if they are at the top then they are the equal to this. Then they can return to their normal life, feeling good about themselves. They cannot just live, they cannot just look, they must own what they see."

"Wow. I never thought of it like this. But what about women, they climb mountains too?"

"Si, but not so many. It is mainly men. But you are right, I cannot only say men."

"But it is true, you make me think of my Dad when you say this. All my life he loves to achieve, he cannot stay still and just watch. He has to be the hero, and often he is. He has done so much. But I sometimes wonder why. So much of his life has been away from us, he goes away to be a hero but then we never see him. When we do it is like we do not know him."

"I could see the expression on his face when I first saw him. Then I heard you were going without a guide. I felt worried for you. He looked like this was more than just a mountain to him."

"Yeah, he has been obsessed the last six months before we came here. And then the first few weeks out here he was not easy to be around. I couldn't believe he was my father some days."

"I think you are both very lucky to come back down again. But I think your father is like many men, he doesn't know who he is unless he is winning."

"Wow. I hadn't ever thought of it like that."

"We see it here all the time, the men who come and climb. I always ask myself why they do it. Who is it for? What do they seek up there at the summits? Does it make them happier or does it make their lives harder?"

"How do you mean?" Jonno asked, looking around him and finding it hard to reconcile the fact they were having such a deep conversation in a chicken and chips restaurant.

"Well, think about it. If you only feel alive at the top of these mountains, if you only feel alive when you have extreme danger and risk, then what is normal life like? How can you cope? I wonder if it makes these men feel even more dead when they go home. The white summit, it is like a *droga* for them, an addiction. They need it, they need the buzz to feel alive again. Without it maybe their life becomes meaningless."

"And maybe it is not only climbing mountains as well?" Jonno added, pleased to finally be able to contribute something, "Maybe the mountains can be other things too? Like a career, success, making money, being famous, being seen to be the hero. I see this in my father, I saw it so clearly this trip. It is like he needed some sort of victory to be at peace with himself. And that almost killed him, could have maybe killed us both."

"Pues, eso, I think we are both agreeing. And this is the problem of the world, people feel lost and so they need to feel good about themselves. They seek winning to make themselves feel powerful and in control. But in doing so they hurt others who happen to be in the way. I think men are more vulnerable to this, but you are right it affects women too."

"Are women different do you think?"

"*Si hombre,* so different. The world is a different experience for us. Each month we know what it is to die, to have the potential of life and then lose it again. We bleed part of our bodies back to the Pachamamma every month. Men cannot know this, they lose nothing of themselves in how their bodies are, they simply attempt to become bigger and stronger and then don't die until they are at the end of their lives. Women, we know life and death as it is part of our bodies and how they work. We are physically closer to the rhythms of the earth than men are, our bodies are closer to how creation works. Men only know how to create, but their bodies don't experience death so they do not know. Because of this they believe they can be immortal, and they chase this. Men will never know childbirth and the deep pain of true creativity, and this makes them ignorant of life. And people who are ignorant are dangerous. To themselves and everyone around them."

Jonno was silent, not fully understanding what Magdalena was saying but hoping that he could remember enough of it to come back to it at another time, as what she was saying seemed to speak to him.

"How do you know all of this?" He said finally.

"*Hombre,* I don't know this, I live it. And if you live something then you just know."

"But you haven't given birth?"

"Haha, OK, *verdad* it is true. But I read, I study. Like I said, I do not want to live here forever. But unless I take charge of my life, I cannot expect any different."

"And you, what then do you want?"

"*Dios Mio,* good question, I ask myself this all the time. I am not sure. Perhaps I too want these things, and it makes me angry that I cannot have them. It makes me angry that as a woman it is harder to live in the world, that men seem to have the power and control. That they tell us how to live and how to be, and if we do not do this then we are seen to be the ones that have the problem. I want to live in a world where I can feel free, I can be myself without fear."

"But who doesn't want that?" Jonno laid his cutlery down on his finished plate careful not to make a sound.

"*Como*? How do you mean?"

"Well maybe it is not just women who feel trapped. You know, to be a man is not always easy. There is a world that we feel under pressure to enter and make a success in. No one ever tells us what being a man is, only what being a man isn't.

We must not be weak, we must not cry, we must not be lost in emotion, we must not look stupid or fail. There is pressure as well, to be a man is not easy, it is not defined. But everyone knows how *not* to be a man."

"But this is madness," Magdalena shot back, "to be a man simply means to be strong when you need to be, and then be simpatico, gentle, the rest of the time."

"You make it sound so simple." Jonno pleaded, "but it is not that easy. So much seems to be expected, to become someone. And men are hard on each other, in my country anyway. To be gentle carries risks. It is easier just to be strong, to look capable, to be the hero."

"Easier perhaps, but at what cost? What damage can this attitude cause?"

"True, I agree. But I think maybe you are too hard on men. I can promise you, trying to be man is confusing. It is to me anyway!"

"Haha, but this is why I see you as different amigo, I see this in your eyes when you arrive. You are not trying to read someone else's script; you are not trying to be like the Marlborough Men in the adverts. I feel that you are honest, because you know that you don't know. You are not acting, just trying to live. I love this in you!"

Magdalena stopped, and they both looked momentarily deep in each other's eyes. The *"Polleria Los Angeles"* seemed to become intensely silent for a split second as they both stared at each other, finding no end-point onto which their gaze could settle. The silence was neither embarrassing nor awkward, but simply one of curiosity and surprise. Eventually she smiled and broke the silence, and with it the chatter and noise of the restaurant roared back into both their ears.

"OK *chico*, I think we have eaten enough chicken and chips. If we eat more maybe they will cook us and sell us to the next people. I can't take the looking of the jealous men anymore. Time to go dancing!"

"*Vamos*!" Jonno said heartily. Half pleased with himself for his ever improving Spanish and half annoyed that he had managed to sound like his father yet again.

***

"What to drink gringuito?" Magdalena asked loudly above the booming music of the bar.

"Err...what do you suggest?" Jonno replied, putting his head as close to hers as possible while also trying to allow some personal space.

"Are you sure they will serve me? I am not eighteen yet." Jonno asked.

"What sort of country do you think this is amigo?"

"Ha OK, I just wondered."

"OK, I think you have the Pisco Sour, you know it?"

"Oh, yes, I read about it. But it has egg in it?"

"Haha, que huevos tienes tio! Si, it has egg in it, it will make you big and strong!"

"Ha! I thought that was the sort of attitude that was making the world go wrong!"

"Ha, funny gringo, this time I let you off!"

Magdalena leaned forward and caught the barman's attention who was busy chatting to a group of young locals at the end of the bar, "Si?" he said gruffly, sweeping his eyes over the two of them. Jonno did his best to puff out his chest and look as over eighteen as he possibly could.

"Dos Pisco Sours por favor" Magdalena said in a mellifluous hypnotic way that seemed to take the barman under its spell, she looked him straight in the eyes and his body appeared to soften slightly, as though his knees might buckle.

"Two Pisco Sours, I bring them," he then said, looking straight at Jonno as if making a point he knew that he wasn't a Peruvian and could speak English.

"Gracias!" Jonno retorted determined not to completely be the cultural outsider.

"Ha!" the barman snorted and turned his back to them to begin making them.

They had arrived in the local dance hall after a detour through some of Magdalena's favourite haunts. Jonno had been amazed at how many people she had known and said hello to on the way. Some had been friendly and others had given the same narrowed eyed suspicious look that he had seen earlier. He had been impressed at Magdalena's ability to not let it ruffle her and just let it wash over her.

By now he had had a couple of beers and was beginning to feel a little lightheaded. He still hadn't fully grown used to the thin air of altitude and remembered the warning of the guidebooks to be careful when having a drink, "one's tolerance at sea level was not the same up high," they had said. The last thing Jonno wanted to do was make a fool of himself in front of Magdalena as they were getting on so well. But the alcohol in his system and the fact they were having a great time together meant he was starting to feel more relaxed and playful. It was his last night in Peru, he had thought, it has been an incredible trip, so then it deserves an incredible send off.

Bob Marley was "*Jammin*" in the background and Jonno felt his feet tap at the floor. He loved music, loved the expression, loved that fact he could be wrapped up in it like a warm blanket. For a moment he lost himself in the thick but gentle baseline letting his thoughts wander back to the mountains and the spectacular summit day with his father. He had listened to Bob Marley that morning and the Jamaican's soulful voice had accompanied him through the deep snow that day.

"Haha, dancing again, I think you are born to dance," Magdalena tapped him on the shoulder bringing him back from the white sparkling summit to the dark and intimate club they were in.

"Oh, sorry. I was just..."

"I know; you were back on the mountain; I could see it."

"Huh? How...?"

"Like I say, I see this look a lot from the men who come here. I just see it in you."

"Who are you? Are you really human?" Jonno asked smiling, "I mean you talk like you have been alive for a thousand years, not eighteen. I am not sure I can cope!"

"Ha, like I say, I just read a lot. Not just books, I like to try and read people too, it is one of my favourite things."

"Read them like how, how do you know you are right?"

"Oh come on, people are like books too. *Venga*, look. Everyone is speaking all the time. Their bodies are telling stories their mouths do not have the courage to. Each time someone moves, they tell you something. Each time they speak, they tell you something. Not in the words, often the words are not true, but the sound of the voice, this is harder to hide. We are telling each other the stories of our lives all the time. I love this, I learn so much."

"OK. So tell me about me then, what do I tell you?" Jonno stiffened his back slightly as the words tumbled out, wondering whether he really wanted to know what she could see.

"Ha, pues, you, Señor gringuito, what do you say? Well I see you often do not say what you think, your words are correct but your tone of voice says you want to say something different. Also I think right now, you are half here, half somewhere else. Maybe you are more nervous than you want to be, but this is only when you think too much. When you relax, like when I see you with the music, I feel like you become part of the place and you are calm. I see you with your father before climbing and maybe there is distance between you, your body looks so tight and rigid with him. I see you talk but you do not say the things you want."

"Wow. Seriously, who are you? This is too much, OK well let me try the other way with you then?"

"Haha OK, but I warn you, it is never safe to have two experts sitting at the same table!"

"Ha OK. Well I see someone who has lots to say about everyone else but says little about herself. I see a person who puts lots of energy into the lives of others and trying to understand them, but who is also angry."

"Angry! Me?! *Como*!" Magdalena snapped back.

"Haha, maybe you just proved my point. I listened to you in the restaurant, and I thought "wow, this is a side you do not show the world." I think the world makes you mad but you have learned to hide it. In the hotel it looks like you are the happiest, most relaxed person in the world, but actually you carry a lot of rage."

"Oh...you have found me..."

The drinks arrived interrupting the flow of conversation, the barman put the Pisco Sours in front of them, lingered slightly longer than was perhaps necessary before sidling off back up the bar to the conversation he was having with the group when they had first arrived. Magdalena lifted the drinks and motioned to go sit down at a small wooden table, raised up to about chest height with stools to sit, just outside the dancefloor. The club was just starting to get busy, and they had to skilfully weave through the people milling about to get to it.

"It's popular this place, no?" Jonno began.

"Si. This is the place we all love to come. Always such a mix, old and young, local and gringo. The nights here are amazing. I love it."

"You love to dance?"

"Yo? Si *amigo!* It makes me so happy. I love to lose myself in the music. For all the things I complain about in Peru, *la musica, la salsa,* oh I love it so much."

"We don't hear much salsa in the UK, but I love it. It makes your feet move without even trying."

"Can you dance? You know salsa?"

"Oh no, I have no idea, but I like the sound."

"OK! Well later I will teach you, it will be fun."

Jonno's heart beat a little faster. He felt an unusual safety with Magdalena, that he could be himself, that she would listen. He also found her extraordinary and he wanted to listen to her more.

"So why do you want to leave, where will you go?" He asked.

"*Oh tio,* I don't not feel like I am from here."

"But you are not Peruvian?"

"Si! But actually only half. I never know my mother. She was a gringuita, from Europe. From Spain. But the story is so sad, she met my father and they married. Lived here together. But then one day in Lima, maybe she was not paying attention, but there was a car accident..."

"She died?" Jonno couldn't believe what he was hearing.

"Si. Oh it is so sad, so sad. But I never really knew her."

"So Adriana? She is not your mother?"

"No, but she is a very good person. My father met her after and they fell in love. I don't feel jealous and I am happy for him. But yes, I never knew my mother." Jonno saw a distance appear in Magdalena's eyes for the first time that evening. For the first time he saw her to be thousands of miles away.

"Oh. I am so... well I don't know what else to say... but I am so sorry."

"Thank you *chico,* but you know it was a long time ago, and really I never met her so I am only missing someone I imagine, not someone I actually know. It is confusing, you know?" Magdalena's eyes came back into the present and held his gaze.

"Wow. I just don't know what to say. I would have never known."

"No, it is OK. You know no one really knows. Mamacita's family live very far away and there were problems between them and her. So I never really knew them. So this family I have with my father is my real family, but..."

"It is like something is missing?" Jonno offered.

"*Eso.*" Magdalena answered softly. "Part of me is from here, and the other part, from so far away. So far away I might never know."

"Will you go to Spain?"

"I am not sure, I think about this a lot, but I do not know. Maybe it is better to imagine where we are from then to see the reality of it?"

"Ooof, this is hard to listen to. I don't know what to say." Jonno breathed out as he spoke. Leaving a little silence that was filled by the thudding baseline of the dance music that was currently holding the attention of all those lost to the latest European dance music out on the dancefloor. "No wonder," he continued "you find living here so hard."

"Si. It is a strange life for me *chico*, I am not from here, but I am not from there. So where am I from?"

"I don't even know where I am from half the time, so there is no way I can answer that."

"How do you mean, you have your family, your blood?"

"Yes... but I sometimes look at them, all of them and wonder how I ended up with them. I feel so different to my father, yet occasionally we are so similar it hurts. I look at my sister who I both love and hate in equal measure. And then there is my mother, who is constantly amazing but I even have moments when I feel she is a stranger. I love them but I don't want to necessarily be like them. Especially not like Dad, I don't want to make his choices."

"How do you mean?"

"Well he is so driven, to the point that he is always chasing the next mountain, the next peak. I wonder if he even knows what mountain he is ever on. His eyes are only ever on the summits, looking upwards. It makes him miss out on the people he is climbing with, miss out on the view. I think sometimes he wants to achieve to feel good about himself, not because the thing is worth achieving."

"So you are not close? That is sad."

"Well, we have become closer I think. This trip especially, given all that has happened. Maybe he will change after this accident. Maybe he will have to. Growing up the last few years I have felt very distanced from him. But then, it is not so simple. This trip, in the mountains, I have for the first time seen him not only as my father, but as a person. His own father, my grandfather, died recently and it has really hurt him I think. But he is like so many men, he doesn't talk. He keeps it in and goes chasing new successes to numb the pain. But in a funny way, I have seen this now and it makes me feel something for him, not just anger. He is a person, not only my father. I never really thought of this before and I don't really know what to think of it now, but it is something I need to think on. If you know what I mean?"

"Haha, I think you say these words very nicely chico." Magdalena smiled attentively at him. "But, listen, the music is changing. The salsa...si, it is time!"

"*Vamos chica!*" Jonno blurted out almost as a reflex, smiling to himself at his own capacity to get it so right and so wrong all at the same time.

"I think you are really speaking Spanish now!"

And with that, she grabbed Jonno's hand with a mixture of tenderness and power to the dancefloor. Ducking and diving she led him to the centre. Surrounded by the heavy throng, she indicated for him to follow her, first her lightly tapping feet, then the movements of her legs. Jonno, at first, found it hard to keep up with her effortless matching of the beat and seamless capacity to allow her body to mirror the music. But he soon found his own rhythm and his mind relaxed enough to let his body move as it wanted to. Magdalena smiled, leaned forward and yelled over the music in his ears that he was looking good. Jonno looked up and smiled, putting his thumbs up. The consequence of which meant he spent the next song unable to dance as his mind went into meltdown about his persistent efforts to continually avoid being uncool.

As that part of the evening unfolded, their bodies began to move in harmony with each other, and Magdalena taught Jonno a few spins and moves that allowed them to dance together. They moved in time to the music, pushing their young bodies close and then separating, spinning as though they belonged together but were then strangers, independent beings. The energy of the dancefloor seemed to intensify with every move, as those who shared the space with them also seemed to drop into a deep rhythm that controlled them rather than the other way around. Couples moving in time with each other but who were not of each other. Freedom and shared experience moving to the beat of the drums, piano and voice of the singer. Everything seemed to pulse, throb and vibrate to its own frequency. For a moment again, there were no separate beings, but simply a purity of energy that rose up generating form, and then fell away creating space.

Finally, the music switched back to some type of rap, which broke the trance. The floor cleared as those on it returned to their individual bodies, heading back to the tables or the bar where they could sit and rest and take stock. Jonno and Magdalena returned to where they had left their drinks but saw that the table had been taken. Out the corner of his eye, Jonno saw a small corner with comfy seats that had just been vacated and he pointed it out to Magdalena.

"Grab that, I'll get us more Pisco Sours!"

"Si Señor," her eyes flashed.

Jonno proudly headed for the corner, with the new Pisco Sours in hand, still slightly incredulous at how easy it had been to buy them. The barman hadn't even taken a second look at him, but seemed more interested in having a conversation with a group of women at the end of the bar. The Pisco Sours had arrived in quick time.

He squeezed in past the table next to Magdalena who had successfully commandeered the corner spot, which gave them a good open view of the club, and he settled down next to her onto the comfortable seats.

"Gracias gringuito."

"*No pasa nada*" Jonno replied, with no idea as to where he had learnt that phrase or how he had managed to access it so quickly.

"Ha! You really speaking Spanish now." Magdalena smiled taking a sip from the white drink.

"I have no idea where that phrase came from," smiled Jonno.

"Haha, you are so honest *chico*, I like this."

"One question," Jonno carried on, having not really paid attention to what Magdalena may or may not have just said to him, "why gringo? Why this word? What does it have to do with being foreign? Part of me likes it, and another part doesn't like to have an easy label."

"*Ah si... los gringos.* So as I think is the truth, it comes from Mexico from a long time ago. There were problems with them and America and they had a war. The American soldiers wore green and the local people would shout "*Green, go!*" to them as they wanted them to leave."

"No way?"

"*Si pe*. I think this is the truth. Maybe there are other stories too, but this one I like."

"Wow, but is it a bad word, when people say it?"

"Ah, good question. This is hard to answer. For me, it is a friendly word, an easy word to call someone. But maybe for some it is a bad word, maybe it depends on experiences with gringos, you know? But I like it, because I think it is important to meet new people and learn new things. If you only stay with *Latinos* or *Latinas,* maybe your world is not so big."

"True." Jonno added, not knowing what else to say. For a moment they both sat there quietly as the staccato baseline of the unintelligible rap music pumped through the room. He looked out across a sea of young people all enjoying their night out, lost in a combination of conversation, strong drinks and loud music. There was something safe about how loud it all was, as though you didn't have to listen to one's own thoughts or perhaps even the conversation of who you were with. A brief freedom from the noise in one's own head. He then looked to his side and looked at Magdalena and saw her looking at him. For a moment the surrounding clamour seemed to die down and it felt like it was only her and him sitting in the room. Her eyes looking deeply into his and he felt totally comfortable looking back into hers. The rest of the world seemed to fade away into a silent movie that was playing out unwatched in the background.

As though in perfect harmony, they both leaned towards each other. Nothing was said but both heads moved softly but with purpose until their lips touched. Jonno was surprised at how tender Magdalena's lips were. How inviting and gentle they were. Their noses brushed lightly against each other's. As their skin touched Jonno felt a surge of relief wash through him, as though he was finally home and he could now relax. They lingered there for what seemed like an eternity, like there was nowhere else to be. Until suddenly, without warning, Magdalena pulled her face away, almost tearing at his lips in the process. Jonno awoke as though from a beautiful trance to see Magdalena facing away from him, hunched slightly forward.

"Hey...what... are you OK?" Jonno suddenly felt very raw and completely unaware of what was going on. They had been having such a good time up until this point. His mind screamed with confusion as to what was happening, what he may or may not have done.

"Sorry. You must forgive me, I am sorry." Magdalena seemed to be saying, even though she was facing the other way and Jonno struggled to hear her.

"It's OK, honestly. I am sorry. I didn't mean to upset you."

"No, no, this is how I feel, I am sorry."

"Hey... please... it's OK. We don't have to..."

"I am sorry *chico*," Magdalena turned back to face him, Jonno could see the strain in her eyes and pallor had come over her smooth features, "I am sorry but I cannot."

"It's OK, please, don't worry." Jonno offered, not totally meaning what he was saying but unsure what else to say.

"I am sorry... it is..."

"You have a boyfriend?"

"Ha, *tio*. No, it is not this. No..."

"Then you are married?"

"Ha, you are so funny. No, it is... well..."

"Please, you are killing me here." Jonno didn't know what else to do but make a joke out of what was happening, it was that or just run away as fast as he could.

"It is just..." Magdalena drew in a deep breath, "it is just... well, I like you too much. So I cannot do this."

"Sorry?" Jonno spluttered.

"I mean, oh how to explain, my English makes this harder. I mean, I like you, Juanito, I like you so much..."

"But..." Jonno did his best to avoid adding any extra growl into the sound of the word than he had to.

"But, I am sorry chico, but I like you so much. But I also do not want you to break my heart. I have enough sadness in my life already to fall in love with a gringo who is leaving mañana."

"Go on."

"It is, oh, *que dolor,* I must protect myself. I don't know what you think. I think you like me too, I think we have a great time together. But tomorrow you go, maybe I do not see you again. Maybe to you I am just another story to tell your friends. Maybe I am another mountain that you can climb and put your flag. I do not want to be this story."

"Woah, that's not what I was thinking at all." Jonno grabbed his drink and took a hurried swig.

"I think you are a good person, I don't think you think this. But I cannot allow myself a broken heart, not now, I have too much to do. If we kiss, then I know I will crumble, and when you go, I am not sure I will be able to rebuild myself quickly. I am sorry."

"Hey, please, it's OK, it's fine honestly." Jonno said as softly as he could, given that the music was still thumping in the background.

"But I want to stay in contact with you, I want to know you more. I want to see you again. But now, I cannot do this."

"Please relax, don't worry. It's not a big deal." Jonno dug his nails into his palm.

"You are OK?" Magdalena said wiping the tears away from her large brown eyes with the cuff of her cardigan.

"Magdalena, I think you are amazing. I have never met anyone like you before, but I don't want to upset you. We were just having such a good time, it felt like the right thing to do."

"*Verdad*...I want to kiss you more, so much Juanito, but I cannot. It will break me, and I cannot do that to myself, not now."

"I understand." Jonno replied sinking back into the soft seat.

"But I want to stay in contact, I want to know you more. And then, in the future, who knows, we might meet again."

"I'd love that."

"I think you are a special guy," Magdalena continued, "there is something different in you that I did not meet before in other guys." She reached out for his hand and held it with hers.

"Likewise," answered Jonno, not in any way resisting this latest development, "I never met anything like you in others guys before" he added, his eyes catching hers.

"Eh, you are...?" slightly relaxing her delicate grip.

"Haha no, I am not. I was just playing. Just trying to make light of this."

"Oh haha. You are big *gringo tonto,* but good that we can laugh."

"It's either that or cry!"

"Ha, so true." Magdalena then leaned forward giving him a small push and then passed her arm through his so that she could hold onto him without being too close.

With that, they both sat back, arms interlocked, in their respective seats and looked out onto the scenes of other people's young lives that were playing out in front of them. No one seemed to be paying them any attention, but everyone was lost in their own story, their own narrative, their own dramas. Time passed as they sat side-by-side looking ahead. The silence between them was unusually comfortable and neither felt the immediate need to say anything else. Jonno felt bruised to have been rejected even if his logical mind could make sense of what Magdalena had to say. Whilst Magdalena also felt bruised that she had rejected not only Jonno in that moment, but also herself and something that a deeper part of herself yearned for. Her own rational mind coming up with plenty of practical reasons not to let herself fall into an emotional abyss that her heart was longing her to do.

The time passed with neither really knowing what to say, either to themselves or the other. Eventually Magdalena stirred and pulled her arm away from where it had linked in with Jonno's. The sudden disruption broke Jonno from his thoughts and he turned to face her. Both their faces the same distance as just before their lips had met the first time.

"*Vale gringuito,* we have a choice."

"We do?" Jonno asked.

"*Si*. We always have a choice. In this moment we can feel sad because we cannot have what we want, or we can dance! And I know you love to dance!"

"Ha, you still want to dance?"

"*Si hombre,* there is no life to have if everyone sits in sadness all the time. We are both still here, there is much to celebrate!"

"This is true." Jonno answered, his jaw feeling tight.

"*Venga tio,* I hear the sound of salsa calling!" Magdalena smiled.

Jonno paused and heard the familiar piano riffs fill the air, and a slow migration of those in the club who had been put off by the last music come out of hiding to return to the dancefloor. He saw his feet starting to tap and felt his shoulders begin to lift and fall, even though this was not a conscious request.

"Let's do it *chica*, a bailar!"

"Ha, I think you are Latino now!"

And with that Magdalena lightly but purposefully took Jonno's hand and led him back to the dancefloor. Again squeezing their way through the assembling crowd to the centre. There the old rhythms began to take over and they merged into the crowd for as long as the music played. Jonno initially found his body to be a little heavy as he struggled to reconcile his old wants with the current reality, but this began to seep away as he let himself lose himself to the music. As he did, a flow of thought and emotion washed through him as the realisation that this trip was soon coming to an end. And what a trip it had been. This was his last night in Peru and while it might not finish as he wanted, he was still having fun with someone he thought was amazing. As the mass of bodies heaved, spun and stepped their way across the floor he found himself needing to be nowhere else than he was at this very moment. Life by no means felt perfect, and it was tinged with confusion and chaos, but it was definitely exciting due to it being in no way predictable. He looked up from his dancing feet and saw Magdalena lost in her own tempo and smiled, feeling a warmth flood his body and mind.

They danced until closing time, saying little but simply enjoying each other's company and the chance to have someone else to dance with to the music that kept playing. And then it was over, the last song came to an end, the lights came on and the club began to slowly empty. Magdalena threw her arms around Jonno and gave him a big hug.

"*Gracias Juanito,* that was so much fun."

"Haha, thank you, that was fantastico."

"I think you have *sangre latino,* Latin blood, I think this music is in you."

"Ha you may be right, I love it."

"I am proud to dance with you tonight."

"Me too."

"I think we will know each other for a long time."

"I hope so," Jonno smiled, holding her tight, and bowed his head to rest it on her shoulder.

"OK we must go. I think we are here a long time now."

"What time is it?"

"*No tengo* ni *idea.*"

Jonno reached down to his pocket, pulling himself away from Magdalena in the process to grab his phone and check the time.

"Oh God, it's late! We need to go!"

"What happened chico?"

"I am meant to be meeting my father in the hospital in forty-five minutes to go to the airport. The taxi is coming to the hotel to pick me up. I can't miss this flight!"

"OK tranquilo chico, there is time."

"But I haven't even properly packed yet, it is only half done."

"No problems *tio*, we have time."

"Ha OK, let's go."

They left the club and hailed a taxi. The sun was starting to rise, flooding early morning Huaraz with its generous light. The sky was a mixture of faint pinks and whites which looked so warm despite the air almost biting the skin. Huascaran appeared on the horizon looking patiently down over Huaraz, its face no longer in shadow, but its contours and white faces revealing itself. Jonno looked up at the giant that loomed up in the distance and felt absolutely no compulsion to want to climb it, he was satisfied to simply exist alongside it.

The taxi stopped, and they got in. After some brief haggling which Magdalena did with a combination of subtlety and gentle ferocity, it took them back to the hotel, the older driver kept looking and catching Jonno's eyes in the rear view mirror, smiling in a slightly sinister way, as though he knew their secret. Jonno was too tired for this and just put his gaze out of the window, looking out onto the empty concrete street of Huaraz.

They arrived back at the hotel to find Rodrigo waiting for them at the door.

"Hola chicos, Magdalena, que pasa?" He said sternly, then softening slightly "Yonny, your taxi coming in twenty minutes, you must be quick." And then he said something to Magdalena which Jonno didn't understand but felt it wasn't necessarily congratulatory on having spent the night dancing together.

"Si Papi," Magdalena answered, her facing blushing slightly.

"OK, Yonny, *venga*, por favor.*"

"Si. Thank you. Sorry," was all Jonno was able to answer.

Twenty frantic minutes later Jonno had managed to stuff everything into his bag and made his way down to the lobby. Thankfully his father's bags were already done but he needed to make two trips to bring everything down. Magdalena and her father were waiting there, things seemed to be calmer between them and they were both smiling and joking with each other now.

A white taxi was waiting outside.

"OK Señor, now you are ready."

"I hope so. I think I have everything."

"Haha maybe, but everyone leaves something in Peru, even if they think they have packed everything."

"Sorry?" Jonno asked, not sure what he was getting at.

"Haha Juanito, don't worry. My Papi, he likes to joke. I am sure you take everything."

"Si Yonny, I am sure you take everything, I like to joke. Please give my saludos to your Papi, I am sorry not to say "adios" in person to him, but this morning I cannot leave the hotel, some staff did not come today. But we will see you again, I hope he recovers OK, please send us message of how he his."

"Si Señor, I will. Thank you for everything."

"You must come back. I think people here would like to see you" Rodrigo beamed, looking at his daughter. He held his hand out and shook the hand of Jonno without any extra grip or power.

"Oh Papi, que vergüenza! You make me so embarrass!" Magdalena led Jonno to the door of the hotel away from her father who seemed to respect their parting. "Oh Juanito, it is so good to meet you, thank you. Please, you must write," pressing a small piece of folded paper into his hand, "I hope I can see you again." And with that she flung her arms around him in a warm and full embrace.

"Thank you too," whispered Jonno, aware that her father was still in the room. "I will write when I am home, you must keep telling me how you are, and what you are doing."

"*Si señor!*" Magdalena giggled.

A beep from outside the door prematurely brought the embrace to an end. As their bodies parted, Jonno felt a familiar small pang of sadness enter his heart and begin to set up home. Rodrigo came over to help with his father's bags and bring them out to the taxi.

"OK, vamos!" he said looking up at them, "time to go." With that he skilfully picked up his heavy rucksack and adeptly swung it over his shoulders. Rodrigo picked up his father's as though it weighed nothing and brought it out to the car. Magdalena joined him, staying close to Jonno but not too near. The driver opened his door and jumped out, much more nimbly than his heavy frame might have been predicted. He opened the boot and Jonno put his bag in. "Hospital y despues aeropuerto?" He asked, although probably knowing the answer.

"*Si Señor!*" Jonno responded with gusto, not really knowing how else to be with the full spectrum of emotions still dancing inside of him. Rodrigo patted him on the back and shook his hand again. He heard Magdalena giggle again.

"Please come back soon Yonny, I think someone would like to see you again" He smiled,

"I will. I am sure" Jonno answered.

"Ciao Gringuito" Magdalena flung her arms around Jonno, giving him no time to respond. "I see you online soon."

"*Sin duda*, of course" Jonno smiled back, allowing his exhausted body to be fully crushed in her embrace but also doing his best to hug her back.

"Your Spanish, always improving" she added before squeezing a bit tighter.

The embrace finished and Magdalena stepped back to stand alongside her father.

Jonno then opened the back door and placed himself inside. The driver got back into his seat, shut the door and started the engine. The car began to pull away. He looked back to see father and daughter standing arm in arm waving with their spare arms. He strained to take in one more look of Magdalena. Despite the smiles he was sure he could see small droplets of water over her cheekbones, falling into the grooves of her face carved by her deep smile. The car eventually turned a corner, and she was lost from view.

Chapter Thirty-Two – Departure

The taxi took Jonno to the hospital where his father was waiting. He found him sitting in a wheelchair and talking in seemingly animated terms to the nurse that was with him. He was smiling which helped relax Jonno as he was unsure how he might find his father. He was aware that this was not the way his Dad wanted to be returning home and that there would still be uncertainty as to what the next few months of his life held. Thankfully he seemed to be on good form as he was transferred into the taxi. The nurse gave him a hug before he got into the car and Jonno felt that his father was in a peaceful place.

"Morning Dad, feeling OK?" Jonno asked, turning around to see his father. He was sitting in the front seat to allow his father the back seat to stretch out his heavily plastered leg.

"Morning Jonno, thanks for making it on time. I was feeling a bit stressed about it all this morning."

"I bet," Jonno replied, "I wanted to make sure that we were here for you on time. We don't need any more dramas."

"Ha," responded James, with a slight wistfulness in his voice, "No, I think we have had more than our fair share in the last week or so."

"Yep, let's just hope for a nice easy day. The insurance people have got it all sorted haven't they?"

"Yes they have been brilliant. There should be someone to help me in the airport with wheelchairs and they have even given us upgraded flights on the way back!"

"No way! How come?"

"Because I said to them that there is no way I can sit in cattle class with my leg like this, I would have to lie in the gangway. I have to keep it straight."

"And they bumped us up?" Jonno said with great excitement.

"They certainly did!" James added with a grin. "We might be going home broken and battered, but at least we are going home in style!"

"Sounds good to me Señor," Jonno said, relaxing back in his seat.

The flight back to Lima was an unnecessarily complicated affair with various important and uniformed people disagreeing with how best to manage James in his wheelchair. Rather than a coherent plan, there seemed to be a selection of conflicting ideas that not one person seemed to want to make sense of. He was pushed in one direction, then another. No one really seemed to know what to do with him. Finally, after one particularly awkward exchange between two men in their mid-forties who clearly seemed more proud of the outfits they were wearing than the actual job they were there to do, he was brought through the pre-flight checks to the steps onto the plane. There was no contraption seemingly available to take him up the stairs which meant he had to be hauled up by sheer man power. In a comical but also horrifying sight, two men in front and two men at the back, he was shunted step by step into the plane. The men seemed to take great enjoyment and pleasure from the challenge they had been set, whilst James sat there gritting his teeth trying not to think about what could possibly go wrong as he became farther and farther from the ground. Finally, he was up the steps and given a row of three seats to stretch his leg out on. However, he was placed on the front row of the plane meaning that he was firmly on show to all the passengers who subsequently bordered after him. Jonno, sitting behind, considered cracking a joke about this being First Class to ease his father's flagging mood, but decided against it and sat back looking out onto the runway as the plane filled up.

The flight to Lima gave Jonno one last chance to take in the mountains. The sky was clear and he saw the way the Andes stretched their snow covered spine north and south down this incredible continent that he had his first taste of. He felt a mixture of awe and terror as he saw the mountains stretch out in front of him. He saw the rugged brown ridges of land converge to form white peak after white peak. They seemed endless, yet neither calling anyone to them nor pretending that they were not there. They seemed to simply exist. Once high enough in the air they appeared to then blend in with the rest of the scenery as it became harder to fully appreciate their contours or heights. It was obvious that they were high but the enormity was lost as they blended back in with the ground that supported them. They stopped looking like something that could be climbed and regressed to look like just another part of the beautiful planet, no better or worse than any other part.

James slept most of the way, Jonno had noted how exhausted he looked and that he looked visibly thinner from the experience. In many ways he was quite glad not to have to talk too much as he had so much going on in his own mind. The night out with Magdalena and the half-kiss they had shared. Jonno's mind raced and his heart thumped as he thought again and again of the words she had said. She was the first person he had ever met that had made him feel something for someone else. He felt a mixture of clarity and confusion in his sleep-deprived mind. He felt so much certainty of how amazing she was but then he could not work out how he was going to see her again in the near future. He had another year of school to complete with his exams; there was no way he would get out of that. But then if he didn't see her again soon the connection might fizzle out or she might meet someone else. Jonno's mind spun and spun but he couldn't work out what to do or how to make it work. Eventually fatigue and heaviness in his head forced him to close his eyes, and he leaned back against his headrest.

As the plane crossed from the Andes down to sea level, Jonno drifted off into a momentary but incredibly deep sleep where he was sitting back at the top of Casharaju with his father, mother and Macie having a picnic. They were all looking out over the view, sharing a pasta salad that his mother had prepared, in shorts and T-shirts, despite it being covered in snow. Yet it felt warm and there was no need for any extra layers. As they sat enjoying the meal he looked across the clear view to the other peaks that surrounded the summit. On top of one of the other peaks were two people also enjoying some food, seemingly doing the same thing as them. As he looked closer he saw Magdalena and her father doing the same things as they were, just enjoying each other's company. He called out to her but she didn't hear him. He shouted louder and louder but to no response. Finally, he began to shout so loud that the ground began to shake and the mountains began to rumble, snow began to slip off of the summit and cause small avalanches down the side of the white faces. But still he kept shouting and the shaking increased so much that he found himself thrown forward into the air.

Jonno lurched forward in his seat as the plane hit the runway and he opened his eyes expecting to find himself plummeting down the side of a mountain. To his great relief there was no mountain but just the headrest of the seat in front. He looked to the side and saw his fellow passengers looking at him with an expression of mild bemusement. Before he had a chance to say anything the loudspeaker broke into life,

"Señores y Señoras, Bienvenidos a Lima, Ladies and Gentleman, welcome to Lima."

Chapter Thirty-Three - Mum 2

It was good to be able to catch up with them again before they fly, even if it did mean talking in the middle of the night. James sounded quite low and a bit distracted, like he has a lot on his mind. It can't be easy for him coming back like this. It might be the first trip he has ever come back from where he can't stride heroically back into the house with that big grin of achievement on his face that I know so well. There was a vulnerability to his voice that I have not heard in a while, a sense of rawness underpinning his words. He says he is fine and not to worry, but I hope he is OK. I know how hard he finds it to talk about things that are painful, and this will hurt him I'm sure.

He did say that he has been thinking about a few things that he wants to talk to me about properly when he is home. Part of that makes me feel a bit worried as I am not sure what it could be that he means. He might have been thinking about us, he might have been thinking about himself and what he wants, who knows? I hope they are positive things, we haven't been close for a while and I feel like I do not know him like I used to. He told me not to worry, they are good things but still I hate not knowing. I will worry now until he comes back. I need my security too.

He also talks about how proud he is of Jonny and how amazing he has been on this trip. I really heard his voice lift when he talks of him. He kept saying how if it wasn't for Jonny then he might not be alive, I could hear his voice starting to fragment and break when he said this. That almost brought me to tears as I know their relationship has not been easy for the last few years. I hope this, in its own bittersweet way, has really brought them close again. I know that Jonny has suffered hugely being the son of James recently, and that it has been hard for him. I admire him hugely for taking the risk and going to Peru with his father knowing that they might not get on.

I didn't speak to Jonny this time, he was off wandering the duty-free James told me, but I have noticed something different in him since they got back from the mountains. There has been a slight deepening of his voice. It's hard to put my finger on it, but there seems a solidity to the way that he speaks that I don't remember. Who knows? Time will tell but I am just so glad they are coming home. We have missed them so much.

It has been strange not having them around, although it has been good to spend some time with Macie and catch up together. She is a wonderful person who perhaps gets a little forgotten when the two men are back at home. We have had some lovely moments together and time just to chat and be. I think she is really looking forward to seeing Jonny again but she told me I mustn't tell him! They are funny those two, you can tell they really love each other but it is as though they must not ever show each other. They are so similar but then so different, they always have been. I hope that some time apart will have been good for them. All I want is a happy, peaceful home. I am not really interested in how we appear to the outside world, whether *they* think we are a successful family or not. I just want all of us under one roof getting on and appreciating each other. But then maybe to do this we all have to go out to discover the world to then come back and be able to share it with each other. Maybe we can only let success go once we have it? My father always told me that the true mark of a successful person was not what they had achieved, but how successful they had been in letting it go and moving on. He was a wonderful man; I miss him so much.

But this is exciting. I have missed them all so much. I know Jonny won't be at home forever, he's getting to an age where he will be wanting to leave soon. Especially if and when he goes to university. So this time feels ever precious having them all at home. I can't wait to have them back. The house has felt so empty without them. But I also don't want to wish away time, it goes fast enough as it is these days. I am getting older myself, the days seem to tick by so fast, each one a little faster than yesterday. The sun will be rising here soon and the day beginning. How best to make use of it? This is a question that never seems to get any easier, all I know is it is not to be wasted, my mother was adamant about this. She always used to say that whatever is happening will never come again, it is unique, even if it appears the same or is hard to deal with. So always try and be curious, be interested, look again. I feel I have lost a little of this spirit these last few years and would like to try and re-find it again. I have a few things I would like to talk to James about too, but all in good time. He has a lot to go through when he comes back and I want to be there for him.

Lots to think about, there is lots to come. Perhaps I will go back to bed and try and sleep. Macie is going to school in the morning and I don't want to be too tired. But I definitely feel like something is opening in me, I am not sure what it is, but I feel like things are changing. How exciting.

Chapter Thirty-Four - Take Off from Lima

James put the phone down and stared into the distance, his eye being caught by the arrival of the air stewards and stewardesses marching to the departure gate and setting themselves up to start calling passengers onto the plane. He had been sitting at the gate, waiting for some time now, being stuck in the wheelchair. Jonno had been very dutiful in pushing him around, taking him to the toilet and sitting with him. But he had noticed that he was a bit restless and so told him that it was OK to go off for a walk. Jonno had taken his time and James was starting to wonder where he was. He remembered when he snapped at him in the airport on the way over, how unnecessary that had been. Being forced to sit still had given him a lot of time to think and reflect on things, whether he wanted to or not. He had had a strong realisation he must have loved to keep busy in his life up until now to avoid thinking about things, his life, his decisions, his own inner health. But ever since the accident, he had had almost no choice.

The thoughts, feelings and conflicting interpretation of who he was and how he had been spending his time had kept coming. To the point where he was beginning to feel slightly exhausted from it. But for now, there was to be no escape, he couldn't move and he didn't feel like reading. He had taken to just watching the world to distract himself, which he had begun to find unusually calming. What he kept seeing was that everything around him was in constant movement. Even in times of still, something was always moving and changing. The airport was a good example, it was in constant flux; people with their variety of bright cases and bags striding up and down the shiny floors, off to the next destination, all on to the next place. Then if there were no people, he felt the movement of the non-human world. He had seen the trees constantly sway and bob in the breeze out of his hospital window in Huaraz, the clouds would come and go, days would turn to night and then vice versa. The clocked ticked and ticked, just like his heart would beat and beat, sending warm vibrations through his body. His chest would rise and fall, air would arrive cold to his nose and leave warm and humid. Time being still had made him see the world again. There was a curiosity that had re-awakened in him, an echo of when he was a child and the world seemed so endlessly interesting. A curiosity that had been buried deep down, an inquisitiveness that was perhaps lost when he had realised that acquired knowledge and success were a safe way to gain the respect of those around him. Better than that, this slowing down had made him feel the world again. Yet in doing this, he also had discovered a sadness in his bones that had perhaps been there for a long time and he hadn't wanted to pay attention to. He had discovered a new found honesty and clarity in his perception of himself. This, he was intrigued about, and although he didn't know what it meant or how things might play out when he got home, he felt like change, healthy change, was coming. He had no idea how to articulate any of this as the thoughts and insights had come in surges, rising and breaking on him without warning.

Jonno strolled back and tapped his father on the shoulder breaking his thoughts,

"Hey Dad," he said cheerfully.

"Hey Jonny,"

"I thought I didn't want to be late this time," his son smiled.

"Ha! I was just thinking about that."

"Me too, that seems a long time ago, doesn't it?"

"A lifetime."

Jonno sat in the seat next to his father's chair. The dark heavy sky shone through the high glass windows of the airport, adding an interesting contrast to the bright and well-lit interior. The plane looked like it would be full, as the gate had filled up with people. The public address system then burst into life,

"Ladies and gentleman, welcome to flight 467 to Atlanta. We invite all those in *First Class to come forward and start boarding."*

"I guess that's us," grinned Jonno.

"Certainly is," said James, "only the best for the Coopers!"

"Ha, every cloud I suppose."

"Haha, you could say that."

Jonno stood and wheeled his father towards the front of the queue. He was aware of lots of eyes upon them from the other passengers. But he was also aware that he didn't care. *Let them look,* he thought. He felt proud to be the one helping his father onto the plane, he felt a pride for what had happened on this trip. Even though his father was going to need surgery and had a tough time ahead of him, Jonno felt proud of the part he had played in rescuing him, satisfied that in a moment of crisis he had proved himself. It was a good feeling to be the one in charge for a change, he smiled, looking down onto his father as he pushed him through. He felt only a sense of tenderness and wanting to protect him. Whilst he knew this man was not perfect, and there was still plenty of work to be done in their relationship, he was still a human being and had his own needs. He was not only his father, he was also a person to whom life had its own battles, challenges, and ups-and-downs. Jonno felt a warmth of love flow through him that made him feel utterly protected from the stares of those who were still sitting, waiting to board. *Who knows what they think,* he thought, *who cares? I know the truth and that is enough. Let them look.*

The staff couldn't have been more friendly and polite, showing them to their seats, which were more like beds. He and his father were put side by side in their booths, meaning James could fully stretch his leg out. Jonno noted that it wasn't easy for his father to be so looked after and so tried to help him get settled with as little fuss and comment as possible. Finally, he too sat back, putting his feet out, breathing out and relaxing into his new surroundings. He was by the window and James on the inside, to help him get to the toilet if he needed.

As Jonno looked out of the plane window, his busy mind wandered through some of the aspects of what had just happened over the last few weeks. He had come to this country sure of many things and seemed to be leaving more confused than ever. But instead of being bothered by this it actually seemed to make him calm and happy. Perhaps life didn't really make sense after all, maybe that was never the case he thought. Possibly there is real freedom in just embracing this and just going along with the ride rather than trying to make it all work for you. His mind felt blank, not from lack of thought, but from a lack of any real understanding of the world he was in. There was suddenly so much more to see, experience and learn. Life seemed open and mysterious rather than closed and stale. His body tingled with an almost intoxicating sense of anticipation.

This time being the one to break the other from his thoughts James leaned over to Jonno, gesturing him to bend his head closer to him. Jonno looked at him,

"Jonny, I just want to say thank you. You know, you have saved my life. In ways you might never know."

"Dad, thank you, but you know I really had no choice in the matter." Jonno held his father's gaze.

"Ha!" James retorted, putting his hand on Jonno's shoulder. "But still, thank you."

Both men looked at each other, smiling, before James relaxed his grip and sat back in his chair staring ahead with a grin on his face.

Jonno let himself sit back. Experience had taught him he didn't need to say any more in this moment. And so he decided to just be quiet and not force this into an unnecessary conversation. There was no need for anything else to be added. Deep in his chest he felt a great releasing of tension, a pressure that had been building up for longer than he could remember. He understood what his father was really saying and that was more than enough. It didn't even matter that he called him Jonny again. He felt loved, he felt respected, he felt his father's equal. In fact, he briefly had a deep feeling of being the equal of everyone on this plane, in this country and everywhere else in the world. For now, there was nothing more that needed to be said.

The captain's voice crackled over the loudspeaker preparing the plane for take-off. Time to go home, he thought. As the engines roared and whined, for the first time in his teenage life, the idea of home had begun to really mean something exciting.

Epilogue - Macie 2

So they are on their way back, finally! It seems like so long since we said goodbye and it will be strange to have the house full of people again. Mum has been keeping me updated the whole way through, she has been quite stressed the last week or so. I'm not really sure why, Dad was always going to be in control and make sure nothing bad happened. Even though he has hurt himself he was always going to come back, wasn't he? I never really worried about them, I must admit.

But what I am worried about now is that one of my friends, Tallulah, who lives just down the road and goes to my school, has said that she now fancies my brother! I couldn't believe it when she told me, I felt a bit ill! She said that he was a hero for climbing a mountain and also rescuing Dad, somehow everyone seems to know the story around here, although Mum and her mum are friends too so I guess maybe they have been chatting. She told me she thought he was really hot and wanted to come over and see him when he was back.

This has really stressed me out, I don't want any of my friends fancying my brother. I mean, what!? Come on! He's just Jonny, my lanky, geeky older brother who I love. But I had never really thought of someone else loving him, especially not one of my friends! And she's *my* friend, I have always had to share everything with him and now if my friends like him too, it's too much!

I mean, I obviously still love him and am sort of looking forward to seeing him. It sounds like he really was amazing over there, keeping his head and helping Dad. I do feel super proud of him. But I am not sure whether I want to tell him any of that. I mean it will only go even more to his head and I am not sure that will be a good thing. Then, to have my friends fancy him, he will become so arrogant.

It has been a good time here without them though, good time to be with Mum and have fun together. Apart from the last week or so she has been really happy and we have had some adventures ourselves. We went to the beach one weekend and camped which was amazing, lots of swimming in the sea and walks on the beach. But I bet they don't ask us about that when they come back. I noticed that a lot of people would smile at Mum and she would smile back. I feel like she is a very attractive lady, people often say we look quite similar which is good as I would like to grow up to be attractive too.

I hope Dad is OK and not in too much pain, I am sure he will be OK. One thing he has always been is very strong and determined and so I am not worried that he will not recover. It must have been a shock though to have hurt himself like that and to need surgery when he gets back. I bet he wished he could operate on himself, he would have loved that!

I really hope no more of my friends start fancying Jonny, I really do. I mean I want them to be *my* friends only and not because of him, that will really annoy me. Tallulah said that now he is a mountain hero he is really cool. But I remember only a few months ago we were all laughing at him because he was being such a geek in the house, we all used to giggle when we were around him. It would annoy him so much. Maybe I could start fancying some of his friends to get my own back on him, I bet he would hate that too. He has a friend called Benjie who I have always quite liked actually.

So I find myself in an odd situation; until Tallulah told me this, I was really looking forward to seeing them both and actually felt really proud of my big brother. But now I am slightly dreading that they're coming back as it will affect my life again and I will lose some of the freedom I have just had. It seems a bit unfair that my life is not fully my own! Even when he is not here I am not free. All through my life I have had to follow my brother, he has always got to do everything first, I even had to wear some of his old clothes and play with his old toys when I was younger. Now it seems I can't even have my own friends without him having some sort of effect on them. Part of me doesn't want him to come back any more. I tried to tell mum the other day but she wasn't really listening.

And what if him and Tallulah get together? Yuck, I don't even want to think about it!

ND - #0415 - 270225 - C0 - 203/127/15 - PB - 9781912092208 - Gloss Lamination